MARIE TAYLOR-FORD

Second Chances at Lilac Bay

LILAC BAY
SERIES
BOOK 2

No part of this book may be reproduced in any form or by any electronic or mechanical means, including information storage and retrieval systems, without written permission from the author, except for the use of brief quotations in a book review.

This is a work of fiction and all characters in this publication are fictitious. Any similarity to real persons, living or dead, or actual events, is purely coincidental.

Text Copyright © 2022
Marie Taylor-Ford
All rights reserved

Cover design by Ana Grigoriu-Voicu

–

Author note: This book is set in Australia, and therefore uses British English spelling.

*To the best husband I could ever have dreamed up for myself.
Thanks for riding out every storm with me, and being the sunshine
at the end of it.
I love you, always.*

PROLOGUE

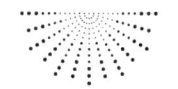

Amy stood at the crest of the slope above Lilac Bay, looking down at the perfect scene below her.

Fairy lights twinkled along the water's edge, reflected in the still, calm waters that stretched into the harbour. The Sydney Harbour Bridge arched grandly over the tableau. A dramatic orange-gold sunset glowed over the city, setting fire to the clouds. Laughter, music and easy Friday-evening conversation floated up to her from the crowd gathered along the shore for the food truck festival that was taking place.

Lyra, Amy's best friend in the world, had just finished a killer set on the small stage at the bay. She'd stood in front of the crowd and sung a brand new song she'd written for the man she loved, baring her heart and soul in the most courageous and vulnerable way. And it had paid off. When Lyra had finished the song, she'd leapt off the stage and into a long-awaited romantic reunion. Amy had been teary-eyed with happiness for her friend.

She'd also never felt so lonely in her life.

She missed Rick painfully. All she could think about was

seeing him, putting her arms around his waist and pulling his tall, muscular body towards her. She missed his kisses, his smile, the feel of his huge hands on her. She missed his easy good nature and his fierce but tender love.

She glanced at her phone again. Nothing. He still hadn't replied.

Amy dropped her arm and took one last look at the scene spread before her. She felt as though an invisible wall separated her from the people enjoying their evening. They all seemed so relaxed, as though they didn't have a care in the world.

As she walked back to her car to begin the drive home, Amy felt sick with fear. She couldn't shake the feeling that she'd left it all too late - that she might have lost Rick forever.

CHAPTER ONE

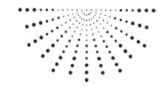

SEVERAL MONTHS EARLIER

Amy didn't notice him at first. She was enjoying her Friday night out with her two best friends, Lyra and Marley, at their favourite bar, the Whistle Stop.

She swept her gaze over the crowd and saw nothing but the expected faces - an eclectic mix of older locals, quiet groups of friends, and teens warming up before hitting one of the nearby nightclubs. But that was why the girls usually chose the Whistle Stop; they could hang out without being hit on constantly. They could chat and actually hear one another. Until the live music started, at least.

Amy was about to respond to Lyra's question to her when he caught her eye. The tall, well-built guy with the muscular arms, strong jawline and twinkling eyes, standing ramrod straight near the booths. He was talking to a couple of friends and nursing what looked like a cola.

He ducked his head shyly after they locked eyes. In someone else, the gesture could have looked like an act. In him, it didn't. He glanced back up a moment later and she gave him a small smile. He returned it. Interested but bashful.

Amy knew she looked good. She was dressed, as usual, in head-to-toe vintage clothing that flattered her curvy figure. Her creamy-blonde hair was styled in pin-tuck curls and she was perfectly made-up. There was rarely a time when Amy wasn't as polished as a new penny.

She also knew she stood out, not least among her two best friends. Lyra had a natural but understated, girl-next-door type of beauty. And Marley... well, Marley's dress sense was unique to put it mildly. Right now, she was wearing several clashing prints in a dizzying mix of colours.

Amy tore her eyes off the guy at the booths, turned back to the girls and asked Lyra to repeat what she said.

"How are you supposed to get new clients anyway?" Lyra asked her, puzzled. "Are you meant to go around insulting people's current interiors?"

Amy was a senior designer at Edgerton's Design Firm, where she'd worked for the last six years. Recently, her boss had been putting pressure on the team to bring in new business.

Amy chuckled. "I've been calling my existing clients, seeing if they have any projects coming up. Maybe I can make something happen that way."

"But I thought you were already snowed under with work," Marley said.

"Yeah, I am. We all are. That's Beaumont for you though." Amy sighed as she thought of the late-fifties, perma-tanned and botoxed owner of her company. At one point, Beaumont had been a mentor to Amy, someone she looked up to and respected. Those days were well and truly over. She wasn't sure if he'd become more demanding as he got older, and whether he'd just begun to tell off-colour jokes - or she simply hadn't noticed those things about him before. She had the feeling she'd outgrown him, and possibly his company, somewhere along the line. It was an unsettling thought.

Her eyes were drawn again to the guy near the booths. Her heart picked up a beat as their gaze caught and Amy wondered how long it was going to take him to finally come over and say hello.

"I can speak to the other people in the building where I work," Marley offered. "Maybe I can hand out your cards to them or something."

"Thanks." Amy smiled at her. "That's really sweet. I actually don't want to try *too* hard, though. Beaumont wants the business, but none of us have capacity to take it on. It's a bit dumb."

"I was going to say, we can have a little stand for your business cards on our food truck," Lyra said. "We get a lot of the Lilac Bay commuter footfall. But I don't want to usher you towards a burnout, so forget that."

"Thanks anyway. Honestly, it's something he should be doing himself, in my opinion." She twisted her mouth. "But it didn't go down that well when I suggested it." She flicked her eyes in the direction of the guy at the booths and saw him deep in conversation with his friend.

"Thank God I don't have to try and drum up business for Dr. Martelle," Marley said, referring to the GP she worked for.

Lyra smiled. "What would that even look like? Going around coughing on people? Carrying a vial of bacteria with you?"

Marley laughed. Out of the corner of her eye, Amy saw the guy at the booths push himself upright, set his drink down and walk towards her.

"This conversation might have to wait, ladies," she said under her breath as the girls exchanged grins. Amy checked her watch. It had taken him longer than most to work up the nerve to come over.

"This is awkward," he said when he reached her, his voice deep and rich. "But you've been staring at me for so long that I wondered if you recognised me from somewhere?" The words sounded light, but the pink tinge to his cheeks gave him away.

"I think I saw you on Australia's Most Wanted," Amy quipped. "I've been wondering whether or not to call the tip hotline." Lyra and Marley tactfully pretended to be absorbed in their own conversation.

"Please don't turn me in. I can explain the whole thing."

"Stealing underpants off clotheslines in three states?" Amy arched her brow. "This is going to be one hell of a story."

He laughed and she immediately liked the sound of it. Deep and warm.

"Thing is, I lost a pair, my great-grandfather's actually. They were a family heirloom. Made it through three wars. His lucky underpants. They're worth millions now, but there's only one person in the whole world who can correctly identify them and it's my 90-year-old gran. So I bring them to her and she checks if it's them."

"Any luck yet?"

He shook his head sadly. "None. But I live in hope… speaking of which, can I get you another whisky? Glenfiddich, right? 12 years? Hold the rocks?"

Amy was impressed. "Either you bribed the bartender, or you actually checked their drinks menu and that's the only single malt."

"There's a lot of other whisky on there, so you at least have to give me credit for knowing you're a single malt kind of girl."

"What type of credit are you looking for?"

He dipped his head, smiling, but didn't answer. When he brought it back up, he held out his hand. "Rick Ford."

"Amy Porter," she said, taking it. Electricity passed between them in that touch, and set Amy's heart on an uneven rhythm.

Another hour and he asked to walk her home.

"Well, actually I have to catch the bus," she said. "A walk would take around three hours. And in these shoes…" She lifted a pink heel.

"I can drive, I haven't been drinking."

Amy tilted her head at him. "You don't *look* like a serial killer. But that would be the perfect disguise for a serial killer, wouldn't it?"

Rick grinned. "Good call. I'll leave my car here, catch the bus with you, walk you home, then come back and get it. If that's okay with you?"

"That's a lot of public transport." Amy thoughtfully tapped her chin with a manicured fingernail. "There's no pot of gold at the end of this rainbow tonight, let me forewarn you."

Rick almost looked as though he was blushing. "I'm not after *that*." Amy raised an eyebrow and he broke into a grin. "Well, okay, I wouldn't turn it down. But escorting women home like a gentleman is kind of my thing. *I* don't use the word superhero." He put a hand to his chest. "But I can't help it if they do."

Amy suddenly very much wanted this man to walk her home. She kissed the girls goodbye, Lyra mentioning to Rick that she could trace Amy's location via her phone. She tapped a few buttons and held her screen up to prove it. There was the "Amy" pin, right there at the Whistle Stop.

Rick held his hands up and swore to get her home untouched. Amy hoped he didn't mean that *too* literally.

"I'll see you tomorrow for my big move, right?" Marley asked, a note of anxiety in her voice.

"Wouldn't miss it," Amy promised, not nearly as enthusiastic about the prospect of hauling boxes around on a Saturday morning as her smile might have indicated.

She and Rick put their jackets on and left the bar, walking side by side to the bus stop. Now and again their arms brushed and the contact set Amy's heart thudding.

"Your friends really have your back," Rick said, as they boarded the bus to Bondi Beach.

"They're the best." Amy felt a huge surge of love towards them.

They took a seat towards the back of the bus and Rick surveyed their fellow passengers: a teen couple furiously making out, a drunken old man almost falling off his seat with each turn, and a lone guy in army uniform.

"I forgot how, uh, *colourful* public transport is."

Amy chuckled. "I drive to work every day, so the odd bus ride is kind of fun. And gives you way better stories than a taxi."

They sat, deep in conversation until they were almost at the beach. One stop before Amy's, the man in military uniform stood to get off, locking eyes with Rick and nodding as though in farewell. Amy frowned.

"What?" Rick asked, catching her look.

She shrugged. "Whenever I see someone in that uniform, I think of one of my poor clients. She was a military wife and honestly, I couldn't imagine anything worse. Constantly packing up and moving, losing friends all the time, not really being able to have your own career because you never know what's coming. We had to scratch everything halfway through the project, because they had to leave." Amy shook her head. "It just isn't the life for me. Oh! This is our stop."

They stepped off the bus opposite a cosy cafe and stared

through the window at the couples and groups of friends inside, snuggled in the warmth.

"Want to go in?" Rick asked.

"How about we get some hot chocolates to go and walk along the beach, instead?"

"I like that. My treat. I've had enough of you saying I don't do anything for you." He nudged her playfully with his elbow and she laughed, enjoying his sense of humour.

Once they reached the beach, Amy removed her shoes and hooked two fingers through the backs of them. The sand was cool, but not unpleasantly so. Almost like a relaxing spa for her feet after they'd been pinched into heels all evening.

Despite the fact that it was autumn, the beach was dotted with small groups of people drinking, talking and playing music. Rick and Amy sipped their hot chocolates and wandered down to the shoreline, where the sand was firm. Amy felt so relaxed that it was difficult to believe they'd only just met.

Rick regaled her with tales of the clumsy apprentice who was part of the crew on a house he was building. The lad, in his early twenties, had fallen through the ceiling right as they'd finished plastering it, on the same day he'd walked through fresh concrete for the veranda and managed to burst a pipe. Amy's stomach hurt from laughing when Rick was through.

He asked about her family and, though she normally avoided the topic, she found herself opening up to him. She confided that her father's compulsive gambling problems had led to him losing their family home when she was small. He'd gone to prison for fraud after forging signatures on some deeds and Amy's mother had needed to take on extra shifts at the hospital where she worked in admin. Amy had gone to live with her grandfather. It was a story she had told almost no one beside Lyra; a secret she jealously guarded.

Not only because it was painful, but because Amy took great care in cultivating a certain image and she felt like the story cast her whole family in a trashy light.

As they left the beach and meandered towards Amy's flat, she slipped her shoes back on, taking Rick's arm to steady herself. She already felt comfortable doing a lot of things with Rick that she wouldn't have dreamed of with another man. There was something reassuring about him, something that made her feel completely at ease in his presence.

"Do you speak to your dad?" Rick asked her, as they strolled past the surf pavilions and turned onto Campbell Parade.

She shook her head. "Not really. He reaches out sometimes, sends letters and cards through my mum. He also sees my Pop sometimes, so I get small updates if I ever ask for them. But I don't want a relationship with him. I can't forgive him. I've tried. What gets me the most is the lies. They're what caused all the issues in the end. If he'd been honest with Mum at any point, we might have still had a home. And a family."

Rick looked thoughtful. "Maybe he was trying to protect you?"

"Oh, I'm sure he thought he was! Look, you can't make any excuses for him that he hasn't made for himself over the years. But still, wouldn't you rather swallow your pride and keep your family together, with a roof over their head?"

Even after all this time, the topic was painful for Amy. It always would be. She knew it wasn't healthy to carry this much anger towards her father, but she wasn't really sure how to deal with it. Rick let the subject drop.

They strolled along in silence for a while, until he reached out and took Amy's hand. His palm was huge and slightly rough, engulfing her much smaller one with a warm strength. Amy had never known holding hands to be so exciting, and butterflies tickled her insides as she smiled up at him.

When they reached her block of units, a cool evening breeze was rustling through the trees. It blew strands of Amy's hair around. As Rick shyly reached out to tuck one behind her ear, Amy felt an excited kind of nervousness in the pit of her stomach. Something she hadn't felt for a long time.

"Thanks for walking me home. I had fun."

"It was my pleasure." He smiled in a way that made her feel a little light-headed. "I like this," he added, running his eyes appreciatively over her. She was wearing her blush-coloured, cinch-waist coat and Rick tentatively drew his hand over its faux fur collar. "I like the way you dress."

"Thank you," Amy said, realising she couldn't exactly say the same about him. He was wearing jeans, a brown button-down shirt and workman's boots. It was perfectly functional - inoffensive even - but not exactly stylish. It was unusual for her to be attracted to someone with so little flair. Rick was tall, friendly-faced and shy - at least he had been shy at first. Perhaps he wasn't Amy's usual type, but she was quickly realising that didn't seem to matter to her at all.

"Can I get your number?" He bit the inside of his cheek.

Amy feigned shock. "Do you honestly think you can just walk around with me for three hours being brilliant company and letting me bare my soul to you, and I'll hand over my number like that?" She snapped her fingers.

Their eyes met and he grinned. "But I bought you that hot chocolate. That's got to be worth at least two of the digits."

"How will you figure out the rest?"

"I'll go back and buy four more hot chocolates."

Amy nodded slowly, as if she was weighing up the pros and cons. "Tell you what, I'll make you a deal."

"Anything."

She pretended to fuss with the collar of his shirt, using it as an excuse to close the gap between them. "I'll give you my number if you kiss me." Amy wrapped her arms around Rick's neck and looked up at him.

"Miss Amy, you move *fast.*" He put his hands around her waist and pretended to be scandalised. "We haven't even shared a yoghurt yet."

Amy threw her head back and laughed. During the walk, they'd discovered they were both huge *30 Rock* fans, and Amy loved that he'd found a way to reference the show.

"It's just that I like you." She tilted her face to his again. "And I'd like you to kiss me now."

He was looking down at her with such intensity that she felt her knees might give out. "I like *you*," he said huskily. "So I'll go ahead and do this."

He leaned down. Their lips met and the kiss was sweet and lingering. Slowly, it started to heat up and when Rick cupped her face with his hands, Amy felt as though parts of her were on fire. They finally broke apart, breathless, and Rick leaned his forehead on hers before pulling her tightly to him.

"I'll take that number," he whispered in her ear, sending a thrill down her spine.

"I don't see any hot chocolates." Amy's voice came out wobblier than she expected.

Rick smiled and she opened her handbag to take out her gold fountain pen, scrawling her number across his hand in her best writing. Rick looked at it and immediately fished his phone from his back pocket to snap a picture of it.

"This is a real work of art. I knew you were a designer, but you even made something little like that beautiful."

She smiled, appreciating the compliment. "You're a builder and I'm a designer. You make things and I make things pretty. A good team, don't you think?"

Rick's smile twitched for a fraction of a second and a look flashed across his features that Amy couldn't quite read. She thought he was going to say something, but instead he tightened his arms around her and buried his face in her hair for a moment. "Good night, Amy. I'll see you very soon."

Amy leaned into his chest, her arms encircling him. "Night."

They kept their fingers laced together until their bodies were too far away and their hands broke apart. Amy walked into the warm foyer of her apartment block, turning several times to look back at Rick, who watched her through the glass front door.

She went up the stairs to her first floor flat, the grin on her face spreading from ear to ear. It had taken all her willpower not to invite Rick inside. She had a feeling she wanted to take things nice and slow with him.

As Amy stepped inside her flat and locked the door behind her, her phone buzzed. She pulled it from her handbag.

Hi, the message read. That was all, and it turned her insides to jelly. She leaned against the door, her cheeks hurting from the smile.

Maybe she wouldn't take it so slow with him, after all.

CHAPTER TWO

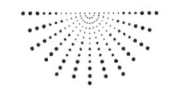

Amy spent the next evening at home, indulging in her favourite 'me time' activity.

She had taken extra care when she'd remodelled the bathroom after buying her flat. She'd fallen in love with the bones of the place and had been able to look past the hideous colour scheme, cheap and tacky kitchen and bland but functional bathroom.

But there had been a *lot* of work to do to make it fit for one of the most popular interior designers at Edgerton's.

The bathroom had been transformed into a luxury oasis complete with terrazzo flooring, white floor-to-ceiling subway tiles, brass fittings, a marble countertop and a custom ceramic sink. Amy had invested heavily in the fluffiest towels and bathmats she could find, and finished the room off with a vintage claw tub. It was still the most popular "before and after" in her flat's tour on *Apartment Therapy*.

Now, she drew a hot bath of Epsom salts, lit several candles and poured herself a generous glass of red. She sank into the water with a groan that reminded her of the noise her grandfather made getting out of his armchair.

The last thing Amy had felt like doing after a long week of work and her evening stroll with Rick was helping Marley move into a new flat. But Marley was short on funds and Amy knew Marley would do anything for her. So she had found herself that morning - a Saturday morning no less - in a pair of tailored slacks and a beret, standing beside a moving van with Marley and Lyra.

Now, not only were her legs, arms, shoulders and feet aching, she kept reliving the hair-raising moment when she'd almost toppled backwards down the stairs with two boxes stacked in her arms.

Her phone started vibrating, skittering along the edge of the bath. She just managed to catch it before it joined her in the tub. It was Lyra.

"Are you basically dead?" Lyra groaned.

"Oh God. I'm in *pieces.* I have never wanted to break an ankle so badly in my life as I did today. I can barely hold the phone to my ear."

"She owes us big time. I kind of want to move apartments just so she can help me."

"You know she would though," Amy sighed. "That's the only reason I said yes in the first place."

"Yeah, I know, I know. I'm going to hell for complaining about helping her."

"I'll see you there, then I guess. All I've done all evening is curse her name. I'm in the bath right now and you might have to keep your phone handy in case I can't get out."

Lyra laughed. "Well, I'd be no use to you. I'm face-down on my bed... It was great to see her looking so happy though, right?"

"Yeah." Amy thought tenderly of their friend. Marley had arrived in Sydney two years earlier from some tiny country town and Amy had met her at a painting class soon after. It was a stroke of fate - Marley had never painted before, and never did after. In fact, Amy couldn't hand on heart say that what Marley had done to the canvas that evening could be called painting either, but they'd had a ball getting to know one another. Back then, Marley had been living in a hostel, nothing but a suitcase to her name. She'd eventually progressed to a flat-share a few months later and now Amy was delighted that she had her own place.

"What are you calling for, anyway?" Amy asked. "Making me strain my arms this way."

"I've got a case of the willies about Wednesday night."

Lyra was a singer and Amy had offered to update her website for her that Wednesday after work, adding a fictional manager named "Margot" to the bookings section. People kept telling Lyra they needed to speak to her manager before they booked her for a gig, but Lyra didn't have one and couldn't afford one. Amy found this profoundly unfair, especially since Lyra was genuinely incredibly talented.

Amy made the drunken suggestion that Lyra should answer her phone without saying who she was. If they asked for Margot, she would say she was Margot. If they wanted Lyra, she was Lyra. She could also call "as" Margot and negotiate bookings for Lyra.

Amy sighed. "Which specific willie is haunting you?"

"The willie about lying and saying that I am a singer with a manager when I am in fact a singer without a manager. And the part where I say I *am* a manager." Amy could hear the stress in her friend's voice. "What if I get found out?"

"Do you think the police are monitoring your website?" Amy joked.

Lyra managed a tight laugh. "No, but, ugh I don't know. We had the idea when we were drunk... maybe it's not a good one."

"It's a *really* good one," Amy said firmly. "Look, all we're going to do is add Margot's name to the page. Once you start getting gigs, you can remove her or whatever you want. It's only to give everything a kick start. That's all we're going to do."

Actually, Amy had also tentatively organised a gig for Lyra and her keyboard player Mick, at her Uncle Rusty's pub. She was planning to have Lyra ring the pub as Margot on Wednesday and make a booking. Amy realised now that she'd have to ease Lyra gently into that one.

"Okay, okay," Lyra said. "That makes sense. Right, willies deactivated. Let's get back to being exhausted."

Amy hung up the call and dropped the phone onto her bath mat, picking up the glass of red and taking a long sip. She sunk deeper into the water, sighing. The phone rang again and she groaned, sure it was Lyra with another hesitation. She contemplated ignoring it, but when she looked down at the screen, Rick's name was flashing up.

"Well, hello," Amy answered, the hint of a drawl in her voice.

"Hello yourself." Amy could hear the smile in his voice.

"A phone call. How perfectly old-fashioned." She slid down in the bath a little so she could fully relax, tilting her head against the edge of the tub and closing her eyes.

"It's called courtship and it isn't dead yet. Not on my watch."

"I'm very glad to hear it. Where are you?"

"Where are *you*?" he threw back. "It sounds echoey."

"Why, in my bathtub."

"A bathtub. But that means…"

"Mmm-hmm. As the day I was born."

"Lord have mercy," he whispered.

Amy's heart was pounding and her cheeks were flushed. Rick seemed to do something to her insides that was simultaneously terrifying and thrilling. "I take it you're *not* in a bathtub then?"

"You assume correctly. I'm whatever the opposite of floating in a relaxing bathtub is."

"Sinking in a stressful one?"

They laughed. Amy pictured his face as they spoke. Clean-shaven with a strong jawline and a deep dimple on one cheek, the whole thing framed by a short haircut.

"Do you have plans for this Wednesday night?" he asked.

"Yes. I'm helping Lyra improve her website. But..." Amy would usually be more coy about agreeing to dates, or even suggesting them, especially so early on. But things felt different with Rick. "What about Thursday, or the weekend?"

"Oh, I wasn't asking for a date. I was just checking what you're doing."

"Tease!" Amy laughed. That sense of humour...

"You're the one naked in a bathtub," he said and Amy's heart flipped. "But seriously, are you giving me a choice of evenings?"

"It appears so."

"Then I'll take all of them, please."

The website design session turned into a drinking session and Amy suffered the next morning. Her hangover was so bad she almost had to pull the car over on her way to work to be sick. Amy reminded herself she was far too mature to be drinking on school nights - she was thirty three after all! She detoured past a fast food drive-through and grabbed a strong black coffee and some hash browns, wolfing them down while sitting in the parking garage at work. As she ate, she scrolled back through the text messages she and Rick had sent one another the previous evening.

Everything had gone perfectly with Lyra; the website was updated and the gig at Rusty's pub was booked. And all through the evening, Rick had peppered her phone with exactly the right volume of text messages. Amy loved that he didn't play games and hold off replying to her for hours, nor did he bombard her with every passing thought.

You're a perfect texter, she'd written, and reading his reply again now brought colour to her cheeks: *If you think I'm good at that...*

Amy sighed, clutching the phone to her chest, then realised the time. She felt slightly better now the food had hit her stomach, but the detour had also made her very late for work. She speed-walked up from the garage to the open-plan office as fast as her pencil skirt and stilettos would allow and was surprised to find it empty.

Puzzled, she headed for the boardroom and inwardly groaned when she saw through the glass panels that everyone was inside.

Beaumont had evidently called *another* spontaneous meeting. He called them so often that Amy and her colleagues had secretly dubbed them "yachting meetings", because: *we need all hands on deck, folks!*

Usually, Beaumont had nothing much to say and simply enjoyed the attention and sense of importance the meetings brought him. But today, there was a young woman standing at the front of the room with him, so Amy realised he must have called everyone in for something other than his own amusement.

She slipped into the back of the room beside Martha, her best work friend. The young woman standing at the front of the room locked eyes with Amy, giving her a small smile. She was pretty, slender and petite with long brown hair that she wore in two braids. Amy smiled back, having absolutely no idea who she was or what she was doing there. Amy noticed Kyle from her team making eyes at the woman and made a mental note to tease him about it later

"Kristina Lucas," Martha whispered, answering Amy's unspoken question with a discreetly pointed finger. "She's joining our team."

Amy was surprised, but not altogether unhappy to hear that a new designer was being added. Maybe it was a sign Beaumont had realised the competitive, strained atmosphere lately, and was doing something to change it.

She couldn't help thinking that it would have been nice to have a heads up, or be involved in the hiring process in some way. Usually, Beaumont let potential new joiners spend the afternoon with the existing team, so they could get a sense of how they'd fit in. It had been something Amy had pushed for and Beaumont had grudgingly agreed to. He must have been very sure about Kristina if he'd hired her without that input. Amy wasn't sure whether to be impressed or concerned.

When the meeting broke up, Kristina headed straight for Amy and Martha, sticking her hand out. Amy and Martha shook it, introducing themselves and welcoming her to the team.

"Is that your motorbike parked in the garage?" Kyle horned in on their conversation. Kristina nodded, not looking overly impressed with the interruption. "Cool," he said, grinning goofily.

"Excuse me." Kristina tipped her head to the girls in a farewell gesture, before walking back to her desk, which was distant enough from Martha and Amy to make them feel safe discussing her as they sat back down to work.

"Beaumont described her as a *wunderkind*," Martha whispered. "But she looks so young. We need to watch out for her."

Amy felt an unwelcome spike of jealousy at Martha's words. *She* was used to being the apple of Beaumont's eye. So, Beaumont had hired Kristina sight unseen for the team, hauled her up in front of a yachting meeting to show her off *and* described her as a wunderkind. Maybe Martha was right about them needing to be on guard. Still, Amy resolved to give Kristina the benefit of the doubt.

CHAPTER THREE

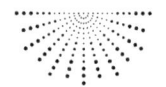

Lipstick? Perfectly in place. Hair? Flawless. Dress? Spotless. When Amy had finally finished her appearance check in the rearview mirror that Friday night, she got up the courage to exit the car.

It was her stepfather's birthday "soiree" - as the invitations had read - but Amy could think of a thousand things she'd rather be doing with her evening. Seeing Rick was top of the list. She'd tried to rope one of the girls into coming with her, but had never really expected them to accept. Amy couldn't blame them. Her mother, Diana, had once told Lyra that running a food truck was an "interesting occupation, if there was absolutely no other option", and had asked Marley whether she was colour blind after icily appraising her outfit.

Still, Amy knew if she'd pushed the issue, one of them would have joined her out of loyalty. She just hadn't wanted to put them through it.

An unexpected issue at work had kept Rick busy since Thursday. He'd be stuck working on it the whole weekend, so they'd rescheduled their date for the following Tuesday.

Even if he'd been free, she would have kept him away from tonight's event. There was no guarantee it would go smoothly, and every chance she'd end up sobbing in her car later.

Bill, Amy's stepfather, had seemed nice enough when she'd first met him eight years earlier. A bit dull, but then Amy wasn't dating him so that wasn't really a problem.

Slowly, Amy had come to realise she hated Bill. He was snobby and boring, and often made snide comments about Amy's dad. She assumed he was jealous, although why he'd be jealous of a gambler who'd lost his wife, daughter, house and freedom was beyond her. They'd argued about it many times and Diana had pretended not to hear. Another thing Amy hated Bill for - he'd slowly turned her down-to-earth if distant mother into a poser like him.

Amy picked her way across the lawn since the driveway was packed with shiny, expensive cars, and hesitated at the door.

Her phone pinged with a text and warmth spread through her chest when she saw it was from Rick. *You got this.*

He knew she hadn't been looking forward to the evening and his message made her feel like she wasn't in this alone. She texted a heart emoji back and rang the doorbell, shuffling Bill's present between her hands. She knew he wouldn't like it, because she'd chosen it deliberately to upset him. It was a coffee table book called *Icons of Architecture*. Bill had been an architect pre-retirement, as he told anyone who stood still long enough, and had told Amy he thought interior design was like "dressing up a doll" while architecture was more like sculpture. The book was to remind him that even if he considered himself an *artiste*, he wasn't one the world was going to remember.

Diana answered the door, dressed in an elegant yellow gown that brushed the floor and showed the hollows of her clavicles and the rounds of her shoulder sockets. She was flawlessly made up, her brown hair in a French roll and her thin arms weighted with gold bangles.

"You made it." She air-kissed Amy and gave her the briefest of hugs.

"Wouldn't have missed it," Amy said, and followed her mother into the marble-floored, high-ceilinged living room where small clusters of guests stood sipping from champagne flutes and delicately selecting canapés from the flying buffet. There was a bar set up in the corner, attended by an older man in a tuxedo, and a pianist played on a baby grand off to one side of the room.

Several guests turned to Amy, smiling as she entered the room, but she could read the shock in their faces. *Who's the big one?* she could almost hear them thinking.

Diana took the present from Amy, laid it on a crowded table and handed her a glass of champagne. She steered her towards Bill, who was talking to a gaggle of elderly white men and one Black woman about his golf swing.

"Happy birthday, Bill," Amy said flatly as they faked a hug. She wondered whether Bill and Diana's marriage was as bloodless as their shows of affection. It was a good thing they hadn't had children together - Diana would probably have given birth to a statue. Amy sipped her champagne and enjoyed the discomfort her presence seemed to bring to the group.

"Bill tells me you're a painter," one of the men said, his tone slightly patronising.

"Interior designer," she corrected, and she felt Diana shift uncomfortably beside her.

The man, who was wearing a bowtie, raised his eyebrows. "I have an old friend who runs a design firm. Where do you work?"

"Edgerton's. In Lilac Bay."

"Well, that's him!" Bowtie said, as though it were the most incredible coincidence in the world. "He's a devil, that old Beaumont," he added, chuckling fondly.

"He's something alright," Amy agreed.

Bill seemed irritated with the turn of the conversation. "Didn't get the talent from her father, I think we can safely presume." The group chuckled as Bill pulled Diana close to him. "Must have come from this one." He planted an awkward kiss on Diana's forehead as she beamed at the group and discreetly shot Amy a warning look. Amy bit back the nasty comment that was on the tip of her tongue and instead took a long sip of her champagne.

"I must say," began a man dressed in a tweed jacket, "I don't see the resemblance." He pointedly looked Diana and Amy up and down and Amy felt colour rising to her cheeks. "You're definitely more…powerfully built than your mother." He smiled at Amy as though he'd meant to compliment her.

"Amy, I don't think we've met. I'm Loretta." The Black woman cut through the circle by extending her hand. Amy took it and smiled genuinely for the first time since arriving at the party. Loretta had warm eyes set off by the gold of her cocktail dress. "Would you mind helping me choose a whisky? Bill tells me you're something of a connoisseur."

Amy and Loretta peeled away from the group and headed towards the bar.

"Sorry about Fife," Loretta whispered to Amy.

"*Fife*? What kind of a name is that?"

"My husband's. And mine. It's his last name, but he goes by it. I hyphenated."

"Oh, God. Sorry. Which one was he? They all look exactly the same." Amy grinned slyly, sensing a kindred spirit in Loretta.

Loretta laughed. "You're absolutely right. Oh, that's a depressing thought." She glanced back over her shoulder at the group. "He didn't look like that when I met him back in our uni days, I swear. He's the one in tweed."

Amy's eyes bugged. "You're married to him?"

"Don't look so shocked."

Amy shook her head. "Sorry, it's only that you look like a real person, and he…"

"Fife's a real person, too. But he is a little different when he's around this crowd, I'll give you that."

At the bar, Amy helped Loretta select a smooth blended whisky, perfect for the uninitiated. Loretta sipped and looked pleased with Amy's choice, as they fell into easy conversation. When the topic turned to work, Loretta asked about Beaumont. Amy must have made a face because Loretta looked thoughtful.

"Have you ever thought about going out on your own?"

Amy shook her head. "Dreamed about it maybe, but it's nothing I'm ready for yet."

Loretta reached into her clutch and pulled out a business card. "If you ever do decide to do that, give me a call. I could be your first client. Well, some of my clients could be your first clients," she said with a smile. Amy wasn't quite sure what that meant, but she took the card and thanked Loretta sincerely, tucking the gold-embossed square into her dress pocket. Loretta shrugged as though it was no big deal. "There are few things more satisfying than working for yourself," Loretta added.

The soiree made for a difficult evening overall, even more so since Amy only had a single glass of champagne so she could drive home. But whenever she touched the card in her pocket, she felt soothed.

When she was leaving several hours later, her mother pulled her aside at the door and stuffed a letter into her hand. "From your father," Diana whispered, glancing back to make sure Bill hadn't seen.

"Thanks." Amy always put the letters into a shoebox in her wardrobe. Once a year, on his birthday, she read them all. It was never a good day.

When she finally got home, she kicked off her heels and added the letter from her father to the pile. Then she took Loretta's business card and reverently set it on her bookshelf - a reminder of their conversation about how fulfilling it was to work for yourself.

In bed, she hesitated with the phone in her hand but couldn't resist texting Rick a goodnight message.

Did it go well? he replied.

It wasn't a total loss, she texted truthfully, thinking of Loretta.

I'm going to make sure you're a bit more enthusiastic after our date next week ;)

Amy's face split into a huge grin. *Can't wait to see what you've got…*

You're making a grown man blush over here.

Amy sighed, hugging the phone to her chest. She fell asleep thinking of Rick.

CHAPTER FOUR

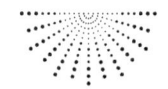

Amy had offered to drive to Rick's neighbourhood for their date, but he'd felt bad about needing to work over the weekend so he'd insisted on coming to her. An early start the next day meant he wouldn't be drinking or staying the night.

Amy was disappointed, but also relieved. The evening would be free of all the usual "will we, won't we" pressure, and she and Rick could concentrate on getting to know one another better.

Standing in front of her closet, she picked out a forest green, long-sleeved wrap dress that fell to mid-calf and was tight in all the right places. She brushed her hair out over her shoulders in loose curls and added a string of vintage pearls around her neck. She finished the outfit off with a pair of cream peep-toe heels.

They'd chosen a cosy Vietnamese restaurant not too far from her apartment for the date. When she arrived, Rick was standing outside holding a small bouquet of native flowers. His face lit up as he handed them to her, his dimple flashing.

Amy realised then exactly how much she'd been looking forward to seeing him again.

"Oh, I love these!" She took the flowers and stood on tiptoe to kiss him. "Banksias are my all-time favourite flowers."

"I'm glad. You look beautiful." He traced his eyes over her and she marvelled that he managed to say things like in a way that made her insides melt, but somehow sounded wholesome.

"Thank you."

Amy still wouldn't have described him as handsome, exactly. He was dressed in a pair of black trousers and a grey button-down shirt, an outfit Amy was fairly certain her date had worn to their end of school formal dance. Still, there was something about Rick that she was beginning to find irresistible.

He held his elbow out and Amy hooked her arm through his, enjoying walking into the restaurant that way. Like a couple. They took a seat by the window and ordered a bottle of sparkling water to begin with, having fun with the people-watching they could do from their vantage point. A candle flickered inside a red paper lantern, casting a flattering, warm glow over them.

"That guy there." Rick pointed out the window to a man with an overly pumped upper body swaggering past. "He's on his way to meet his mates for a marathon *Sesame Street* binge."

"Hey, don't knock The Street," Amy said.

Rick grinned. "I only made the joke because that's what *I* do with my mates."

"I would have thought you'd all be more into *Bob the Builder*." Rick gave her a puzzled smile. "Because you're builders!" she clarified, surprised he didn't get the joke.

"Oh, right." He flashed a tight smile and cleared his throat, picking up the menu. As he scanned it, a frown deepened across his brow. "I haven't heard of most of these things," he said finally, sounding sheepish.

"Let me help you. I know food."

There was a time, and a type of guy, that Amy would have hesitated to make that comment to. Her mother often moaned about Amy's weight and had done so as long as Amy could remember. For most of her teens and twenties, those comments had made Amy ashamed of her body. Her confidence was newfound, but it was strong. It was refreshing to notice that with Rick, she didn't think about weight at all.

Rick laid his menu on the table and Amy leaned forward, running a red-manicured fingernail down the paper as she briefly explained the dishes. Rick seemed mesmerised by her hand and halfway along the menu he gently picked it up and kissed it, holding her gaze.

Her heart thudded out of rhythm and her chest heaved. They stayed that way for a long minute, tingles spreading from Amy's hand to her tummy, where butterflies were taking flight. She cleared her throat and pulled her hand away, pretending to study her own menu.

"Sorry," Rick said, embarrassed. "That was a bit weird. Who am I, Pepe le Pew?"

Amy laughed and they continued studying their menus, but she couldn't concentrate. She looked through her lashes at his strong jaw clenching and unclenching as he frowned at the menu, his huge hands tilting it a different way to throw more light on it.

"You know what?" Amy said a moment later, her voice slightly unsteady.

"What?" He smiled as he looked up.

"It turns out I'm not super hungry at all…" She raised her eyes to look at him.

The corners of his eyes crinkled, but his gaze was smouldering. "You know I can't stay the night?"

"I have never cared less about anything in my life."

A waitress approached the table, smiling warmly at them. "Are you ready to order?"

"It's the dumbest thing," Rick said, throwing a twenty dollar note on the table and moving to stand. "We just remembered we left the stove on."

"We're so sorry," Amy added, as the waitress gave them a sceptical look. "It's a bit of an emergency."

Giggling, they ran up the hill to Amy's flat. At her door, they started kissing and Rick picked Amy up as though she weighed no more than a feather, her back pressing against the door as her legs wrapped around his torso. She kept one arm around his neck and reached behind with the other to try and open the lock. She kept missing, scratching the key around the handle as their kisses heated up. It must have been making a racket because a moment later, Amy's neighbour Wilma opened her door and peered down the hall.

"Amy?"

They broke apart and Rick quickly lowered her to the floor. Amy's red lipstick was smeared all over his face. "Sorry Wilma. I - my key wouldn't fit."

She raised an eyebrow at them, shaking her head. But she was smiling. When she waved goodnight, Amy quickly opened her door, yanking Rick inside. Once it was safely closed behind them, they exploded into laughter.

Later that night, Rick and Amy were sitting on the sofa, snuggled under a chunky knitted blanket, an episode of *30 Rock* coming to an end. Rick was wearing only his boxers and Amy was enjoying resting her head on his broad, toned chest. She reached a hand up to his hair, combing her fingers through it.

"You'd suit growing your hair longer," she said, looking up at him. "Have you ever considered it?"

There was an odd look on his face. "No. We... they. It has to stay short for work."

Amy frowned. "Oh, really? I didn't think there were rules like that. You could always tie it in a ponytail under your helmet hat thing if it got too long."

"Yeah, maybe." Rick traced a finger over her cheek. "I really wish I could stay tonight."

"Is the build so far away?"

"Huh?"

"The build," Amy repeated proudly. "I have an uncle who works in construction and he filled me in on a bit of the lingo."

"Oh, right. I have a long drive in the morning and a really early start, that's all."

"Sounds like you need to be off then, young man," Amy said, smiling up at him.

He leaned down and kissed her gently, his brows furrowed in a slight frown. "I hate that it's after our first time, that's all."

Amy wrapped her arms around his neck and tilted her head up for another kiss. "Well then. We just have to make sure it's not our last."

CHAPTER FIVE

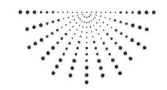

After an intense day at work which left her with a pounding headache, Amy was still looking forward to her regular visit to her grandfather.

"Evening, Amy!" Carol, the overly-friendly receptionist who worked at the retirement village waved her in. "Ooh, don't you look happy?"

Amy ducked her head, thoughts of Rick bringing immediate heat to her face. "How is he?"

"Raising hell as usual!" Carol answered, shaking her head and chuckling.

"Glad to hear it!"

When she knocked on the open door to his room, Pop was in the middle of a jigsaw puzzle and didn't immediately respond. It could be hard to break his concentration once he was absorbed in something, a trait Amy had inherited.

"I got your favourite sweets." She tossed a bag of Clinkers onto his neatly-made bed and leaned to kiss his cheek. When she got no response, she took a seat at the foot of the bed and watched him for a moment, her heart swelling with love. Pop himself had chosen to move to the aged care facility, or the Sunnywoods Lifestyle and Retirement Village, as it was officially known. He'd wanted people to play cards with regularly and figured he'd get constant company at Sunnywoods. Amy was relieved he was thriving here and had all the staff wrapped around his pinkie finger. She even suspected he was having a fling with Hazel, a retired barrister six years his senior who lived two doors down.

Pop's room was kitted out with a comfortable single bed, a small private bathroom, cosy lounge area with twin recliners and a wall-mounted TV, and a little round table with two chairs where he could choose to eat his meals if he didn't want them in the common room.

As Pop sat hunched over his puzzle, Amy noted he was due for another trip to the in-house salon. His hair was poking up at odd angles like it did when it got too long, and she marvelled once again at the thickness of it. Aside from the silver colour, the hair looked like it belonged to a much younger man.

"Aha! There's the little beggar," Pop said suddenly, lifting a jigsaw piece triumphantly into the air. As he snapped the piece into the puzzle, Amy stood to admire his handiwork and realised the puzzle featured a Lady Godiva-style naked woman on horseback, her long hair barely covering her breasts.

"*Pop!*" She slapped him playfully.

"Oh, don't be such a prude, Amy Beth," he said, grinning at her. Pop was the only one who used her middle name and she loved it. "Gimme my Clinks." He snapped his fingers in the direction of the lolly bag. Amy grabbed it and sat opposite him in the other chair at the little table, sliding the bag to him. "You touched her boobs," Pop said as he opened the bag, and Amy couldn't help but laugh.

"Her hair's over them, how could I? And don't eat all

those at once, I don't want you having a heart attack or staying up all night."

"Oh, the women here'd love that." He gave her a cheeky wink.

Amy grinned and reached out to grab one of the candies, snapping it in two with her front teeth. "Pop, when did you know about Nana?"

His eyes lit up. "Ah. Thought there was something different about you. Spill!"

Amy laughed. "There's nothing to spill yet, I just…" She twirled the remaining candy half between her fingers. "Did you know right away?"

"Absolutely," he said firmly. "Moment I saw her."

"Really?"

"Yeah," he said tenderly, his expression misting over. "We met at a wedding. Some cousin of hers, marrying a school buddy of mine. She was there with another fella, but as soon as I spotted her, I knew. I asked if I could walk her home and she said yes. Ditched the other bloke cold. Never left her side after that."

Amy sighed. "That's beautiful, Pop. I can't believe I never knew that story."

Pop tossed a Clinker into his mouth, grinning cheekily. "Course, there were tons of times I regretted it. She had a hot temper, my Nellie. Sometimes wished I'd let her walk home with the other chap."

Amy burst out laughing and then turned as she and Pop heard a voice at the door.

"You're a terrible liar, Percy," Hazel said.

She was leaning against the door frame, smiling at them and holding two mugs of coffee. Hazel was a petite and elegant woman, well-spoken, gentle and whip-smart. Amy secretly wondered what she saw in Pop. Not that she didn't fiercely love her grandfather, but she couldn't for a moment imagine what they had in common. Perhaps he had a "wrong side of the tracks" type appeal to her. Amy imagined Hazel had lived a life surrounded by decorum, sophistication and reserve, now here was the brash bad boy of the nursing home showing her the rough parts of life she'd missed out on.

"Come on in, Hazel," Amy said warmly, standing to give her the seat at the table. Amy moved to the bed as Hazel set the coffee mugs down and took a seat.

"Where'd you get these?" Pop snatched his cup up gratefully and blew before he took a sip. Caffeine was normally banned after 3pm at Sunnywoods.

Hazel winked at Amy. "I have my sources," she said mysteriously.

"You're a tramp, that's what," Pop said, and they both laughed at Amy's shocked face and sharp intake of breath. Amy sat for a moment, gathering herself as Hazel examined some of the puzzle pieces and held one up to catch more light on it, before delicately adding it to the area where the woman's thigh met the horse's back. She paused to daintily sip her coffee.

"Close your mouth, Amy Beth," Pop said.

She snapped it shut. "Sorry! I…"

"Didn't think a barrister could tolerate your Pop's off-colour language?" Hazel looked at Amy with a smile in her eyes.

"I guess not. Sorry."

"Oh, it's fine. At least you only underestimated my sense of humour."

"What do you mean?" Amy asked. "What else do people underestimate?"

Hazel gave her a look. "I was a female barrister who started practising in the seventies. What *didn't* they underestimate back then? But now…" She smiled at Amy.

"Now people often think I'm a sweet, dottery old lady and nothing else."

"What else do you wish they knew?" Amy asked.

"That I'm co-owner of Sunnywoods, for a start."

"Wow," Amy breathed, feeling a little awed. "So that's how you get hold of contraband coffee."

Hazel smiled. "I was sick of living alone and couldn't find a place I liked. So I made one."

"Smart, ain't she?" Pop winked at Hazel.

"She is," Amy agreed.

"Not too smart. I still hang around with your stinky butt."

Pop guffawed as Hazel tittered sweetly. Any ideas Amy had had that Hazel was an innocent drawn to her Pop's bad boy persona vanished. She was worse than him!

Amy stayed another hour, finishing off the bag of sweets and working on the jigsaw puzzle with Pop and Hazel.

She drove home and collapsed onto the sofa, the headache that had been bugging her all day finally hitting with full force. In the kitchen, she gulped down two headache tablets and decided on an early night. She was already dreading work the following morning, which was an unusual feeling for her. She couldn't help thinking about Hazel. How wonderful the world must be when you had enough money to simply create the environment of your dreams.

CHAPTER SIX

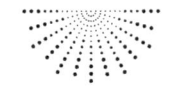

Rick drove out to Bondi that weekend and he and Amy decided to take a leisurely walk along the beach. When Amy had again offered to drive to his place, he'd vaguely suggested he had relatives staying with him so he preferred to get out. He didn't know the beach well and Amy was delighted to be the one to show it to him, this time in daylight.

They walked down the hill from Amy's apartment, stopping at her favourite ice-cream vendor on the way for double-scoops in waffle cones. Then they strolled hand-in-hand along the shoreline, heading from north to south.

Only minutes into their walk, Amy felt the sea air blowing the cobwebs from her head and the stress of the work week from her shoulders. "I can't wait to show you Icebergs."

"Is that that nice building down there?" He raised his chin toward it.

Amy nodded. It was her favourite pool and clubhouse in Sydney, and arguably also one of the busiest. From above, the ocean baths looked like a walled-off part of the sea, filled with crystal clear, aquamarine water. It was sea water, but it somehow looked even purer and more dazzling than the Pacific Ocean it bordered. It was Olympic-sized and overlooked by the beautiful white rendered-brick clubhouse. Amy was a member there, and filling out the paperwork had been one of the highlights of her move to Bondi.

"We going for a swim when we get there?" Rick asked. Amy looked up at him. He was wearing terrible sunglasses, the wraparound kind that Pop usually bought from the Cancer Council. Somehow, they suited him. Or he made them work. Amy was beginning to realise that one of the special things about Rick was his complete lack of self-doubt. He was shy, sure. But he wasn't seeking anyone's approval. He wore whatever the hell he wanted, and he wore it with his shoulders squared. Much like Marley. Rick knew what he brought to the world, and Amy liked his blend of confidence without arrogance. It was a rare trait.

"I didn't bring my swimming costume," Amy said. "And sadly, it's the kind of place where nudity is frowned upon."

"Oh, one of *those* places, huh?"

Amy laughed. "Do you swim much?"

"Not really. I mean, I can, of course. But I grew up pretty far inland, so I was late to the party. Do you?"

Amy nodded. "Not a ton recently, I've been too stressed with work. But an early morning swim makes me feel so grounded. It's been way too long since I did that, now that we talk about it."

"What's happening at work?"

Amy sighed, crunching into the last of her waffle cone. "Competition, I guess."

"Isn't that supposed to be good?"

"Argh. Maybe if you're competitive." She grinned. "I'd

rather just be the top cat and not have to worry about anything else, to be honest."

"That sounds kinda boring if you ask me. Someone challenging you and trying to bring out the best in you... I think *that's* inspiring."

"Well, I *didn't* ask you." Amy shoved him playfully. "And it sounds like I need to challenge you to a swimming contest then."

"Oh yeah? You think you could beat me?" He stopped in the sand, gripping Amy's hand so that she had to stop too. He had a huge smile on his face.

"Pssht," Amy scoffed. "I thought we were talking about *competition*." Before she could say anything else, Rick started dragging her by the hand into the water. "No!" she cried, laughing. "I'm not dressed for it!"

"You didn't specify terms!" He grabbed her around the waist and lifted her off the sand. She squealed as he waded up to his knees, holding her above the water. The sea was calm, but the waves were still licking up at her feet. She was wearing a vintage sundress and thongs, nothing that could get completely ruined if she really did get wet...

"Okay, first one to stop swimming loses," Amy said, jumping down from his arms. She pulled her thongs off and tossed them towards the sand, diving under a shallow wave. She'd forgotten about her sunglasses, which pushed hard up against her nose with the pressure of the dive. She stood up again, tucked them into her sundress pocket and burst into freestyle.

She'd only done about ten strokes when she heard Rick calling her name as she turned her head for air. She turned, treading water as she looked back at him. He was still standing where she'd left him, laughing.

"Come back!" he called, beckoning her with his arm. "I

was only kidding. You're insane," he added, once she was back by his side. He slipped an arm around her waist and pushed strands of wet hair from her face, bending to kiss her.

A second before his lips pressed hers, Amy drew her head back, out of reach. "I'm the top cat," she said. "Say it."

He smiled, and then pulled her even closer. "You're the top cat," he murmured into her ear, kissing her as waves broke around them.

They took a rain-check on the trip to Icebergs and went back uphill to Amy's place so she could shower and change. She wrapped herself in her fluffiest bathrobe, leaving her hair wet and her face makeup free. She couldn't remember a time she'd ever felt comfortable letting people see her like that. Even her best friends had rarely seen her this way.

When she padded into the living room in her fluffy slippers, she found Rick standing in front of the games section of her floor-to-ceiling, custom-made bookshelf. He tapped a huge bucket, looking like a kid in a candy shop. "Is that full of Lego?"

"What gave it away?" she replied, grinning. The lid was shaped like a huge piece of Lego.

"Can we play?"

"No one ever asks me that!"

She plonked herself down beside him on the carpet and emptied out the bucket.

Rick immediately picked up a base plate and started building. "I haven't built Lego stuff since I was a kid. I used to spend *hours* at it."

"It's kind of addictive, isn't it?" Amy grabbed a base and began, as she always did, to make a room. "Most of it is house and city type stuff. I love playing around with the layouts of the little houses. It's so much easier than in real life."

Rick looked up at her with an excited expression on his face. "Man, I wish this was my job."

Amy laughed. "But that more or less *is* your job, isn't it?" He smiled vaguely, but didn't answer. "Shall we order takeout and do this all evening?" Amy asked, selecting a tiny table and chairs from the rubble.

Rick nodded, beaming. Amy watched him as he hunted for the perfect piece to add to his creation. More things to like about him: his child-like sense of wonder and his spontaneity. She couldn't remember ever having this much fun with a guy before.

"Shall I stay here tonight?" he asked later, as they sat cuddled up on the sofa. Amy paused the TV and shifted to look up at him in surprise.

"What about your relatives?"

Rick's eyes widened. "Oh, they're pretty self-sufficient."

"You don't want to see them? You've already been away from them most of the day."

He avoided her gaze. "We're not really close or anything. But you're right, I should probably go."

"You know you could have asked me to come out to you," she said slowly, "I'd have liked to meet them."

Rick paused. "I just wanted you all to myself, that's all."

"You've had me all to yourself since we met." Amy was blindly groping her way through some emotions that were new to her. Namely, the desire to know more about Rick. To fit him into the picture of his life, surrounded by the things and people he was with when not with her. It was a somewhat frightening feeling - she was used to pushing guys away after the second date.

"That's what it's usually like when two people first meet," Rick said, a slight edge to his voice.

"All I'm saying is that I haven't met a single other person in your life. You didn't even introduce me to the guys you were with the night we met. You met my friends."

"I came over to you," he pointed out, "and by the time we went to leave, my friends were gone. Besides, it's not like I've met many other people in your life. You didn't officially invite me to your stepdad's piano thing."

Amy bit her lip. He had a point, but it was still bothering her that he barely even spoke about his life when he was away from her. There were anecdotes, of course, but they usually talked about other things, or he listened to her. It struck her now how odd that was, and she wondered why she hadn't noticed it before. Then again, maybe she was coming across as needy. The last thing she wanted was to push him away with any clinginess.

"I knew you were busy," she said, biting her lip. "Anyway, trust me. I did you a favour."

"And I'm doing you a favour now, with my relatives." He took her hand and looked earnestly at her. "Do you not want me to stay? Is that what this is about?"

Amy shook her head. "God no. I like you staying." She decided to drop the whole thing. "I don't want them to resent me. It'll be awkward when I meet them."

Rick's jaw muscle worked as he gazed at her intently. "No one could ever resent you." He ran his hand down her cheek and then leaned and kissed her so tenderly that Amy tingled all over. Slowly, their kisses heated up, until she found herself pushing him backwards onto the sofa.

"Well, I guess that's settled then," he whispered in her ear and she grinned down at him. His heavy-lidded gaze made her blood hammer and she couldn't believe she'd tried to talk him out of staying over.

CHAPTER SEVEN

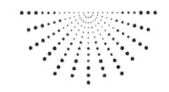

"Could you stop that?" Martha asked Amy, halfway through Wednesday.

"Stop what?" Amy asked, turning to look at her in surprise.

"You're heaving a huge sigh every couple of minutes and you've been doing it all week. I thought that one was going to blow a roof tile off."

Amy knew it was true. She trudged into the office each morning, plonking her bag on her desk and flopping into the chair. She felt ill-prepared for everything and wasn't sure why.

She forced herself to smile at Martha. "Sorry. I'll try to stop."

"Do we need a supply cupboard meeting?"

Martha and Amy often used the cupboard as a place to hold quick, private conferences, away from snooping ears and prying eyes.

Amy shook her head. "No, I just need to get my head in the game." She turned back to her computer. "I seem to have lost my mojo, and I have so many clients, I honestly don't even know where to start."

Martha winced. "I'm the same. I'm supposed to be part-time, but at the moment, the only thing part-time is my paycheck." She rolled her eyes and then something seemed to catch her attention over the other side of the office. She paled and looked at Amy in panicked concern.

"What?" Amy turned to follow her gaze. There, leading *Amy's* client through the office to one of the meeting rooms, was Kristina. "What the *hell*?" Amy said through gritted teeth, moving to stand up. Martha yanked her back down into her chair and jerked her head to indicate Beaumont, who was headed straight for Amy.

"Don't you cause a scene now." There was warning in his voice.

Amy's cheeks burned with indignation. What was Kristina doing with her client? Amy glared hotly at them and it took a moment before they caught her eye.

The client flushed, averting her eyes. Rebecca Evertree, owner of the Evertree bakery chain had been a loyal client of Amy's for over five years. Kristina didn't look the slightest bit abashed as she marched Rebecca through to a meeting room and shut the door.

"Gonna keep you on your toes, that Kristina," Beaumont said, slapping Amy on the back like they were pals on the golf course.

"Are you *seriously* going to let that happen?" Amy's voice shook. Everyone in the office was looking at her. Her heart pounded with humiliation.

"Looks like someone's out to steal old Amy's crown." Beaumont shrugged and walked off without a further word.

Amy turned to her screen and bit her lip hard, fighting tears. She wouldn't give everyone the satisfaction of letting them flow. She swallowed hard a few times, but forced herself to stay in her chair, pretending to work while struggling to get her breath and heart rate back to normal.

After a moment, Martha gently spoke. "You *did* say you had too many clients..."

Amy whipped her head to glare at her, but Martha's face was soft and sympathetic. Amy realised she was trying to take the sting out of the situation, so she choked back the threats she'd been about to issue and forced a smile instead.

"Fancy a drink this evening?" Martha asked, as they were getting ready to head home several hours later.

Amy considered for less than a second. "Sure, why not."

"Do you know the Whistle Stop?" Martha asked as they headed down to the parking garage.

"Know it?" Amy grinned. "I practically live there."

Amy and Martha slid into one of the vinyl booths near the entrance of the Whistle Stop, rather than sitting at one of the oak barrels. They felt it might be better for private conversation, and they both needed to let off steam.

"When did it get this bad?" Martha asked sadly, slumping her head into her hands.

Amy shook her head, trying to flag down a thin young barmaid who was pointedly ignoring them. "I don't know. I think it happened gradually. Maybe Beaumont's going senile."

Martha giggled, then her face fell again. "Seriously, it's beginning to feel unbearable. But I'm really hesitant to start looking for something else. There aren't that many part time jobs in this field."

"I know," Amy said sadly. A bartender wandered over to their table to take their order and Amy sighed inwardly when she realised it was Miles. He was relatively new to the Whistle Stop, and was supposed to be having a "thing" with Lyra. But Amy didn't like him for her best friend - didn't think he was good enough. She also suspected he preferred the attention he got from Lyra rather than the idea of actually being with her. It was all very frustrating.

"Hey, Annie," he said, beaming at them.

"Amy," she corrected bluntly.

"Right, right." His tone indicated he couldn't care less. "What can I get you?"

They ordered their drinks and Miles wandered away, veering off towards a table of young girls. Amy heard them giggling and narrowed her eyes.

"What's up with you and that guy?" Martha asked.

"He's supposed to be interested in my best friend."

"Oh," Martha said, and winced as she watched Miles openly flirting with the table of young girls. "Maybe he's after tips?"

"He's after something that rhymes with that," Amy said, and they giggled. She peeled her eyes off Miles and looked thoughtfully at Martha. "How are you going about drumming up the extra business Beaumont's asked us to?"

Martha's shoulders dropped. "Ugh. I haven't done anything about it yet. I don't even know how he thinks we can take more work on."

"That's exactly my point." Amy fished into her handbag and pulled out Loretta's business card. She'd started carrying it around with her; it had become something of a talisman.

"What's that?" Martha took the card as Amy held it out. "Loretta Goodman-Fife," she read, then raised her eyes to Amy. "Who's she?" She turned the card over. "It doesn't even say what she does."

"I met her at my stepdad's party. I think maybe she's loaded and has a few ventures running. Well, that would be my best guess based on most of Bill's friends," she added wryly. "That's just like a visitor card or something. She told me to look her up if I ever start my own business."

Martha's eyes bugged. "Are you thinking of doing that?"

"No." Amy shook her head, taking the card back and carefully tucking it into her handbag. "And I know I should probably call her and convince her to work with me at Edgerton's if she has clients who use interior designers… or if she does herself. But…"

"But what? Amy, we're all supposed to be bringing in new business. You have her card right there! That would get you major points with Beaumont."

"I know. But she specifically said to call her *if* I started my own thing. I don't want to hand her over to Beaumont. I probably wouldn't even get to work with her if I did."

Martha exhaled, gratefully taking the drink that arrived at that moment. "You're absolutely right. God, I used to love my job so much."

"Me too." Amy took a sip of her whisky.

"How did it come to this?"

Amy had no answer.

CHAPTER EIGHT

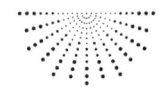

Rick smelt shower-fresh as he hugged Amy on arrival at her place the next night. Officially, this was only their fourth date, but that wasn't counting the endless phone calls and text messages they'd shared since meeting. It felt to Amy like they'd known one another much longer. She didn't say anything to Rick, but she'd realised today marked a month exactly since they'd met and she'd done a little cooking to celebrate.

Rick caught her as she all but jumped into his arms and they leaned up against the door, kissing deeply.

Amy was tingling as she led him to the sofa. "I'll be back in a second," she said.

She returned with a tray of bacon-wrapped dates, a little Spanish omelette and some grilled green *pimientos de Padrón* peppers. She set it down beside a small, beautifully-wrapped box on the coffee table that hadn't been there a moment ago.

"What's this?" Amy sank onto the sofa beside Rick. He shrugged as though he had no idea where the present had come from.

"Why am I getting a present?" She broke into a grin of delighted surprise.

"You should probably be given presents every day of your life." He traced a finger down her cheek. "But I'm a mere pauper. Once a month shall have to do."

"It's been exactly a month since we met. I know that, I just didn't know we would celebrate with presents. I cooked, but I feel like a horrible girlfriend because-"

"You said it!" Rick yelled triumphantly, cutting her off and standing up to clap like he was at a football match. "You said girlfriend!"

Amy rolled back on the couch, laughing and covering her eyes. "No! I didn't! I didn't!"

"Ohhhh, yes you did," he said when she peeped through her fingers. "You admitted it first. That makes me top cat."

"Okay, well *fine*." She grinned up at him. "I said it. What are you going to do about it?"

"What am I going to *do* about it?" he asked, manoeuvring himself so that he was on top of her on the sofa, easily holding a plank position. Her wrists were gently pinned in his grip. "Oh, I'll show you what I'm going to do about it."

He lowered himself to plant a delicate kiss into the crook of Amy's neck and she shivered.

"What else?"

"She's greedy, this one."

"Insatiable."

"This is what else." He slowly planted tiny kisses all around her neck and across her jaw and cheek.

"What else?" Amy whispered, her heart hammering in her chest as he lifted himself back up and looked at her.

Rick slowly lowered himself back down and stayed there, the gift forgotten.

Later in the evening, as they flicked through her streaming services for something to watch, Amy remembered the perfectly wrapped little gift box.

"Oh my God." She sprang up to get it. "I can't believe I forgot."

She was wearing her dressing gown and marvelled once again at how completely and utterly relaxed she felt in Rick's company. It really was a kind of heaven to spend time with him and she'd never felt so deeply, so quickly about someone before.

"You really didn't have to get me anything." Amy kissed the tip of his nose.

"Of course I got you something!" His close-cropped hair was sticking up at the top from where Amy had run her hands through it, and he was wearing a pair of cosy track pants he'd left at her place last time. His feet were up on the coffee table and he looked totally at home. "I'm not a Neanderthal."

"I guess that makes me one then." Amy snuggled beside him on the sofa and opened the box slowly. Inside sat a beautiful enamel brooch of a red banksia. It was exquisite and incredibly thoughtful. Amy remembered having told them they were her favourite native flowers, but it had been an off-hand comment and she hadn't thought any more about it.

"It's absolutely beautiful," she gasped, immediately pinning it to her dressing gown. "I'm going to wear it with everything. Thank you so much, I love it!"

"You're welcome." His face was glowing with pleasure at her happiness.

Amy leaned in to kiss him and sighed contentedly as they hugged tightly.

They spent the rest of the evening watching *30 Rock* and

chatting, cuddled up in one another's arms. Amy's fingers kept straying to her new brooch, and a huge smile would break out again.

She realised with a jolt how late it had gotten. "Are you going to stay here tonight?"

He ran a hand down her arm, sending tingles into her stomach. "I've got a really early start tomorrow. I'd need to leave here around 4:30… would that bother you?"

Amy shook her head. "Not unless you expect me to be conscious and say goodbye. Is it the same build?"

"Hmmm."

"Is your company big?" she asked, trying tentatively for a little more detail about his life. Or the life he had when he wasn't with her.

"God, please don't make me talk about work." He dropped his head into his hands with a groan. "I hate discussing it."

"Sorry. I love talking about my work so I assumed…but everyone is different, I guess. I loved hearing the stories about the apprentice. I guess there's a lot of hazing that goes on for the poor thing."

"I never do anything mean!" She arched an eyebrow at him and he relented. "Okay, I *did* send him to the hardware store for striped paint once," he admitted.

Amy giggled. "I knew it. See? I don't really get why you don't talk much about it."

"Tell me more about your work." He slung his arm back over Amy's shoulder and faced her. She hit pause on the remote.

"Well, I had a client stolen yesterday."

"What? Like they were kidnapped?"

Amy threw her head back and laughed. "No. They've always worked with me and now it seems they're working with a new colleague instead."

"Oh." Rick frowned. "Does that mean you don't have enough work now?"

"Not exactly, I still have more than I can handle. It's the principle of the thing."

Rick nodded slowly. "I sort of get it. But did your colleague steal them on purpose?"

Amy screwed up her face. "I don't know. To be honest it wouldn't surprise me if this was something our boss did to stir things up."

"He sounds like a bit of a knob."

"He is," Amy agreed. "He really is."

She told Rick a few choice Beaumont stories and he shook his head as he listened, a frown knitting his brows together. "He sounds horrible. If it makes you feel any better, there's lots of politics where I work too. It's not only an office job thing."

"I guess it's everywhere," she conceded. "I've managed to avoid it until now."

"Well, if you want him taken care of, just give me the word." He winked.

She grinned. "Don't tempt me."

As she leaned into him and hit play on the remote again, there was a strange feeling in the pit of Amy's stomach. She wasn't entirely sure whether it was caused by thinking about Beaumont and Kristina, or by the fact that Rick seemed determined to avoid telling her more about his life.

An hour later, all doubts about Rick were gone from Amy's mind. When his arms were around her, when he stroked her hair so tenderly, when he listened to everything she said with complete and utter interest, when he'd spring off the sofa to get her water if she said her mouth was dry, when he looked at her the way he looked at her... Amy knew she was inventing problems where there were none.

As they prepared for bed, Amy hooked her dressing gown on the back of her wardrobe door, the brooch still pinned on. She ran her thumb over it, smiling.

"Do you really like it?" Rick asked, so uncertain and hopeful that Amy's heart surged.

"I honestly do." She hoped he knew it was true. "I love it, and I'll treasure it. It will go with so many things in my wardrobe."

"I thought that too." He paused, as though deciding whether or not to say something. "Look, I'm sorry I don't like to talk about work."

"Oh, it's fine." Amy waved her hand dismissively. "But if you ever do want to talk about it, I'm all ears and I'm genuinely interested."

He nodded slowly, staring at her with an unreadable expression on his face. She smiled and turned to leave for the bathroom.

"Hey," he said, and she turned back to face him. He still had that expression on his face.

"What is it?"

He opened his mouth and closed it a few times, but nothing came out. Then he shook his head, giving her a sheepish smile. "Nothing," he said finally. "I wanted to say thanks. That's all."

CHAPTER NINE

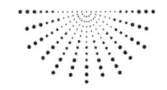

A few weeks later, Amy found herself with a different problem. It was the Monday following Lyra's gig at Rusty's pub - the gig Amy had encouraged Lyra to book posing as her own manager - and which turned into an unmitigated disaster. A huge fight broke out after the first set when a rowdy group of drunken men had kicked off at one another.

Three people had ended up in hospital. One of them was a barmaid from the pub who'd broken her leg. The other was one of the idiot group of men who'd started the punch-up in the first place. They'd been rowdy from the moment everyone had arrived and had seemed eager for a chance to cause a fight. The third was Mick, Lyra's keyboard player - a grizzled rocker of an older man who was more or less a father to Lyra. He'd thankfully been released the following day, only kept in for observation.

The pub itself was a different story, one that Amy was afraid to hear about. She'd left with Rick shortly after the incident, driving Lyra to the hospital to check on Mick. So she hadn't had a chance to see the extent of the damage to

Rusty's pub. She knew she needed to call her uncle and check what she could do to help, or maybe even just let him vent. She'd given him all day Sunday to get his blood pressure back to normal and hopefully stop cursing her name. But she was still having some trouble dialling his number...

Amy spent an entire hour taking deep breaths and pacing her flat, knowing she was going to be late for work. Finally she snatched up the phone and dialled Rusty's number.

"Uncle Rusty. How bad is it?" she asked as soon as he answered.

He was silent for a long moment. "It's not *as* bad as you might be thinking. But it's bad. I'm going to have to pay a worker's comp claim for Michelle, the one who broke her leg, not to mention being short-staffed while she recovers. We lost a lot of glassware and one table, and there's actually a hole in the floor we're going to need repaired. I have no idea how that happened."

Amy slowly let her breath out. She'd been expecting much, much worse. "I'm so sorry, Uncle Rusty. Is there anything I can do to help?"

"Insurance is going to cover some of it, but I'll lose my no claim bonus of course. However," he added, "it doesn't seem to have been *entirely* bad for publicity. Someone filmed me breaking up one of the fights and your cousin tells me I'm going viral as 'Pub Hero'."

Amy laughed. "I'll have to try and find the video! So you don't want to kill me?"

"Nah, love," Rusty said. "It wasn't your fault. I don't think I'll have Lyra and Mick in here again though, if it's all the same to you. Might need a word with that Margot lady who booked 'em."

Amy's pulse began to gallop. "Oh, I can talk to her," she offered quickly. "And don't worry, I think Lyra will understand that she can't play there again! She's sorrier than you can imagine, Uncle Rusty."

"Ah," he said, softening. "Don't let her get hung up on it. She didn't cause it!"

They chatted a few more minutes and by the time Amy hung up the phone, she felt reassured. She was also praying the whole debacle wasn't a bad omen for Margot's future.

She couldn't help feeling slightly irritated with Lyra though. She knew her friend was sorry about everything that had happened, and it absolutely hadn't been her fault, but still... Lyra hadn't reached out to Rusty at all, and hadn't followed up with Amy to ask how things had worked out. She'd even sent her older brother Silas over to collect her and Mick's equipment, not bothering to turn up herself. Amy knew Lyra wasn't doing these things on purpose, but she was still a little annoyed. Surely Lyra knew what a pickle the whole thing had put Amy in.

One positive thing had come of the evening, at least as far as Amy was concerned. She'd had a chance to meet Alex, a guy who was most definitely interested in Lyra, and who Amy thought would be a much better choice for her best friend than Miles.

Alex had not only turned up to watch Lyra sing, which was more than Amy could say for Miles, he'd also appeared at the hospital to make sure she was doing okay after the brawl.

Amy knew Lyra had been afraid that Alex was trying to put her and her brother Silas out of business. The siblings ran a popular pie truck along the Lilac Bay shoreline - not too far from Amy's office - and Alex had suddenly appeared beside them with a rival food truck. Poor Lyra and Silas had been through a horrible time a year earlier, when escalating tensions with another vendor had caused them to flee their previous spot in the city. But one look at Alex, and Amy had known he wouldn't hurt a hair on Lyra's head. In fact, quite the opposite...

She hoped Lyra could see that too. She always wanted the best for her friend, even when she was irritated with her.

Amy was still full of adrenaline from the call to her uncle when she walked into work. Kristina immediately approached her, a determined look on her face, and asked whether Amy was free for lunch.

"Uh..." Amy stalled, setting her bag on her desk and frowning. Maybe Kristina had an explanation for what had happened with Evertree and she should hear her out.

"Amy and I have plans," Martha said curtly, spinning to glare at Kristina before Amy could respond.

"I'd like to explain-"

"I'm free!" Kyle piped up eagerly from beside Martha.

"Sure, whatever." From the corner of her eye, Amy saw Kristina shrug as Kyle's face lit up. Once Kristina was gone, Martha glared at Kyle.

"What? She's the *wunderkind*."

Martha and Amy groaned in unison and Amy shot Martha a look of gratitude. She knew it likely wasn't Kristina's fault about Evertree and she resolved to hear her out sooner or later. But not today. It wasn't easy, being knocked off Beaumont's pedestal.

Rick called that night as Amy was painting her toenails and nervously asked whether she wanted to go away for a spontaneous long weekend with him. Amy's heart went haywire, imagining three glorious days with Rick all to herself, and she eagerly agreed.

"Where shall we go?"

Rick was coy and said she'd have to wait and see.

Amy was grinning as she emailed Beaumont the next day, informing him she'd be taking a personal day on the following Monday. She could easily have taken the ten steps into his office to tell him face-to-face as she usually did, but she was avoiding him after the Evertree incident.

With the email sent, Amy launched into a charm campaign with her clients. She called each and every one of them and held long, bubbly conversations as she checked whether they had any projects coming up, whether they'd think of her if they did, whether they had any feedback they wanted to give her. She was relieved when they all emphatically confirmed they loved her work and used her exclusively. She also spent time in the evenings secretly stalking Kristina on Instagram, terrified she'd accidentally hit the little heart button on one of her rival's pictures. Kristina's following was fairly large. It was odd that Amy hadn't heard of her before and she briefly wondered whether Kristina had heard of *her*. Amy had been profiled a few times in design magazines and was often called up by journalists for online platforms, to be the "design guru" in articles with names like *Five Ways to Cheer Up a Rental without Losing your Bond*.

Kristina's style was the complete opposite of Amy's - lots of clashing patterns and chaotic colour schemes that somehow all came together. Amy found her work strikingly original, though it had taken her half a bottle of wine to admit that even to herself.

The calls to clients took an emotional toll and by Friday, Amy was completely drained. The long weekend with Rick couldn't have come at a better time.

CHAPTER TEN

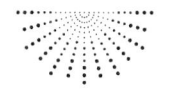

Rick picked Amy up early the next morning and they ate junk food and sang road trip songs the whole two hour drive to their long weekend destination. When Rick pulled up outside their hotel, Amy turned to him, open-mouthed. She realised she'd been half-expecting something terrible, like a hiking trip or a cabin with no Wi-Fi and lots of horseback riding.

What she hadn't been expecting was Hotel D'Montvue. It was an expansive cream-coloured building, only two storeys high but spread in a wide, square U shape against the backdrop of the majestic Blue Mountains. It looked as though it might have served as cloisters at some point in history. The lawn was manicured to a deep emerald green - the kind of grass that made Amy want to run across it barefoot or sink into it for a nap. Or at least it would, if it wasn't so cold.

"How did you find this place?" she asked, her eyes wide with delight.

"A buddy of mine stayed here a few weeks ago with his

missus." Rick looked pleased by her reaction. "I thought we could try it out."

"I get a whole three days here?"

"You do."

"And what will you do?" Amy chuckled at her own joke.

Rick swatted her. "Just for that, you can carry your own suitcase."

She feigned a wounded look and he resisted for all of a second before pulling her close for a kiss. As it deepened, Amy lost all sense of time and place, melting into him until they both heard a crisp rap at the window. They sprang apart and Amy hid her face in her hands as Rick cleared his throat and pressed the button to roll down the window.

"Hi?" Rick was slightly out of breath but admirably pretended to have no clue why a uniformed hotel worker would be banging on their window.

"Shall I park the car for you, Sir?" the man asked politely.

"Thank you." Rick rolled the window back up, then turned to Amy and they giggled like schoolchildren.

As they handed their luggage to the porter, Amy looked at their gear. She had packed her vintage cognac leather suitcase and it contrasted with Rick's beat up khaki duffel, the kind Amy had seen in army surplus stores. But then, their whole look contrasted.

Amy was dressed in a midi-length, belted floral dress with three-quarter sleeves and a deep v neckline. Her hair was in finger waves and she wore rose-coloured kitten heels that matched her jacket. Rick was dressed in a plain cotton button-down shirt tucked into greyish slacks. All perfectly neat and tidy, clean and crisp. But it was almost like a uniform for him.

Amy found herself wondering whether over time, if they stayed together as she hoped they would, Rick would change his sense of style and dress so that they fit together more, visually. She wondered whether it would bother her if he didn't, and stole a sideways look at him as they entered the hotel.

Objectively speaking, he might not have been the most handsome guy in the world. But he was tall and *very* well built and there was something about his face that grew more beautiful the longer she knew him. He flashed her a quick smile that showed his dimple, and grabbed her hand. Her heart banged against her ribcage and she realised right there and then that even if he wore nothing but head to toe form-fitting lycra, he'd still be the one she wanted. He'd still be able to melt her with a single look.

In their room, Amy walked directly to the huge bay window opposite the bed and yanked back the filmy curtains.

"Whoa," she breathed.

The view from their room, in the back of the hotel, could not have been more different from the front. It seemed the hotel was built right on the edge of the escarpment. From here, the world appeared to drop away below their balcony, before scooping through the low, deep slope and back up one mountain and the next and the next until they all overlapped in the distance, as far as the eye could see. The trees changed colour from golden up close to a rich green in the middle ground and finally to their signature blue - the effect of eucalyptus vapour mixing with the atmosphere. The mountains were bare and craggy in places, the exposed basalt outcrops looking gilded as the light hit them.

Amy moved from the bay window and slid the door open to take in the view from the large balcony. She leaned onto the railing and breathed in the air, so different from the salt of the sea or the fumes of the city. Rick stepped onto the deck behind her. A moment later he snaked his arms around her waist and rested his chin on her shoulder.

Amy sighed with contentment and leaned back against him. "This view is incredible."

"You should see my view," he growled suggestively.

She giggled, turning to face him as she reached her arms up around his neck.

"Seriously," she whispered, "This is totally amazing and I couldn't love it more."

"I know it isn't the fanciest hotel," he began, a note of insecurity creeping into his voice. "I'm sure you've been taken to better places…" Amy's heart surged. He was worried it wasn't good enough. She stood on tiptoe to cut him off with a long, lingering kiss.

"Ricky, it's *perfect,*" she said, when they finally broke apart. She looked him in the eye. "I'm sorry if I haven't made this abundantly clear to you. Whatever you do is more than enough. You *never* need to worry about that. Ever."

Rick tore his eyes away from her and looked into the distance, his jaw muscle working. Amy knew he was struggling with his emotions and didn't push. When he finally looked back at her, he nodded once and smiled.

"You've convinced me." He reached to tuck a strand of hair behind her ear, his hands radiating with warmth. Then he shook his head, letting out a short exhale. "I have no idea how in the world I got this lucky."

"You walked up to me at the Whistle Stop." Amy shrugged and made a cute face. "You coulda been anyone!"

He grinned, and then in one motion swept her off her feet and into his arms. Amy squealed, feeling light as a feather as she kicked her heels off. She wrapped her arms around Rick's neck and buried her face in his chest as he carried her back inside the room and tossed her gently onto the bed.

"We're going to miss our massages!" Rick said, sitting up in alarm sometime later. Amy stretched and rolled onto her stomach, propping herself up on her elbows to look at him.

"There are *massages?*"

"Yep. And the day after tomorrow," he booped her nose with his index finger, "we're going skydiving!"

Amy tilted her head. "Oh really?" She didn't believe a word but decided to play along. "We're going skydiving? That's cool."

He exhaled. "Is it? I was kind of worried how you'd react." He grimaced.

"Wait. Are you serious?" Amy sat up. "Did you book for us to go skydiving for real?"

He nodded, biting his lip and frowning at her in concern. "Is it too much? I should have asked, right? I should have asked."

Amy eyeballed him.

"Make up your mind if you're going to hit me or kiss me," he said, reading her mind. He stepped out of the bed and strolled towards the bathroom. "We need to be at the spa in twenty minutes for those massages!"

Amy followed him into the bathroom, dragging the whole sheet with her and clasping it together behind her back.

"Richard Ford! Did you seriously volunteer me to jump to my death without running it by me first? I would have said goodbye to my Pop! I would have called Lyra. Oh my God, Lyra. What will she do without me?"

Rick laughed as he turned on the shower, the water fizzing over his muscular body. He winked at Amy and then pulled the curtain across. "She's got Marley and Silas." He raised his voice over the noise of the shower. "She'll be fine!"

Amy stood silently for a moment, shaking her head and

then her fist at the curtain. She was terrified at the idea of jumping out of a plane, but she had to admit, she was also a little excited. It wasn't *pure* horror. It definitely wasn't the kind of thing she would ever have booked on her own initiative, but now that someone had done it for her... Well, if she was honest, she didn't totally hate the plan.

"You could at least have booked the massages for *after* the jump," she sniffed. "My shoulders are going to be up around my ears until I land back on solid ground!"

Rick peeped his head out from behind the shower curtain. "We have massages booked for every day we're here, Ames," he said, like it was obvious. "Do you *really* think I don't know my own woman?"

"Hmph." Amy fought to keep a smile off her face. Then she grinned and tugged back the shower curtain. "Make room for me in there."

Amy opened her eyes before Rick was awake the next morning, nestling herself into the curve of his body and putting her hand on his chest to feel it rise and fall. His whole body was muscular, firm, taut. She'd never dated anyone as brawny as him before. His size made her feel delicate and she loved the feeling of his huge, powerful hands on her. Her breath quickened as she thought about the night before. She was full of pleasant aches, and she half-expected to find scorch marks on their bedsheet.

"Morning," he mumbled, eyes still closed.

"How did you know I was awake?"

"You're breathing heavy." He wrapped an arm around her and pulled her closer. "It's super creepy."

They laughed and Amy lay still for a moment, locked in

his tight embrace, breathing in the heavenly scent of him. "Rick?"

"Mmmh?"

"I was thinking about having a little party. To introduce my friends to your friends. What do you think?"

Amy felt his body stiffen and he opened his eyes, frowning at her. The questions hung in the air for a long time. Far too long.

"You don't think it's a good idea?" she prompted finally.

"It's a great idea." His cheery tone was clearly forced. He ran a hand down her arm and goosebumps broke out where he touched her. She moved her arm away, not wanting to be distracted.

"But?"

He sighed and rolled onto his back. "Ames, my mates are rowdy. Remember that fight at your Uncle Rusty's? Like that but maybe louder."

"Your friends are Neanderthals who couldn't even go one night without putting each other in the hospital?"

"No!" He laughed and it rang hollow. He rolled onto his side, head propped on elbow. "Why don't you come out to my place or something? Meet them first."

"I'd love to. I've never been invited. I don't even know who you live with."

His brow furrowed. "It's not some big conspiracy or anything. I know we talked about this before, but it's not like I've met your mum yet or anything."

"I'm not talking about my mum. I'm talking about my girlfriends - who you *have* met, several times - and your mates. A little mixer."

"They're hard to pin down, is all."

"Then we send out invites well in advance, tell them to block a Saturday night."

"Saturdays are hard. I mean, we all only really only get together then for camping trips and stuff."

"Even your flatmates? Even Deacon?" Amy mentioned the one friend she'd heard him refer to a couple of times. "When do you all see one another then?"

He propped himself up on his elbow, watching her carefully. "Ames, where's this coming from?"

Her heart was beating heavily. She'd asked him about the mixer as a kind of test. And he was failing. "I've said this to you before. I mean, do you think your friends won't like me or something? Or I won't like them?" She paused. "Are you ashamed of me?"

A look of horror crossed his face. "God, *no*. I swear to you, I will organise a week-long meet up when we get back. I'll parade every single friend I have in front of you. I'll... bring you home to have dinner with my mum. I'll take you to my dad's grave. I'll even let you meet my horrible brother. Just don't ever, *ever* think I'm ashamed of you."

She stared into his wide, earnest eyes for a moment, and felt the familiar flutter of desire. As though he could read her mind, he ran his hand lightly up her thigh and leaned in to plant small kisses along her hairline. It was suddenly very hard to remember why on earth she was wasting their precious vacation time arguing with him.

"Okay, okay," she relented softly, pulling him close. "I'll drop it. We can talk about the mixer another time."

"I'll mention it to them. The mixer is a great idea," he murmured, stroking her hair. "But you know what's an even better idea..."

CHAPTER ELEVEN

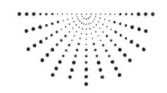

At eleven the next morning, Rick and Amy stood in the middle of a huge grassy field a half-hour's drive from the hotel. There was nothing around for miles besides a huge air hangar and a few parked cars - a fact Amy found very reassuring. Dreams of being snarled around a telephone pole, dangling precariously over a busy flow of traffic had haunted her sleep.

Their skydiving instructors and future tandem jump partners had come out into the field to greet them as they pulled up. Amy's was called Damien and they were struggling to get along.

"So, when I tap your shoulders like this, Amy," Damien briskly double-smacked the tops of her arms, "what do you do?"

"Kill him in cold blood?" She pointed at Rick, who snorted.

"No," Damien sighed, shaking his head. "You open your arms. That's the signal for the arch position-"

"And we're in free fall. Yes, I know." Amy resigned herself

to the fact that joking was obviously off the table with Damien.

Rick had sailed through the prep part of the morning and was already zipped into his flying overalls, clear goggles perched on his head. His tandem buddy, a tall, stocky man named Biff, of all things, had spent the whole of about 45 seconds "teaching" Rick. He'd disappeared somewhere shortly after, promising to be back in time for take-off, and Rick didn't seem the slightest bit concerned.

"What if Biff's off snorting drugs or something?" Amy asked Rick, while Damien went in search of some laminated pictures of their poses. He seemed not to believe that Amy had ever held her arms out or tucked her legs up before. Rick chuckled. "I'm *serious.*" Amy tugged on his sleeve. "The man's name is Biff. *Biff!* Not one sensible person has ever had that name."

Damien returned then, so Amy had to drop it. Rick watched on with amusement as Amy struggled with her instructor, who clearly didn't have a humorous bone in his body. Amy had imagined all skydivers as yahooing cowboys one sandwich short of a picnic, but Damien had smashed the mould into a thousand pieces. She thought he could easily have been mistaken for an accountant with his calm demeanour and neatly-combed hair. Amy wondered what his 'do would look like after the dive. Probably exactly the same. It was snap-on, Lego-piece perfection.

"Okay. When we're coming in for landing," Damien enunciated very carefully, "what do you do with your legs?" He tapped his finger on a picture of a person tucked up in a ball.

"I tuck them up," Amy answered with equal emphasis on each word.

Damien nodded and she could almost read his thoughts. *There's hope for this woman yet.*

"Amy, you are cleared for take-off." He gave her an enthusiastic thumbs up and grinned like he'd made a joke. Amy looked to Rick, who shrugged, and then she showed Damien her teeth. It was the closest she could get to laughing at his joke, after he'd ignored all hers. "Let's go and pick you a suit."

"Ooh. What are the colour choices?" Amy asked eagerly, following Damien towards the hangar that also held all the protective clothing as well as a tiny toilet that had probably suffered a very difficult life.

"Black. Or the colour Richard is wearing."

"Would you call that beige or boring?" Amy joked.

Damien shot her a confused look. "We usually refer to it as off-white."

Amy rolled her eyes at Rick, who shrugged again. If she *was* about to die on this skydive, she really didn't want to do it fastened to Damien.

"Can we swap buddies?" Amy whispered to Rick, dropping back to walk beside him as Damien powered onward.

"You want Biff?" Rick sounded surprised.

"I'd rather they jump together, actually, now that I think about it. Then we go."

"We would definitely die then."

"Oh, come on. It's not that hard. You just open your arms and tuck your legs." Amy grinned. "Damien even said there was an automated thingy on the chute in case he carks it mid-air."

"So you *were* listening!" Rick jabbed her playfully on the shoulder.

"Yes!" she whispered loudly. "Didn't you hear the man? *This gal*," she pointed two thumbs at her chest, "is cleared for take-off."

They laughed, although Amy's was mostly the nervous

kind. Rick was cool as a cucumber. Before they entered the hangar, Amy held up a finger to Rick to wait. She pulled her phone from her pocket - they were going to have to leave all belongings behind in a locker for the flight - and swiped to make a quick video for the chat group she had with Lyra, Marley and Silas.

"This may be my last message," she began in a serious voice. "Rick organised for us to go skydiving. I'm not sure exactly how long he's been planning to kill me, but if you don't hear from me again, please assume I am in a better place. Even though I'm probably not." She winked. "Go visit Percy often. Tell my mum I love her. And girls, you're responsible for making sure Rick doesn't move on too quickly. I want *grief*. Silas, you know what to do if that's not the case-"

Rick jumped into frame then and wrapped his arms around Amy, kissing her hard on the cheek. "She is being *such* a good sport about this." He beamed into the camera. "And she nailed it in training."

Amy burst out laughing and Damien stuck his head out of the hangar, frowning. She managed to get him slightly in frame as he called out. "Amy. Please come and select a flight suit."

"Duty calls, team." She gazed solemnly into the camera. "To infinity and beyond!" She made a peace sign and ended the video. Rick was shaking his head. "What?" she asked, clicking to send the video into the group.

"My girlfriend's an idiot."

"That's a coincidence!" Amy walked past him and slapped his bottom. "So's my boyfriend."

A my and Rick made the same jokes Damien and Biff must have heard a hundred times when they were readying for take-off.

"Why are we jumping out of a perfectly good plane?"

"At least if the plane crashes, we have parachutes. Hahaha."

"This is probably the only time we'll be okay if the engine fails."

Both men smiled and laughed along with Rick and Amy, allowing them their nerves.

"Where's the door?" Amy asked, as the engine started up and the propeller cranked to life. "No, really. Where's the door?"

The side of the plane was completely open and as they bumped off down the runway and no one answered Amy's question, she realised they were simply going to fly like that. She reached over to grip the metal rail that ran the length of the plane for dear life, terrified she was going to be sucked out.

Once the plane had gained some altitude, Rick tried to say something to Amy, but she couldn't hear him over the roar of the propeller, the rush of the air and the pulse of blood in her ears. Damien knelt behind her, fiddling and clicking and snapping.

Rick was looking at her in genuine concern for the first time since he'd had this idea. He crawled over to her and shouted in her face.

"You don't have to do this!"

"Now you tell me!" she screamed back.

Biff reached forward and tapped Rick on the shoulder, jerking his thumb towards the open side of the plane - it was time for them to do their jump. They'd agreed Rick would be the first to go. Rick leaned forward to kiss Amy, struggling to get his arms between her and Damien for a hug. The blasting wind whipped her hair around and over his face.

As Amy re-tightened her hair into a bun, Biff fastened himself to Rick - securing, tightening and double-checking all the straps. One look at Biff's focused face told Amy she needn't ever have worried about his conscientiousness. He looked born to do this.

She locked her eyes on Rick's as he and Biff shuffled to the open side of the plane, and Rick tore his eyes from her as they got closer to the exit. They turned to line up with the edge of the plane and Biff's position blocked Rick from Amy's view. Rick held his arms out wide and gave her a thumbs up, and then the two of them tipped straight out of the plane and out of sight. Amy gasped and squeezed her eyes shut. Her heart was hammering against her ribcage, she was struggling to get her breath under control and her hands were slicked with sweat.

So this is what it feels like to know you're going to die. The thought looped through Amy's brain on repeat.

A moment later, it was Damien and Amy shuffling low on the floor towards the open side of the plane. Amy slipped her goggles down over her eyes and adjusted them as she thought about how what they were about to do contravened every natural impulse in the human body, every survival urge.

They were completely mad and, if she landed safely, she would definitely be making good on her promise to murder Rick.

Damien reached forward and squeezed both her hands. She squeezed them back and then he let go and it was as simple as tipping forward, taking her with him. Amy closed her eyes and screamed louder than she ever had before in her life, amazed that she could still barely hear herself. She found the weightlessness sickening, especially because the air pushing into her mouth, flapping her cheeks around and bellowing past her ears told her they were plummeting toward earth at breakneck speed.

Damien tapped her shoulders and she faintly registered that she was supposed to do something. He tapped again and without thinking, Amy opened her arms into a T shape.

She finally closed her mouth, opening her eyes to a nauseating sight. The farmland all around the jump zone looked like a green patchwork quilt from this height. Entire pastures were no bigger than her palm, stitched together at odd angles as ant-cars drove past ant-houses on a crayon doodle of a road. And it was all rushing up at them so quickly.

After the first shock of terror was over, a strange sense of calm came over Amy. She felt Damien reassuringly strapped to her back, keeping them steady as they plummeted towards the earth. The howling of the wind stopped feeling so dangerous and she concentrated on the sensation of weightlessness. It was no longer sickening, it was somehow magical. Amy was already positive this would be the first and last time she did something like this, so she resolved to try and enjoy it.

She felt Damien wave off and knew then that they were reaching five thousand feet and he was about to deploy the parachute. It popped up and Amy felt her full weight for a split second as they jerked to a complete halt in the air.

"Oh my God," she gasped, letting out a high-pitched, manic laugh.

"It's something else, isn't it?" Damien asked joyfully from behind her. She could see his hands on either side of her, holding the chute strings.

"I guess you could say that!"

The world was suddenly eerily silent but for the quick, rhythmic flap of the wind rippling the edges of the parachute. She could have heard a mouse sneeze back on earth. Below them, Rick was coming in to land. The green quilt patches were slowly getting bigger, and Damien pulled first one string, turning them gently in a wide arc to the left, and then the other. He tugged both at once and they hung for a second, completely suspended in the air.

"You want to try?"

She took the ropes, feeling brave. They were heavier and harder to manoeuvre than she had anticipated and she struggled with them for a few seconds, terrified she'd lose her grip and kill them both. Damien didn't remove his hands completely until Amy had gotten the hang of it. She worked up the courage to try turning them in large, slow circles. She started to whoop with joy and Damien chuckled at her enthusiasm.

"That's one of the biggest mood turnarounds I've ever seen!"

He took the reins back as they prepared to come in for landing. The ground rushed up quicker than Amy expected and she tucked her legs up high as Damien pelted along the grass once they made contact. Amy could hear the parachute sighing and relaxing behind them and soon Damien was unclipping her. As soon as she was free, she was running unsteadily toward Rick who was jogging in her direction. They both had grins spread from ear to ear.

Rick caught Amy and spun her in a huge circle. She could feel him shaking with exhilaration as he gripped her tightly.

"I can't wait to do that again!" he yelled, and Amy clung to him.

"I am not doing that again, not even if you give me a million years to get over it."

He pulled back and looked at her face. "Did you hate it? Did you really hate it?"

"No! I actually kind of loved it. But I don't want to do it

again. Not ever!" She let out the same anxious laugh she had earlier and it came out sounding like machine gun fire. It was a noise Amy didn't feel completely in control of. It made Rick chuckle and soon they were both doubled-over, gasping for breath as they laughed. Amy had never felt closer to another person than at that moment.

CHAPTER TWELVE

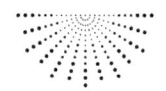

Amy's glow from the weekend away disappeared at exactly 9am on Tuesday morning, when she walked back into the office. She felt a surge of gratitude to Rick for so thoroughly taking her mind off things with the mini-break that she'd almost managed to forget she had a job.

She was planning on meeting Lyra and Marley at the Whistle Stop after work for a few drinks, though she was tired from the weekend. She couldn't wait to fill the girls in on everything that had happened. The hours at work seemed to drag by and she was pondering ways to sneak out early, when Beaumont spontaneously called another yachting meeting. She and Martha discreetly rolled their eyes at one another and reluctantly headed to the boardroom. Beaumont stood at the front, pressing his hands together in a steeple gesture. He caught Amy's eye as she took a seat and smirked. Her stomach dropped.

"Thanks, everyone. I've pulled you in here for a quick but important announcement. Kristina, would you come to the front?"

Instantly, Amy knew the announcement would be about Evertree, the client Kristina had possibly stolen. Beaumont wanted to rub Amy's nose in something. She took some deep, bracing breaths and plastered a smile on her face, determined to keep it there no matter what.

Kristina looked reluctant to be called up. She stood beside Beaumont, her cheeks pink and her eyes fixed on the floor.

"Evertree has announced a huge expansion and a massive refresh of their interiors across all existing branches. This is a considerable piece of work, and I'm delighted to announce that they've put Kristina in the lead! Round of applause." Beaumont turned to Kristina and kicked off the clapping.

The rest of the company slowly followed. Kristina kept her eyes glued to the ground, as Amy's colleagues cast puzzled glances at her, knowing that Evertree had been her account. But no one was applauding more loudly and enthusiastically than Amy herself. She hoped they couldn't see through her facade and that her feigned joy might even make them think she'd been the one to suggest the account change. It was unlikely, but if Amy was ever going to win an Oscar, it was for the performance she gave in the boardroom that day.

She forced herself to stay glued in her seat the rest of the afternoon and made a show of seeming engrossed in her work. She even managed to be witheringly polite to Beaumont when he stopped by her desk later that afternoon to ask an unrelated question.

Since Beaumont had made a huge fuss over Kristina and Evertree, something Amy had never seen him do before, she was now almost positive that he'd been the one to give Evertree to Kristina, rather than Kristina having deliberately stolen the client.

She held it together until she left the office and was on her way to the Whistle Stop. Once she'd parked near the bar, Amy allowed herself a little breakdown. For exactly five minutes, she let the tears flow. Then she wiped them away, reapplied her makeup and fixed her hair.

She dialled Rick and he picked up right away.

"Miss me already?" he joked, but his tone switched to concern as she struggled against fresh tears. "Ames, what's wrong?"

She leaned back against the headrest. "I had a crappy day. My boss was being a jerk."

"Don't let him get you down," Rick said fiercely. "You have more clients than you can work with. And you told me you're the most requested designer he has. Nothing can take that away from you."

Amy let out a shaky breath. "You're right," she said, "I have a perfect track record over six years."

"Exactly. Plus, my offer still stands to get rid of him if you tell me," he joked.

Amy laughed. "Thank you, Rick. I needed to hear that. I mean the bit about how good I am. Well, actually, *and* the bit about you taking care of Beaumont."

Inside the Whistle Stop, Miles the creepy bartender made a beeline for Lyra, getting both Marley and Amy's names wrong - again, in Amy's case. Lyra smiled pleasantly as she gently corrected him and Amy felt a prick of irritation at her friend for being so eager to please.

As they waited for their drinks, Amy filled them in on some of the choicer details of her getaway with Rick. But she found she didn't have the energy to do the trip justice and instead the conversation drifted around to work - where Amy's mind was stuck. She told the girls about Kristina now, choosing her words carefully to cover the embarrassment of Beaumont giving away her client.

"Maybe your colleague can do something for Silas and I," Lyra said thoughtfully, "our place could seriously use some styling."

Amy felt like she'd been whipped. "You've *never* asked me to do that for you. Why would you ask a random stranger and not one of your best friends? Isn't my work good enough?" She was taken aback at the anger in her voice, more so when Lyra looked mortified. Amy tried to keep her blood pressure down, reminding herself it had only been an off-handed comment. But it wasn't just Lyra's remark that was bothering her - she was still miffed about the way Lyra had handled the aftermath of the gig at her Uncle Rusty's pub. Lyra still hadn't brought it up again, or offered to somehow make things right, and Amy knew she should have a private conversation with her friend about it. She didn't have the headspace right now.

Miles arrived at the table carrying a tray of random drinks, confidently acting as though they were what the girls had ordered. Lyra was determined to cover up his mistake, gratefully taking the drinks from him and all but forcing Amy and Marley to do the same. Amy felt her irritation at her friend rising again. Why was she squashing and bending herself around this guy?

"Who's singing tonight?" Amy asked Miles. Her question was calculated. The Whistle Stop often featured live music and Miles was in charge of booking the singers. They were inevitably pretty young things with limited talent. He had yet to offer Lyra an appearance, despite the fact he knew she wanted one, and despite the fact he was supposedly romantically interested in her.

Miles mentioned some other young female singer, one

who was making "avant garde" music. Marley commented on the fact that Miles always seemed to choose beautiful young women to sing and Lyra's face fell.

"Thanks, Marley," she snapped when Miles left the table. "For being so rude that you chased him away."

"How on earth was she rude?" Amy asked. "You're being ridiculous about him. You should see yourself, bending over backwards. It's embarrassing. What is happening to you?"

Lyra's face was burning and Amy regretted the words as soon as they were out. She didn't feel completely in control of her emotions tonight. She took some deep breaths and tried to get herself back on an even keel.

They saw the singer enter and Lyra chewed her bottom lip, her eyes big and worried. The singer was exactly as Marley had predicted - young and beautiful. Amy wanted Lyra to see how Miles was manipulating her, making her feel unworthy - the same way Beaumont was with Amy. She tried to bite her tongue, but the words spilled out of her.

"Oh look," she said sarcastically. "It's Avant Garde."

Lyra stood up as though Amy had slapped her, tears welling in her eyes. "I think I'll head off," she said and Amy couldn't bring herself to stop her. She was being a bad friend and she knew it, but at that moment, her mind was torn in so many directions that she couldn't think of a way to fix it.

"You were kind of mean to her," Marley said to Amy, once Lyra had gone.

"You didn't stop her either," Amy said.

Marley winced. "I know. I think she's being stupid about Miles, too."

"I wish she could see that he's not worth it." Amy dropped her head into her hands. "Crap. I'll text her later and apologise."

Marley tilted her head. "Is everything okay with you?"

"Yes, of course," she lied.

"Shall we get out of here before Avant Garde starts up?"

"Yeah, I think we should. In this mood, I'm liable to throw a drink over her."

"And Miles," Marley added.

"Especially Miles."

CHAPTER THIRTEEN

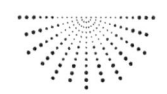

The frostiness between Amy and Lyra hung in the air, so present Amy could almost see it. She didn't know how to reach out, even though she knew she was at least partly in the wrong. Lyra didn't reach out either. It seemed like such a stupid, small thing - the disagreement had blown up out of nowhere and over nothing. They'd both been having bad days, that was all. Still, almost a fortnight later, they hadn't spoken and it was bothering Amy a lot.

During those two weeks, Rick visited Amy every couple of days. He usually stayed the night, but got up so early to leave that Amy didn't even hear him go, most of the time. She was sometimes dimly aware of him planting a gentle kiss on her lips as he left, but otherwise she simply woke up to an empty bed.

She loved falling asleep beside him, his strong arms around her, his breath on the back of her neck as they spooned. Sometimes she woke during the night and turned to face him. She would watch his chest rise and fall in the half-light, tracing her eyes over the slight frown he wore in his sleep. Then she'd lift his arm and curl under it, soaking up the delicious warmth of his body against hers.

There were moments when they were hanging out where Amy had the feeling he was going to tell her something big. He'd look at her in a funny way, as though working up the nerve for a huge announcement. He never ended up saying anything, but it happened often enough that Amy noticed it, and it preyed on her mind.

While it was convenient that he always came to her, Amy still hadn't seen where he lived. She'd tried not to bring it up, remembering his promise on their weekend away to speak to his friends about the idea of a little get-together with her girlfriends. But he never mentioned it again. He never invited her over, still hadn't introduced her to anyone else in his life.

She tried to relax as they sat on the sofa one evening, watching TV and eating takeout, but it was no use. She hit pause on the TV and turned to him. "So, do you have a family hidden back at your place or something?"

Rick froze, his fork halfway to his mouth. He slowly lowered it and looked at her, frowning. "Does it bother you that I'm here again?"

"Don't make it about that, Rick. You know that's not why I'm asking. I always want you around and that's kind of the problem. I'm up to my neck here. And this is a weird feeling for me. I know I might come across as full-on by saying this, but this whole thing," she moved her finger back and forth between them, "it's new to me. And I can't shake the feeling you're hiding something."

"Hiding what?"

"Well, what about everything we talked about on the trip?"

"That's still bothering you?"

"Well, yes. Because nothing's changed! Did you ask your friends about meeting mine? About a mixer?"

He took her hand. She had noticed that whenever this came up, he tried to distract her physically. It wasn't hard, she found his touch exhilarating and distracting. She pulled her hand back, determined not to let that happen this time.

He chewed his lip, his brows furrowed and his expression earnest. "Amy, there isn't any mystery here. My place? It's a dirty bachelor pad I share with two other guys. We could go there, for sure. But then I'd have to leave you crazy early in the morning and you'd be by yourself in the middle of nowhere with a long drive ahead of you."

"We could go there on a weekend though, when you don't have to get up so early. What about that? Even once. I want to see where you live."

"You know there's no Egyptian cotton there, right? And don't even get me started on the thread count of my sheets."

"I'm being serious."

Rick heaved a sigh. "I like getting away from there, it's a bit depressing. But okay, if it means so much to you. I'll ask the boys to throw out the pizza boxes, disassemble the garbage sculpture and chase out the rats."

"You'd do that for me?" Amy clutched a hand to her heart, mock-swooning.

He leaned in close to her, running his hand through her hair. There it was, the physical distraction. He grazed his lips across hers, running them along her cheek and kissing her hairline as he pulled her in closer. Her heart beat quicker and her mind began to unravel. She loved the scent of him, the firmness of his body, the bulk of his muscles. It was intoxicating and it made her greedy.

"It might take a couple of weeks, but we'll get there," he murmured and she felt her whole body respond to his touch. "Soon, I promise. Happy now?"

"Happy," she whispered, her heart pounding as their lips met. She wasn't. Not entirely. But she supposed it could wait for now.

A while later, Rick hit pause on the TV. "Hey, how's Lyra?" he asked suddenly. "I haven't heard you talk about her for a while."

"Ugh. We kind of had a disagreement…" Amy's shoulders slumped. "I feel bad about it. It was really stupid, basically over nothing but I haven't found a way to reach out to her."

"What happened?" He sounded concerned.

She dropped her fork into her bowl of pasta. "She's really into this slimy bartender from the Whistle Stop. I hate to say this, but I *really* don't think he's that into her. I think he likes the attention. He's sort of stringing her along for a gig there, and honestly, I get a bad vibe about him."

"So, you said something to her?"

"A little bit." Amy winced. "I'd had a *really* hard day at work and she said something that set me off, but I know that's no excuse."

Rick nodded, chewing slowly as he considered. "I wouldn't let some dumb guy get between me and my bestie if I were you. Remember how scrappy she was with me the night we met? Making threats about being able to trace you and all that? Lyra loves you like crazy."

Amy put the pasta bowl onto the coffee table and sank back onto the sofa, turning her head to look at Rick. His dimple was showing and she ran her hands over his clean-shaven cheeks.

"You're absolutely right. I'll call her tomorrow. I'm embarrassed I let this much time pass. You're smart. Do you know that?"

"That's my best quality?" He raised an eyebrow.

Amy smirked, leaning over to kiss him. "It's your second best," she whispered, and he all but threw his bowl to the ground, diving onto her as she giggled.

Spurred by Rick's comments, Amy spoke to Marley the next day and they agreed to go to the Whistle Stop and invite Lyra. Rick joined them.

Lyra looked almost sick with nerves as she walked in and Amy felt a huge pang of guilt.

It took just a few drinks for all the walls to come tumbling down. Amy was even gratified to see that Lyra seemed to be brushing Miles off, and hoped it meant she was finally seeing his true colours. She was about to ask about Alex, when Lyra dropped a bombshell about him.

"I caught him in a restaurant eating steak. Eating *actual* steak," she said. The table fell silent.

Rick looked between the three of them. "His crime is... he eats meat? I don't get it."

"He runs a food truck called *Meat is Murder*," Amy explained. "He's been putting up militant vegan billboards trying to damage Lyra's business. Then he eats steak in a restaurant? He's a liar," she added flatly. "He's out."

"He was never in!" Lyra protested, a little too loudly.

Rick stared at Amy. "Wait! We don't know what this guy lied about, or if he even lied at all."

She frowned at him. "I just explained the whole thing. He sounds like a liar to me. At the very least a giant hypocrite."

"What if he thought Lyra would only fall for a vegan?"

"But I work in a meat pie truck." Lyra sounded reluctant to point out the gaping hole in Rick's reasoning. "He literally only knew me as the woman selling meat pies."

Rick tried a few more angles until Amy snapped. "Are you trying to find reasons why a lie is acceptable? Because there *aren't* any!"

He shrugged and dropped the subject. Miles strayed by their table and offered them a round of whatever they wanted. He was certainly more attentive to Lyra when she was frosting him out. Amy liked her like this and she was happy seeing Miles squirm.

They ordered a round of shots and, as Miles walked away, Marley seemed thoughtful. "He's really into you all of a sudden, Lyra."

"Only because she showed *zero* interest in him," Rick laughed. Amy leaned over and kissed him, feeling bad about having snapped at him. She saw Marley and Lyra roll their eyes, but she snuggled into Rick anyway. She smiled at her best friends, feeling like everything was right in the world. She was lucky to be with someone who considered her friendships so important, and was grateful Rick had given her the nudge she needed to fix things. She vowed never to let petty disagreements and bad moods come between her and her friends again.

CHAPTER FOURTEEN

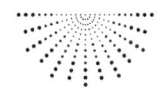

Her father's birthday fell on a Sunday that year and Amy couldn't have been more grateful. It was always an emotional day for her, but lately, her mind felt close to breaking point. With everything going on at work, she couldn't have handled it on a weekday. She was tempted to skip observing it altogether for the year, but her tradition was to give him that one single day. A day where she sat and read his letters, reminisced about her childhood, flicked through old photo albums, did everything to bring him to mind aside from actually reaching out to him - and it was a tradition she didn't want to stop.

In the beginning, it had been a coping mechanism. It was easier to squash her feelings down and ignore them if she knew they were going to be released at a certain point. She felt less guilty ignoring his letters and leaving his cards unopened if she knew there was a set date to go through them.

Somewhere along the line, things had changed. Amy no longer needed to cope with her own feelings, because she had fewer and fewer of them. She'd either dealt with most of them, or held them underwater so long they'd eventually drowned. Now, she celebrated his birthday out of a sense of duty. If she gave him no other days, she gave him this day. Even if he never knew about it.

She fixed herself an espresso, set her phone to flight mode, opened the door to her little Juliet balcony to let the sea breeze in, and sat at her dining table with the shoebox in front of her.

Six. That was how many letters she got though this time before the tears came. Her record was thirteen. Six was at the lower end, but Amy told herself it was also to do with her exhaustion at work.

She always started with the baby photos. Sean Porter, beaming at the new-born daughter cradled in his arms, as an exhausted but eager Diana smiled up adoringly at them from her hospital bed. Sean, holding the back of Amy's pink, streamer-handled bike as she looked determinedly out from her oversized helmet. Sean, presenting Amy with a bunch of flowers after her first ballet concert. She flipped through them one by one. This time she noticed something she never had before - Diana's expression as she looked at Sean. It was one of pure love. The same way her dad was looking at Amy.

The letters were harder, because they contained thoughts and feelings from "after". How much he missed her, how much he yearned to see her again. Letters reassuring her he didn't blame her, he understood why she'd pushed him away. Letters written to a future version of her, one who'd forgiven him, one who cared what was going on in his life. One she'd let back in. As she read each letter, she filed it back into its envelope - all marked with Sean's return address and made out to *My Baby Girl from her Adoring Dad.*

It was emotionally exhausting, reading them. Finally, she opened the latest one, the one Diana had smuggled to her at Bill's party. It was full of the usual types of news: tidbits about old family friends she'd known, about how the stray cat he'd been feeding had disappeared, about how he was keeping all the design magazines she'd been featured in. Towards the end, he'd obviously been drinking. She could tell, because the writing got sloppier and the words got soppier.

Your mother gives me what she can, bless her. There never has been a better woman than her. And she tells me all about you. She and your Pop do. Thank god I have them, if I can't have my little girl.

Amy put the letter down, eyes blurring with tears. Her heart heaved and she decided that was enough for today, hastily stuffing everything back into the shoebox, along with her feelings.

She walked around the apartment, blowing out deep breaths and decided to head down to the beach. She tossed a towel and sunscreen into her beach bag, pulled open her front door, and almost tripped over the huge bunch of flowers on her doormat.

Frowning, she bent to read the note. They were from Rick. She dug through her bag for her phone, dialling him and tucking the phone between her shoulder and ear as she brought the flowers inside.

"What are these?" she asked delightedly when he answered.

"You got them!" His voice crackled through the car's speakerphone.

"Are you nearby? Did you just drop them off?"

"I'm in the car. Left about five minutes ago."

"Turn around and come back?"

"I thought you wanted to be alone today. I was only dropping them off to let you know I was thinking of you. I know it's a tough day for you. I don't want to horn in on it."

"Come back and horn, please."

He chuckled. "How can I resist an invitation like that? See you soon."

They walked down to the beach hand in hand, Rick keeping to his promise not to ask her any questions about the day so far. When they reached the water, Amy kicked off her thongs and slipped her sundress over her head.

"Are you sure you don't mind waiting here while I go for a quick swim?"

He shook his head, spreading her towel over the sand. "I feel like having a bit of a rest in the sun today. If you can help it, try not to get into an emergency situation while I'm working on my tan."

She grinned at him. "You think you'd be able to save me?"

"Hell no." He shook his head. "I don't want to watch you make out with a lifeguard after he rescues you."

"Lifeguards are women, too, you know."

"Well, in that case, why don't you see how far you can swim out?"

She swiped at him and he jumped out of the way, laughing.

Amy waded up to her waist and then ducked under, letting the cool waves wash over her. She was happy simply feeling the sun on her skin, the saltwater through her hair, the way the sea supported her and made her weightless. Really, there were few things better in this life than being in the ocean. One of those things was stretched on a beach towel nearby…

A squeal drew her attention to a father and daughter splashing in the waves near her. The dad pretended to be frightened of the approaching waves, and the girl giggled and showed him how easy it was to duck-dive under. But each time, he pretended to be barrelled over by the force of them.

Amy felt tears threatening. Why couldn't she have had a dad like that? Instead of one who, if he wasn't off at the races, had his nose buried in the newspaper or was tuned to a radio station calling out results. A dad who was always disappearing to "see a man about a dog", sometimes coming home with a black eye or worse. A dad who rifled through the filing cabinet in the dead of night, scaring the hell out of Amy if she got up to go to the toilet. A dad who made grand gestures in small doses, and especially when there was a camera or audience - the flowers at the ballet, teaching her to ride a bike - and a lot of nothing the rest of the time.

Amy reminded herself that she had no idea whether the father on the beach was doing those sorts of things either. You could never tell from the outside. No one had known how bad things had become with her dad, not even her own mum or Pop.

Still, the way that father was looking at his girl, the easy way they were laughing together… Amy knew. She knew the girl was going to have a very different relationship with him than hers with Sean.

She looked up to see Rick stripping down to his boxers.

"What are you doing?" she yelled, but he shook his head and kept coming towards her. When he reached her, he wrapped her in a fierce hug.

"I saw you watching them," he said, his voice low in her ear. "I get it. I miss my dad, too. And I know the circumstances are different. But I get it."

Amy clung tightly to him, burying her head in his neck and letting herself be held. They stayed that way until a long time after the girl and her dad were gone.

CHAPTER FIFTEEN

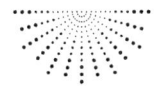

"I think you're looking for issues where there are none," Lyra said, hugging a cushion to her chest as the girls sat on Marley's sofa the next Saturday evening, drinking - wine for Amy and Lyra, juice for Marley - and catching up. They'd been pleasantly surprised that Marley had transformed the space since the day they'd moved her in. She didn't exactly have a huge sense of flair, and her taste wasn't in any way similar to Amy's, but she'd made the place her own and it was cosy. A big, spongy sofa, an armchair, a huge floor cushion and a coffee table made of salvaged crates had transformed the living room into the perfect zone for relaxation.

Amy usually spent weekend nights with Rick, but she'd been missing her girlfriends and felt guilty for not seeing them as often as she had before Rick. She still saw the girls plenty, it was simply that she had less free time since she split it between them and Rick. But she'd still deliberately chosen a Saturday night to suggest a catch-up, almost to prove a point to herself.

"I disagree," Marley told Lyra. "If she feels like he's not telling her something, he's not telling her something."

"But what *is* it?" Amy asked. She'd asked the girls for their advice about Rick. She wasn't usually the kind of woman who needed the opinions of others before settling on her own, but Lyra had asked in passing what Amy thought of Rick's friends, and she'd been forced to admit she didn't know them. "I don't think it's something terrible, like... I don't know, he's an axe murderer or anything."

"Are there still axe murderers?" Lyra asked, trying to keep the mood light. "I guess so, right?"

"Do you think he has another family or something?" Marley asked.

"No." Amy shook her head, wincing. She selected a breadstick from the jar on the coffee table and dragged it through the eggplant dip Marley had opened. "Because I'm pretty sure I flat out asked him that."

"Well, he's not going to *tell* you, if he does," Marley said.

"I don't think it's that. It's something smaller than that, I reckon."

"Maybe he doesn't have any friends?" Lyra said with a shrug.

"He was with friends the night I met him," Amy pointed out.

"Oh yeah, that's right. Maybe he's..." Lyra groped for an idea.

"It's clear he's hiding something," Marley said. "It's a question of what. Can you find out where he's building the current house? Turn up there as a surprise? Sniff around?"

"Sniff around what though? Looking for what? Doing what?" Amy sighed. "He's keeping me apart from the rest of his life and I can't get to the bottom of why."

"I really don't think it has to be a big thing. There might not be a 'why'," Lyra said. "It is clear the man is head over heels for you, Ames. He probably wants to spend all his time with you. I think you're looking for an excuse to end it, like you always do."

"But that's just it. I don't want to end it. I want *more*."

"Get a P.I.," Marley said. "That always works on TV."

Amy laughed. "I'm not getting a private investigator, Marley!"

"Do though," Lyra said, sighing. "Then I can use them as well. I need to know whether it was Alex who booked me for that wedding that's coming up next weekend."

"Oh God, yeah," Amy said. "Can't you find some way to ask him?"

"What like 'Hi Alex, I have a fake manager booking gigs for me, and I'm pretty sure I spoke to you on the phone about this wedding next weekend?'"

"Do you regret having invented her?" Amy asked, an anxious note in her voice.

Lyra firmly shook her head. "It's working. It's stupid really, how well it's working. I should have done it years ago. I wonder where I'd be if I had."

"Have there been any more brawls at your gigs?" Marley asked.

Amy tensed slightly. Lyra's eyes shifted to Amy and she shook her head.

"Ames, I'll be embarrassed for the rest of my life about that. I've been too chicken to call your uncle and properly apologise. I was also afraid he'd ask about Margot the manager. It kind of seemed like he was interested in her."

Amy nodded slowly. It made sense that Lyra was reluctant to call under those circumstances. Amy had also had the impression Rusty was angling for an introduction to Margot. And that was on her. Lyra took a shaky sip of her wine, eyes locked anxiously on Amy, who completely forgave her in that moment.

"It's fine," she said. "Don't give it another thought. Rusty said he went viral after someone took a video. And business hasn't been hurt."

Lyra exhaled audibly and Amy leaned over to pat her arm.

"How's everything going at the doc's office?" Amy asked Marley, wanting to change the subject.

"I really like Dr. Martelle." Marley smiled and grabbed a cushion, toying distractedly with the fabric as she spoke. "She's a fair boss and I find the work interesting."

"I can't believe she was still doing everything on paper," Lyra said. "It's bananas."

"I know." Marley shook her head. "She was a mad professor sitting in the middle of her piles of paper. Weirdly, her system actually worked. She's got such an amazing brain that she can remember patients and their complaints and history."

Amy chuckled. "Sounds like that's a good thing, if she can't even read her own writing! Any interesting patients coming through?" She raised a suggestive eyebrow.

Marley shook her head. "No one looks their best when they come into the doctor's office. And I'm still not interested in a relationship right now. There are quite a few steps in my plan, and I've only now managed to move into my own place. That was kind of a critical piece for it all."

"But if someone came along that was right, you wouldn't say no, would you?" Lyra insisted.

Marley shrugged. "What does 'right' even mean?"

"Someone you can't help falling for," Lyra said. "Even if they weren't what you thought you wanted, when you thought you wanted them."

Marley screwed her face up and jerked one shoulder. "I don't really think there are people like that, but sure."

"Oh, there are," Lyra said. She and Amy exchanged a smile.

The girls worked their way through the bottle of wine until Lyra started yawning. "I'm so sorry, I'm going to head off before we open another bottle and I regret it."

"Shall I leave too, Marley?" Amy moved to get up.

"I'm not tired. You're more than welcome to stay."

They hugged Lyra goodbye and then Marley asked Amy about her skydive on the weekend away with Rick.

"I'd love to do it one day."

"Oh God. Never again for me!" Amy felt a shiver run through her, tossing Marley her phone so she could see the pictures from the jump. They'd been taken from GoPros strapped to Biff and Damien's heads. Rick and Amy had been emailed the files a couple of days after the trip. Amy hadn't been able to look through them herself yet. She still occasionally had dreams about falling from the plane with Damien, but without the parachute.

Marley flicked through the pictures, her eyes widening. "There's a video here, can I watch it?"

"It's going to be me screaming." Amy plugged her ears. She watched as Marley hit play and heard muffled shrieks coming from the phone. She hummed, trying to drown out the sound. A moment later, Marley tossed the phone back to her.

"That was incredible. I cannot believe you did that. What a massive leap of faith."

Amy chuckled, taking her phone back. "It's more like it was sprung on me and I didn't really have a choice."

"But you still did it." Marley looked impressed.

It was after midnight when Amy finally decided to head home. Putting her shoes back on by Marley's door, her gaze fell on an envelope sitting on Marley's sideboard. It was addressed to a "Lena Gibbons" and the top was torn open.

"Marley, you're not allowed to open other people's mail!" Amy spun to look at her friend. Marley blanched as her wide eyes fell on the envelope. "Marley?" Amy repeated, straightening up. "Why did you open someone else's letter?"

Marley put a hand on the sideboard to steady herself. "I forgot that was there," she whispered. "I'm allowed to open it."

"Is that a neighbour or something?"

"No."

"I don't get it. Who's Lena Gibbons?"

Marley looked at her for a long time. Amy could see her chest rising and falling. "I am."

Amy paused. "No, you're Marley Phelps."

"Yes."

"You're going to have to explain. I'm not following at all, and I'm sure it's not just the wine."

"Gibbons was my married name."

"You're *married?*"

Marley didn't answer. They stood staring at one another in silence, Amy trying to put the pieces together, Marley looking like she'd rather be anywhere else.

As the silence stretched out and Marley looked more and more distraught, Amy made a decision not to push any further. Marley had obviously kept this secret for a reason and it crossed Amy's mind that she might be running from something.

"Why Lena?" she asked finally. "Is that a middle name?"

"My whole first name is Marlena. I used to use Lena, and then…" she gulped. "I switched to Marley when I moved to Sydney. And changed back to my maiden name."

"Marley, I don't know what to say. I'm sorry I didn't

know?" Amy shook her head and raised her palms in a gesture of hopelessness, brows furrowed.

"Don't be." Marley let out a quick exhale. "Listen, Amy, there's more I need to tell you. Just not now. And I don't want Lyra to know about this? Okay? I don't really want *you* to know about it, but now you do. I'll tell you the whole story one day, I swear, but I came here to start my life over. It's all coming together for me and I don't want to deal with the old part of it just yet."

Amy nodded slowly, then held her arms out to her friend. Marley stepped forward and Amy squeezed her tightly. "I'm glad you're starting again here," she whispered, and felt Marley nod her thanks. "If you need anything…"

"I know," Marley whispered. "I know."

CHAPTER SIXTEEN

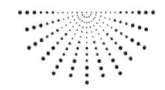

"God, why is *everything* industrial these days?" Amy groaned. She was finishing her work week by clicking through an online catalogue of lighting fixtures as she contemplated what to do with herself on Saturday night. Rick would be away camping with friends, though they were meeting for dinner later that evening. Lyra would be performing at the mystery wedding, and Marley had said she wanted to spend some time alone. Amy had decided on a night of bingeing TV when Kristina approached her, having clearly waited until Martha was in the bathroom.

"Can we go into the supply cupboard?" she asked. "I know that's where you and Martha go when you want to talk about something private."

Amy frowned. "Kristina-"

"Please, just give me five minutes."

Amy shrugged and followed her in. Once the door was closed behind them, Kristina spoke quickly. "I'm sorry I've left it this long before trying to talk to you again. I thought maybe if I gave you some time to cool down. But it hasn't been sitting right with me and I can't stop thinking about it. I've waited until Friday afternoon so if you flip out at me I can take off for the weekend. You have to know, I had no idea Evertree was your client. Kyle told me after I'd been assigned to her. I had no intention of coming in and taking business from you. Beaumont said they needed a new account manager and I assumed he meant they were swapping to us from another company. I'm really sorry about how it happened."

Kristina's face was open and earnest. There was no reason not to believe her. Especially since Amy had already figured out it had been Beaumont's doing.

"It's fine," she said finally. "I won't pretend it didn't sting at the time. I thought Rebecca and I had a good relationship. But if I really think about it, I haven't been paying her a lot of attention, and I've been repeating the same type of look we came up with at the beginning."

Kristina shook her head. "I'm starting to realise that's all we have time for, with the way Beaumont works us." Amy twisted her mouth and nodded. "It's not just me, right? We all have way too many clients?"

"Way too many," Amy agreed.

"Have you ever thought about…" Kristina bit her lip and trailed off.

Amy sensed where she was going and quickly shook her head. "I would never start my own company," she lied. It wasn't something she wanted to talk about with Kristina.

"Okay. Peace?" Kristina stuck out her hand.

Amy shook it. "Peace."

With a single curt nod and the hint of a smile, Kristina walked out.

Martha narrowed her eyes at Amy as she walked back to her desk. "What were you doing with her?" she hissed.

"Beaumont gave her Evertree."

Martha frowned. "She could just be saying that. And she still should have known it was yours."

"How could she know that? Her boss gave her an account, she took it. We'd do the same."

Martha gave Amy a look that suggested she didn't believe a word of it, but turned back to her screen, letting the subject drop.

She met Rick for a sunset dinner on the deck at Icebergs that evening, overlooking the ocean. Amy wore her camel-toned, belted trench against the cold and Rick had tossed on an old jumper. It smelled heavenly, a mix of fabric softener and a new cologne he'd started wearing. They could barely keep their hands off each other.

The view was worth braving the chill for. The sky glowed pink, streaked with fluffy clouds in shades of pale orange. The water was a perfect, clear aquamarine.

They were enjoying a nightcap after their dinner, trying to stretch the time together out as Rick would be heading home to get a jump on traffic first thing in the morning.

"I'm glad you're getting time with friends, but I'm going to miss you this weekend," Amy said.

Rick brushed her hair from her neck and leaned to plant small kisses on her pulse, which sped up as Amy closed her eyes and savoured his touch.

"Same here," he murmured, slipping an arm over her shoulders and nudging their chairs closer together. "So it wasn't Kristina who stole your client, then?"

Amy shook her head. "No, it was our boss. God, Rick. I'm really starting to hate him. Have you ever had a bad... foreman or something? Made you not want to keep working for your company?"

"Yeah, I guess." Rick toyed with a napkin and looked out to sea. "Sometimes people are hard to deal with, that's for sure." He looked back at her. "I wish you didn't have to keep working for him. Is it time to seriously consider going out on your own?"

She sighed. "I don't think so. I really wouldn't have a clue where to start. But everything with Beaumont is slowly building up and I feel like we're going to hit breaking point in the near future."

"What happens at breaking point?"

Amy shrugged. "I have absolutely no idea."

"Ames, you know you can do anything, right?" His voice cracked as he shifted to gaze intently into her eyes. "I don't think you give yourself credit for how incredible you are and how much you've already accomplished." He shook his head in amazement and pride. "I've never met anyone like you."

Warmth spread through Amy's chest as she hugged Rick close. "Thank you for saying that."

"I mean it."

"I know."

Later, heading back to their table from bathroom trip, Amy froze at the sight of a man sitting beside Rick at their table. The two of them were deep in conversation and it almost looked as though they were arguing. She hung back, observing them. Rick was frowning and gesturing and the guy beside him was shaking his head in obvious disagreement.

Rick spotted her and immediately broke off the conversation, beckoning her with a wave. His smile seemed forced and he slipped an arm tightly around her waist.

"Ames, meet my best mate Deacon."

Her eyes widened in surprise and she immediately leaned to envelope Deacon in a warm hug. He seemed a little shocked at first, but surrendered to it, tapping her back awkwardly a moment later.

"I can't believe I finally get to meet you," she said, sitting in the seat Rick pulled over from another table. "I want to know *everything* about Rick."

"You already know all the good stuff," Rick joked.

"I'm so sorry, I really can't stay long," Deacon said, checking his watch. "I was passing by and Rick said you guys were here. I've been wanting to meet you."

"Shall I get us more drinks?" Amy asked.

Deacon shook his head. "Next time."

An awkward silence fell. "Uh...do you work in construction as well?"

"Mmm," he said, studying the wood of the table and nodding slowly. Amy wasn't sure whether she imagined it, but she thought Rick nudged him under the table.

Deacon looked up and managed a smile. "Rick ever tell you how we met?"

"No!" Amy grinned as Rick groaned and dropped his head into his hands. "I can't wait to hear it."

Deacon's face came to life as he told the story. "So we were, what, twelve?" Rick nodded. "And I'd just moved to this tiny town where Rick grew up. I was at the playground a couple of days after Christmas, messing around with my new slingshot." Rick started chuckling, obviously knowing what was coming. "And Rick's there playing with his mates, when this older kid comes over and starts picking on him. Trying to take his...what was it?"

"Remote control car," Rick said, shaking his head at the memory.

"So, anyway, I'm a little ways away and I don't want to get involved, and I'm still learning how to use my slingshot. At a particularly crucial moment-"

"When the bully was making off with my car," Rick added.

"I accidentally slung a stone right at the bully's head."

They both grinned at the memory and Amy put a hand to her mouth, eyes sparkling. "No!"

"Yep." Deacon nodded. "About the only time in my life I got a bullseye with that thing. The bully goes down, Rick grabs his car and then comes up and tells me I'm his hero."

"You were! I thought you'd done it on purpose."

All three of them laughed, and Deacon nudged Rick. "Tell her the best part."

"The bully was my brother!"

The boys chuckled, and Amy smiled along with them. But something in her stomach had turned cold. Deacon was amazing. He was funny and friendly and he and Rick were obviously incredibly close.

So why hadn't Rick introduced them before this? She and Rick had been together for months now. Surely Deacon hadn't been busy that whole time? It didn't add up. She wasn't imagining it. It wasn't her trying to invent problems where there were none, as Lyra had suggested. There was a big blind spot in her picture of Rick. A crucial part, like a piece from one of Pop's puzzles.

Rick walked her back to her apartment block and their goodbye kiss was long and lingering. It reminded Amy of their very first kiss, in the same spot. She felt an inexplicable sadness as she watched him drive off, and sleep eluded her that night. As she tossed and turned, she made a decision. Once Rick was back from his camping weekend, Amy was going to get an answer about the missing pieces in her picture of him - no matter the consequences.

CHAPTER SEVENTEEN

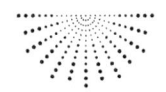

The buzz of her mobile phone confused Amy, who was taking a Sunday afternoon nap on her sofa. She squinted at the screen. It was Rick. She sat up, frowning. She'd thought the camping trip went until Sunday evening and there'd be no phone reception the whole time.

"Hi?" She yawned. "This is a nice surprise. Did the trip finish early?"

There was silence on the other end of the line, followed by what sounded like a cough. "I'm in the neighbourhood," he said finally. "Can I come over?"

"Yes, of course." A strange feeling crept into her chest. They hung up and she paced the flat until she saw him walking the path to the entrance, buzzing him in a millisecond after he rang the bell.

Several minutes later, he still wasn't upstairs. Amy opened her door and gazed up and down the hall. "Hello?" she called gently. There was no response.

Frowning, Amy shut the door and called Rick's phone. It went straight to voicemail. She grabbed her key and shoved

SECOND CHANCES AT LILAC BAY

her feet into shoes, deciding to go down and scan the path to find him.

When she opened her door again, he was standing right outside it and she stifled a surprised scream. He looked so pale that Amy frowned and opened the door wider to let him in.

"What's happened?" She closed the door behind them. "You look like you've seen a ghost."

She wrapped him in a tight hug and felt the tension all through his body. He was like a tightly-coiled wire as she led him to the sofa.

He didn't say a word and sat down as though he was in a trance. It had been a little over a day since they'd seen one another. Her mind raced through the possibilities of what could have happened in such a short space of time.

She sat down beside him and took both his hands. "Whatever it is, I'll help you in any way I can." She watched the muscles along his jawline clench and stroked his hands with her thumbs. "Just tell me what's going on." He got up off the sofa and started pacing the room. "My God, are you *dying?*" Amy clapped a hand to her mouth, tears welling. "Or is one of your family sick? Is it your mum?"

Rick shook his head, and took a deep breath. Then the words spilled out of him all at once. "I don't work in construction, Ames. I'm in the army. And I love being in the army. I never wanted to do anything else. It's caused two breakups in the past and that first night we met, when we saw that guy on the bus, you said you couldn't understand why people got involved with army guys. So when you assumed I was a builder... I didn't want to miss out on getting to know you. I don't know if you believe in love at first sight, but I do. Except it *never* happened to me until I saw you. I meant to clear it all up, but everything was so perfect so quickly that I never found the right moment. It's been eating me up inside and I feel sick. I just hope…" He inhaled sharply and held up his palms, unable to finish the sentence.

Amy sat perfectly still, her mouth open in shock. There it was. The missing piece. Everything made sense now. The fact she'd never been to his house. He must be sharing it with others in the army and there was not enough time in the world to make sure every shred of evidence was gone, or that his house-mates wouldn't accidentally say something to her. The reason he had to leave so early every morning, God the base was almost a two hour drive away! Why she'd never met any of his family or friends. Besides Deacon.

"Is Deacon in the army too?" she asked, and the answer was clear from the look on his face. "You even made *him* lie." She put her hands over her mouth and read in his expression the horror and betrayal in hers. "How could you do this to me?"

He stood on the other side of the room, biting his thumbnail. "I really didn't mean to. I'm proud of my career." He slowly exhaled, his breath shaky. "But there's a lot that comes with it. In the past, it's been too much…"

"Which is *exactly* the reason it should be my choice from the very beginning!" Amy spat the words out.

"I know, I know." Rick looked to the ceiling and back down. "I was - I was worried you wouldn't even want to get to know me. I *so* badly wanted the chance to get to know you, and then when I did." He drew a deep breath. "I was already so in love with you. And the more I got to know you, the more convinced I was that my career wouldn't suit you."

"So you let me believe a lie from the first moment we met, even after I'd told you about my father. And how his lies broke my family up. I know I specifically mentioned that part. And it was after that that you lied to me, I want to be clear. You made a decision to do that probably minutes after

I told you one of the most private and vulnerable details about my life - *about a man who hid the truth from me.*" Amy stood now, pointing her finger at him as she paced the room.

"Yes. I did, and I'm so, so sorry for that. But you and I are *perfect*. We have been perfect, in our little bubble. Didn't you feel that?"

"I did. But now I know the bubble was a lie. How long did you think we could keep that up for? I mean, really? Do you think I'm an idiot?"

"The opposite. You're the smartest, funniest, most beautiful-" He broke off, swallowing noisily several times. "I know you're going to be angry and it's going to take a while for me to build back your trust, but I'm not going anywhere."

She clenched her mouth. "I want to believe I can get over this, but you're right. It's going to take a very long time. I need a break. And I don't know for how long. Or whether it will be permanent."

His eyes widened in disbelief. "How can you talk so calmly and rationally about us maybe breaking up?"

"The same way you've so calmly lied to me the whole time. Would you rather I scream it?"

"Yes!" He threw his hands up. "At least then I'd know you were feeling *something*."

"I'm feeling," she began, and her voice caught. She held up her hand for him to stop as he took a step towards her. "I'm feeling so sad, so *very* sad that the man I'm in love with - the man I thought was in love with me - could treat me this way. You have been deceiving me for *months*." She ran a hand over her face and knew she was probably smearing makeup everywhere, but she didn't care.

"You know I love you," he said firmly, his jaw set and his eyes hot. "Whatever else I've messed up, I love you and I *know* you know that."

When she looked at Rick, she saw her father's face. Why did the men in her life *always* lie? How could this have happened again? What sort of person would keep her in the dark about an entire part of his life? Especially when he knew she had trust issues and had been lied to in the past by the one other man who was supposed to love and care for her. She was angry at herself. She'd known for a long time something didn't add up. Why hadn't she trusted herself? Why hadn't she listened to her gut? Because she was in love with him.

Horribly, irreparably in love.

Your mother gives me what she can, bless her. Amy realised at that moment what the words meant. Her mother was giving her father money. After all these years, after everything he'd done, while she was married to another man. Her mother was a fool. And so was she.

Another thought crossed her mind and she shivered. She looked at Rick. "What made you finally tell me?" Her voice was low and deliberate. "Did someone catch you out? Is that the reason?" His face flamed as he opened his mouth and closed it again. "Oh my God." Amy choked out a laugh, balling her fist and biting the knuckles for a second. "That's it, isn't it? Someone caught you out and forced you to tell me."

"It's not exactly like that!" He held his arms out in a gesture of despair. "I was *always* going to tell you."

"When? After we were married and had kids? On our deathbeds? When?"

"You must know that I'm in love with you, that I have been since I met you."

She laughed tonelessly, the sound bitter even to her own ears. "I can do without this kind of love, thank you. Once was enough. I can't believe it's happened to me twice. I'm an idiot."

"No. " He put his head in his hands. "I am. I am because I might have ruined the best thing I ever had."

"Oh, don't worry," she said coldly, "you still have the army." He clenched his jaw. They stayed that way for a long moment, heat coursing through Amy's body in alternate waves of anger and sadness. "The first time we... *our* first time, when you couldn't stay. Why was that?"

He looked down. "That happens sometimes. We have to go away. Meets, field exercises. That's all."

She nodded. "And all that stuff about the houses you're building, and that apprentice, was that all lies?"

"No." He shook his head, levelly met her gaze. "I'm helping a mate build a house, on weekends and in the evenings. There really is an apprentice there, with the builder. None of that was lies. It just isn't my career."

Amy was silent for a long moment. "I'd like you to leave." She wanted to lash out at him. She wanted him to hurt the way she was hurting. "I need you gone."

He lifted his head, looking up at her so sadly that her heart couldn't take it. She squeezed her eyes shut. "I will leave," he said softly, "because I don't want to torment you. But I am not giving up. I will make this right, Amy. I won't stop until you've forgiven me."

She made no move until she heard him walk past, keeping her eyes closed until the front door latched.

Then she flopped on the sofa, crying, and felt like she'd never get up again.

Amy called in sick to work the next day and spent the entire morning in bed, her heart heavy. She only got up to go to the bathroom and refresh her glass of water between bouts of crying. She had a huge tension headache, and her stomach was growling, but she couldn't bear the thought of food. Everything made her feel nauseous.

She couldn't imagine life without Rick, and didn't want to. But how could she stay with someone who'd deceived her for so long? *Especially* when he knew about her father.

In the afternoon, she texted Lyra and Marley an SOS, briefly explaining the situation. They both came over immediately after work.

Amy answered the door still in her pyjamas, her eyes swollen from crying and lack of sleep. She'd still barely eaten, managing to choke down a piece of toast before the girls came over.

So far, she'd stayed out of her liquor cabinet. But once the girls arrived, Amy found alcohol was at the top of her priority list. She made cocktails and the three of them sat around her living room in silence.

Amy's rotary phone rang for what must have been the hundredth time that day. She went to the wall and yanked out the plug. Her mobile phone was a minefield, exploding with text messages, voicemails and missed calls. She had switched it on only to text the girls, and now it was off, shoved into a shoe at the bottom of her cupboard.

She saw Lyra and Marley exchange concerned glances.

"Ames. What can we do?" Marley asked.

"Let me wallow."

Lyra took a deep breath and Amy could see she was building up to something, something that wouldn't be good. Amy knew how much Lyra liked and approved of Rick, she didn't want to hear it right now. "He did it because he wanted you to get to know him without the assumptions," Lyra said tentatively.

"So, by never telling me the truth," Amy snapped. Lyra winced but Amy wasn't done. "That man completely misrepresented everything he is and everything he stands for. He knew from the first night how I felt about his chosen career, but he duped me."

Marley tried to warn her with a look, but Lyra wanted to get something off her chest. "Well, someone could say that Margot dupes people…and she was your idea."

Amy gasped and slammed her drink onto the counter. "It's not even remotely the same. And whose side are you on anyway?"

The girls were silent and Lyra dropped her head. Amy was fighting tears, and Marley gently rubbed her arm. After that, Rick didn't come up again.

They steered the conversation onto lighter topics and Lyra talked shyly about Alex. They had realised how much they meant to one another and were finally going to do something about it. The vegan food truck wasn't his, he was doing a favour for his cousin. So he wasn't a liar, at least. In fact, by the sounds of things, Alex was pretty amazing. Amy was glad for them, but it made her ache all the more for Rick.

Marley put on some records and danced around the room. Despite herself, Amy smiled, shaking her head at the miracle of these girlfriends, feeling a huge rush of tenderness towards them. The drinks went down far too easily and it was a relief to let the alcohol unplug things in her brain. A relief to switch off from her sadness for a moment.

CHAPTER EIGHTEEN

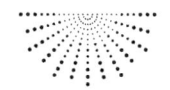

Amy called in sick again the next day, blaming a stomach bug. As she lay among a sea of balled up tissues, with a tension headache nipping at her temples and a hangover roiling through her, Lyra texted to say she and Alex would be going on a date that night. It felt slightly insensitive of Lyra to flaunt that particular piece of information, but Amy tried to muster some happiness for her friend. She spent the day watching TV, avoiding any shows she'd ever watched with Rick. Without reading any of his messages, she switched their chat to mute. At least that way she wouldn't have to hear the special tone she'd set up for him. A tone that had previously triggered a flicker of anticipation.

With heroic effort, Amy made it to the office on Wednesday. She couldn't quite muster the energy for one of her usual hairstyles, and she avoided wearing too much mascara in case she ended up in tears again.

A few colleagues did double-takes as she walked toward her desk, but Amy reminded herself they all thought she'd been off ill. It was probably not a bad idea to be a little puffy-eyed and pasty.

She stifled a yawn as she clicked through a new release of wallpaper from one of her favourite suppliers that afternoon. She had a meeting with a client coming up and needed to present some mood boards, but nothing seemed to inspire her. Her phone lit up with a message and she titled the screen to check. It was from Lyra. Something had gone hideously wrong and she needed the girls at the Whistle Stop.

Amy puffed out a breath and rubbed her temples. She didn't feel like being in a bar. Didn't feel like consoling someone else when her heartbreak was so fresh and she'd had more than enough alcohol for the week. But it was Lyra. And she'd do anything for Lyra. Besides, she could have a soft drink for once.

When she and Marley arrived at the bar, Lyra was a mess. She could barely stop crying long enough to tell them what had happened. She and Alex had gone on one perfect date, then she'd turned up the next morning for a meeting at a national record label - Teller's Music - and the Margot fiction had been blown wide open. To make things worse, it was Alex who'd secured her the meeting as a surprise. Lyra had made him look like a fool and he'd very publicly discovered she had been lying to him about her manager. He wasn't returning her calls.

Amy was overcome with guilt. She remembered Lyra's words: *Someone could say Margot dupes people... and she was your idea.*

"It's all my fault," she said sadly, putting a hand on Lyra's arm.

Lyra shook her head firmly. "That's sweet, but no. It's mine. I should have told him about Margot long ago. When he rang about the wedding. Before, even." She dropped her head into her hands as Marley and Amy exchanged a worried glance.

Miles arrived at the bar, sniffing around Lyra with a concerned expression that didn't fool Amy for a minute. She quickly dispatched him to get them some drinks, though he claimed he wasn't working.

A woman tentatively approached their barrel, staring at Marley in disbelief.

"Lena?" she said uncertainly.

Amy's heart flipped as she looked quickly to Marley, but her friend could have won an Oscar for the poker-faced shrug she reacted with.

"No?" She hit the perfect note of bewilderment.

"It is you," the woman insisted. "I'd recognise you anywhere."

"This is *Marley*," Amy said firmly. "She might look like your Lena, but this isn't her. Sorry for your misunderstanding."

The woman nodded and walked away, turning back several times to look at Marley. Marley mouthed a "thank you" to Amy, and Lyra was too distracted with her own crises to notice.

Not long after, Lyra's eyelids were getting heavy. "I think I need to go home and wallow," she said, gently refusing their offers to walk her home.

Amy and Marley finished their drinks in a sombre mood.

"Poor you, Marley. Two friends down and out on their love luck. So much moping."

"Well, I was almost recognised, so it's not like I'm doing any better." She shook her head angrily. "I thought these clothes would help. That and the changes I made to my hair. I guess not."

Amy tilted her head. "Are you running from something?"

"No. It's more like..." Marley twisted her mouth,

considering. "I felt like my life was paused in Darnee. My hometown," she added. "Paused the whole time I lived there. Then I moved to Sydney and it was like hitting play. Finally. I don't want anyone pausing my life again."

Amy tossed her keys into the bowl on her entry-way side table and headed straight for the shower when she got home - one of her favourite stress-relief tactics. Her emotions swirled as the water ran over her.

She had been the one to suggest a fake manager to Lyra, that was true. But the situations were completely different. Margot hadn't hurt anyone. She hadn't been *designed* to hurt anyone. She was just there to open some doors for Lyra that were otherwise shut, due to unfairness and bias. That was all.

But Margot had also backfired and cost Lyra a potential recording contract, and the man she loved.

Amy knew how innocently Lyra had stumbled into this mess and couldn't help but draw parallels with Rick. For a moment, she could see clearly how it had happened - how he had let her believe he worked in construction, and how that fiction had snowballed.

But seeing it and being able to forgive it were two very different things. Amy towelled herself off and wrapped herself in her thick bathrobe. As she entered her bedroom, she spotted the shoebox of her father's letters peeking out of her cupboard. She kicked the box roughly back into the cupboard and banished all thoughts of Rick from her mind. He was a liar, like her father. If she forgave him, she'd be a fool like her mother. There was no point in thinking otherwise.

CHAPTER NINETEEN

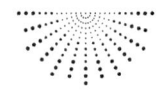

Things went from bad to worse for Lyra. Miles had convinced her to come back to his place the night they were all in the bar - pretending he had a gig for her. Alex had seen her outside, and if he had been going to forgive her for the Margot debacle, seeing her with Miles had changed his mind. Especially since his last relationship had fallen apart after his girlfriend had cheated on him... with Miles. It was a horrible, tangled mess - possibly even worse than Amy's situation with Rick. Not that that brought her any comfort.

Amy's own pain and sense of betrayal was still achingly fresh a week later when she opened her apartment door on a Monday morning and almost stepped on a tiny pale green box tied up with a length of green ribbon. She picked it up, puzzled, and glanced up and down the hallway. No one else was around.

She took the box into her flat and opened it. Inside was a single, pistachio-flavoured macaron from her favourite little French bakery. She immediately knew it was from Rick. She wondered how he'd managed to get into the block, but realised he'd probably seen her punch in the main door code many times. She hadn't exactly tried to hide it from him - there hadn't been any need.

She felt tears prick at her eyes. How like Rick this was. How considerate.

Before the tears could fall, she reminded herself that Rick wasn't entirely who she had believed him to be. He was a man who was also capable of causing her a great deal of pain through his deception.

Anger flickered through her and dropped the box back onto her doormat, stepping over it to leave for the office. She struggled to concentrate the entire day, her mind swirling. She took out her phone to message Rick and ask him to leave her alone, but stopped. There'd been no note with the macaron, no request to get in touch, no plea for forgiveness. Amy realised she was simply looking for an excuse to contact him. She resolutely put her phone away.

The box was still there when she got home that evening, but the following morning it had been replaced with a light brown one. Caramel. Amy left it there again, untouched, and went to the office.

Martha was gathering some mood boards into her leather folio to head out for a client meeting as Amy arrived.

"You look stressed." Amy snapped momentarily out of her funk, glancing worriedly at her friend. "What's wrong?"

Martha bit her bottom lip. "I haven't had enough time to work on this," she said in a low voice, looking around to make sure no one was listening to them. "I had two other client meetings last week, and both were only days after Beaumont gave me the clients. I can't do good work on such short timelines. Especially not when I'm supposed to be part time. I haven't even seen the spaces in person."

Amy hooked her arm through Martha's. "I'll walk you out and you can quickly tell me what you're presenting and what you're planning to say."

After leafing through Martha's boards, Amy helped her polish her pitch a little, but she didn't have a lot of hope that the meeting would go well. The presentation was hastily thrown together and it showed. Amy walked back into the office, feeling a wave of fury at Beaumont. Martha was a brilliant designer and she was being given menial projects and too little time. It didn't even make good business sense to send someone out with half-finished work. It reflected poorly on the firm, on all of them. He must know that.

Amy returned to her desk and logged into her computer, but couldn't sit still. Before she'd even checked her email, she pushed her chair back and headed to Beaumont's office.

She rapped on the glass and he looked up from his desk, beckoning her in with an irritated gesture. He raised an eyebrow at her as she shut the door behind herself.

"You need to give us more time per client," she said bluntly. "Or fewer clients."

He leaned back in his chair and folded his arms. "Is this about Maggie, or whatever her name is?"

"It's Martha and you know it. But no. It's about all of us."

"Oh, I see. Unionised, have you?"

"Beaumont, this is bad for all of us, bad for *you*." Amy held up her palms. "I don't get what you're doing."

He gazed unblinkingly at her. "Running my business. *My* business. Close the door on your way out."

Amy arrived home late and exhausted. The caramel macaron box was still sitting on her doormat, a gentle reminder that Rick was thinking of her. She almost picked it up, but when she thought of his months of deception, she couldn't bring herself to do it. She locked her door, the macaron still on her mat.

Unable to sleep, Amy flicked her phone on and allowed herself to play one voice message from Rick. He'd sent it after she'd met Deacon at Icebergs, when he was heading off on his camping trip.

I'll miss you so much, Ames. Not sure we've actually said this out loud or if it will freak you out, but... I love you. You know that, right?

His rich, deep voice made her stomach clench with desire. Amy set her phone down and fell asleep with tears on her lashes.

Wednesday's box was pale pink, the ribbon around it a bright candy colour. Her mouth watered, thinking about the Turkish Delight macaron inside. She stepped over it as she had been doing every day, carefully avoiding treading on it as she locked her door to go work.

That evening, she drove to visit her Pop.

After hugging her, he held her at arm's length and studied her face. "You don't need to tell me what's going on with you right now. But I want to make sure you're telling *someone*."

She breathed out and shook her head. "How do you always know?"

"Born clever, I guess. You want to talk to me about it now? I'm guessing this is why you skipped last week's visit?"

They moved to the little table and took seats opposite one another. Pop was working on another nudie puzzle, the pieces scattered over the table. Amy was silent a moment, sliding pieces around as Pop sorted some out on his side.

"There's some work stuff going on, which should be more important to me right now, but - Rick..."

Pop clasped his hands in front of himself to give her his

full attention. "You stopped talking about him," he said quietly. "I figured you two broke up and you'd tell me why in your own time."

"It was because he lied to me about what he does for a living. Or, not lied exactly, but let me believe the wrong thing."

"And you saw your father happening all over again," he concluded sadly.

"Yes." Her voice wobbled.

Pop drew a deep breath. "Amy Beth, my son, your father. He's a troubled man. A very troubled man. Always has been, and probably always will be. Breaks my heart."

"I know."

"And you did the right thing to cut him out of your life, don't get me wrong. Much as it pains me to say it. But this fella of yours…did he have an explanation for why he let you believe the wrong thing?"

"He's in the army and he didn't think I'd like it."

"Well, it's not for everyone, being an army wife."

"It's definitely not for me. I know that, even though I wish it was different. But… I want *him*."

Pop watched her closely and was silent for a moment. "Well, that's a pickle and a half."

"Yeah." Amy heaved a sigh.

"How do you both think you're going to get over it?"

Amy frowned at him. "I don't think we can, to be honest. I can't see a single way out of this. And that's after I get over his lie. If I can."

Pop shook his head. "Can't you start your own business that can go free-range? Then it won't matter if you have to move."

"Freelance?" Amy grinned.

"Sure. Or maybe he realises he loves you more than his

career. Or maybe there's something else he can do for the army, something that doesn't involve moving around a lot."

"I don't think he'd be willing to do any of those things, Pop. And I'm not in a position to start my own business, much as I hate work at the moment. Plus, I don't want to go free-range. I want to be *here*. This is it for me, this is the place."

"Well, okay then. How far into solution mode did you two get?"

Amy looked down. "We didn't. I threw him out and I haven't returned any of his calls."

"Ah," Pop said gently.

"I can't yet, Pop. I just can't. And I'm worried he's not going to wait while I figure it all out."

"Is there any sign that he's given up?"

Amy shook her head. "Actually the opposite. He drives to my favourite bakery every morning and leaves a macaron on my doorstep."

Pop looked at her like she was an idiot. "A man who's driving to a biscuit shop, to your place and then to the base. That's not a man who's going to forget you."

"You don't think?"

"I loved your grandmother more than anything in the world. But if she wanted a biscuit even from another room, so help me God she was getting that biscuit herself."

Amy couldn't help but laugh at that, even though she knew it was a lie. "Thanks, Pop."

Hazel appeared in the doorway, holding a tray of mugs and smiling at the scene. Amy squeezed Pop again, then gestured to Hazel to come in. She moved to the bed so Hazel could have the chair.

"Amy, I'm very glad you're here," she said in her tranquil voice, as she set the tray down on a clear patch of the table. "I was talking to the manager here yesterday and we've decided to redesign a couple of rooms."

"Oh?"

"Yes. Starting with the common room. Now, it's obviously not going to be the sexiest project you've ever taken on, but I think you have a vested interest in making it a little nicer than it is now, don't you?" She winked at Pop, who was gazing at her with a fond smile on his face. Amy thought again how wonderful it was that the two of them had found one other at Sunnywoods.

"Me?" Amy asked, confused for a moment.

"Yes, dear." Hazel picked up her mug and warmed her hands around it. "I told them you'd do it."

"But. But - oh. I don't really have time," Amy stammered, completely taken aback. "I have far too much on at work at the moment and-"

"Make time," Pop interrupted, sipping his hot chocolate and raising an eyebrow meaningfully. "This could be the first step to starting your own business."

When Amy arrived home, she found a fat, slow cockroach scratching around the macaron box. Something about that broke her heart. She made a mental note to raise the topic of fumigation at the next strata meeting - cockroaches were the only downside to living in Bondi. Then she brought the box inside and stepped on the pedal to open the garbage bin. She hesitated, then found herself unable to throw it in. Before she could change her mind, she dialled Rick's number.

"Amy," he answered breathlessly after half a ring.

She swallowed several times but couldn't get a sound out.

"Hey," he said gently. "I'm so glad you called."

"I can't," she managed finally, her voice choking. "I can't." She hung up the call.

A moment later, he texted. *It's okay Ames. Take all the time you need. I know how badly I messed up. But I'm not going anywhere.*

CHAPTER TWENTY

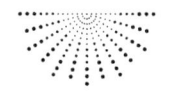

As she stepped out of her apartment, dressed in lilac tweed, Amy saw the pale purple macaron box on her mat. She could almost believe Rick had known what she was going to wear that day. She stooped to pick it up and took it into the car with her.

In the parking garage at work, she studied the box, opening and closing it, pulling the short length of indigo ribbon through her fingers. She imagined Rick's big hands tying it in a bow, although she knew that was ridiculous, they'd have done it at the store. She leaned back on the head rest and stared at herself in the rear-view mirror.

"You should meet up with him," she told her sad-eyed reflection. She sat there for a long time, playing with the ribbon and thinking of him. What would be the point of seeing him? She wouldn't be able to hold herself back from him, they'd end up kissing and they'd tumble into bed. There'd be no solution, no resolution. They were stuck in a riddle right now. She might forgive him for his lie over time, but she didn't want to be an army wife. She didn't want to have to worry when he'd be called to active service or that he might be killed. Or when they'd need to pack up and move next. She didn't want to leave Bondi, move away from Pop and her friends. And it wasn't like Rick would give up the career he so obviously loved - not that Amy would ever consider asking him to.

She sighed, wishing there was a clear-cut answer to it all. Finally, she stuffed the macaron in her mouth and went upstairs to the office.

She was late and growled with frustration when she realised everyone was crowded into the boardroom again. She put her bag down at her desk and surveyed the scene through the boardroom's glass walls. She saw only grim expressions. This was no ordinary yachting meeting.

"What's going on?" she whispered to Martha as she slid into the back of the meeting, ignoring Beaumont's frown.

"He's laying people off," Martha whispered back. Amy's eyes bulged. She shouldn't have sat so long in the car, now she'd missed the start of probably one of the most important meetings in her career. She made a mental note to joke with Rick about it, then her stomach lurched.

"So I don't want anyone to panic," Beaumont was saying. "We haven't made any firm decisions yet. This is a meritocracy, so when the management team sits together and makes these hard calls, we want you to know the only factor we'll take into account is your talent. Nothing else."

He glanced around the room to take in everyone's faces and Amy did the same. Emily from payroll dabbed at her nose with a tissue and Hope from IT looked pale as she rubbed her hand over her growing baby bump. Amy knew she and her husband Connor were expecting twins. Surely her job was safe though. They couldn't operate without IT, could they?

But they definitely could lose a designer here or there and where did that leave Amy?

Once the meeting broke up, she grabbed Martha by the elbow and steered her to the supply closet.

"What did I miss?" Amy demanded, watching Martha's eyes train on the fluorescent light as it slowly blinked to attention. Martha was fighting tears.

"Basically that the market has turned, they can't keep us all on, they don't want to do this, blah blah blah-"

"No *blah blah blah*. I want to know the *blah blah blah*. That's the important part."

"Sorry." Martha squeezed her eyes shut and rubbed her temples, trying to concentrate. "I think thirty percent, they said."

Amy's breath caught in her throat. "They're getting rid of *thirty* percent of us?"

Martha nodded, her eyes welling. Amy immediately wrapped her into a hug. They both knew it would be easier to find a way to cut a part-timer than someone on full hours.

"Maybe that makes you safer," Amy said, trying to sound convincing. "It's cheaper to keep you on, and you more than pull your weight." That part at least was true. Martha brought in a lot of clients who always gave glowing reviews and asked for her again and again. If Amy had to pick someone for a team, she'd start with Martha. And then... mentally she flicked through the people in the design team. She landed on Kristina and her heart sank.

Martha was looking at her. "Kristina?" she asked gently. Amy nodded. While the company itself was relatively large, the divisions were not. Five or six designers apiece. If they were getting rid of thirty percent of the staff, it meant maybe two people being let go from the Commercial Interiors team.

Amy knew that she, Martha and Kristina were the best. But the three others - Walter, Kyle and Amber - had their niches. They were indispensable for their markets.

"She hasn't been here as long as you," Martha said. "Surely if someone has to go, it would be her?"

Amy smiled a little too brightly and nodded. She was going to really have to bring her A game now. Time to stop mooning about Rick and throw herself into work.

That evening, she sent Pop a text message.

Tell Hazel I would love to do the work she suggested to me. And tell her thank you.

At tagore, he texted back and Amy frowned, puzzled. Moments later, he tried again. *Attagirl.* And then one more. *I bloody hate this phone.*

CHAPTER TWENTY-ONE

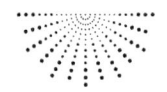

The traffic lights had been red for about a minute when Amy realised the guy in the car beside her was staring at her, open-mouthed. No wonder - she was singing along to *Eye of the Tiger* at full pelt. It was the second round of the song, and she needed it before she could finally work up the nerve to dial her mother through the car's speaker system. When the lights turned green, she floored it, leaving the staring guy in her dust as she zipped along New South Head Road towards her office.

While lying awake in the small hours thinking about Rick the previous night, something had occurred to her. She had a question only her mother could answer. They hadn't spoken since Bill's soiree, but that was nothing unusual. They often went months at a time with little more than a few text exchanges.

"Amy, what a pleasant surprise." Her mother's tone was neutral, as always. If it really was a pleasant surprise, it definitely didn't sound that way to Amy.

"Hi Mum. Listen, do you have time for lunch, or even a

coffee Saturday afternoon? I'll drive out to you. I have a question for you."

"You can't ask it over the phone?"

Amy rolled her eyes, taking a deep breath as she put her indicator on and switched lanes. "I'd rather ask it in person, unless it's too much trouble."

"Oh, sweetheart, don't be like that. Of course it isn't too much trouble."

Then you could sound a bit more enthusiastic, she thought. Out loud she said, "You pick the cafe and text me the details."

They hung up. It was a particularly brutal final few days of the week. Everyone was on edge after Beaumont's announcement and Kyle and Martha got into an argument over nothing, further bringing the mood down. Amy of course took Martha's side, but Kristina was more neutral and Amy could tell that bugged Martha.

Beaumont sent around a memo announcing he was going to hold individual meetings with everyone to go through their accounts and clients. Amy was one major client down now, thanks to his efforts with Evertree, and she wondered how to bring that up without causing an argument with him.

She dragged herself through the last few days at work and woke early on Saturday, heading straight down to the beach for a long walk. The shore was almost empty, a fresh breeze whipping up curls of sand. She hated that Bondi was slightly haunted for her now. Everywhere she looked, there was a memory with Rick. Him wading into the water to hold her while her heart ached watching a father and daughter. Him dragging her, kicking and giggling, into the water for their race. Their walk together on the first night they'd met.

She gave up and came home feeling exhausted. She choked down some toast and drained several espressos before spending the rest of the morning in front of the TV.

In the afternoon, when she pulled up outside the cafe her mother had chosen for their catchup, she groaned. There were so many wonderful cafe choices in her mother's neighbourhood, yet she'd managed to choose the only one with no soul. Even from the front, the best way to describe it was nondescript. Amy could immediately tell this was a place her mother came to often.

She took some deep breaths, reminding herself that this was her mother, that she loved her, and that Amy only had life because of her.

Diana was sitting at a window table. She raised a hand when she spotted Amy. A reserved gesture, nothing too enthusiastic, nothing that would draw attention. Amy thought she'd even lost weight since the last time they'd seen each other. She felt a pang of concern, but reminded herself to avoid any mention of weight. It was never a good idea with her mother.

"How's Bill?" Amy asked, sitting down after giving her mother a quick peck on the cheek.

"Wonderful, thank you," her mother answered, then looked at Amy sharply. "He knew what you were doing with that architecture book, by the way. He isn't stupid."

Amy feigned surprise. "Mum, I just thought it was a cool book. I wouldn't mind if he got me some design books." She showed her teeth in what she hoped was a convincing smile. "Is that why I didn't get a thank you card? I thought that was very impolite."

Her mother pressed her lips together but Amy was saved from her response when the waiter approached. They ordered coffees, and Amy chose a club sandwich for lunch. Diana ordered a naked salad, in what Amy interpreted as a very pointed tone of voice. She swallowed down her assumptions and decided to come right out with her question. In case the afternoon took a bad turn.

"Mum, are you giving Dad money?"

Diana blinked, the faintest tinge of pink colouring her cheeks. "No," she said, her voice impressively level. "Why on earth would you ask that?"

Amy tried to catch her mother's eye, but she seemed suddenly fascinated by the pattern on the cutlery set in front of her. The waiter dropped off their drink orders and Amy let the silence grow between them a little longer.

"Mum?" Diana glanced up, her eyes narrowed. "Are you giving Dad money?"

"How is that any of your business?" Diana snapped.

Amy flinched, frowning. "You're my parents. I'm trying to understand some things."

"Like what?"

Amy drew a breath. "On his birthday, I looked through a bunch of old photos, and I read all his letters."

Diana stirred her coffee, eyes trained on the swirling spoon. "And?"

"And the way that you're staring at Dad, in all the pictures. You were really in love with him."

"He was my husband. That's not exactly a secret, Amy."

Amy winced at her tone. "Mum, I'm not accusing you of anything. I'm asking."

Diana sipped her coffee, finally raising her eyes to Amy. "Yes. I loved your father."

"Do you still love him?" Diana's gaze faltered. "Mum, please be honest with me. I really need to know this right now."

"Yes." Her voice was soft and low, wistful. A tone Amy hardly ever heard. "You don't understand what it's like. He was my first love. He made a lot of mistakes and of course I had to leave him. But love isn't a switch you can flip."

"And you're giving him money, too, right? Money you get from Bill. But Bill doesn't know."

There was a long pause as their food arrived, and Amy thought Diana might not answer at all.

Finally, she said, "I draw the line at talking about that."

The stiff formality of Diana's tone told Amy the conversation was over, but also gave her the impression her hunch was correct.

"Okay. I'll drop it." Amy poked at her club sandwich. Her appetite seemed to have abandoned her lately. And she could pinpoint the moment it left - the night Rick had admitted his lies.

"How are things with you otherwise?" Diana asked and Amy felt a pang of guilt that she didn't visit or call enough. She was Diana's only child and she'd made so many sacrifices for Amy. Amy never really talked to her about what was going on in her life. Maybe she should open up more. Especially since Diana had trusted her to admit she was still in love with Amy's father.

"They're okay, I guess. I was seeing a guy, but…maybe it's over. I don't know. I have some stuff to work through with that."

Diana nodded, her face the picture of concern. She set her coffee down and laid a hand on Amy's arm. "I'm really sorry to hear that, sweetheart."

"Thanks, Mum."

"If you need any weight loss tips, you let me know, okay?" She rubbed Amy's arm. "We'll get you into shape in no time."

Amy's face froze. "What?"

Diana tensed. "That's not why you broke up?"

"No," Amy said coldly. "It isn't."

Diana withdrew her hand. "I'm sorry, I assumed…"

"You assumed that because I'm a few sizes bigger than you, no man could love me?"

"Amy, keep your voice down." She glanced around. "That's not what I meant."

"But that is quite literally what you said." Amy's voice was tight and high.

Her mother sighed as though Amy was being dramatic and, in that moment, Amy remembered with crystal clarity why she never told Diana anything that was going on in her life. Diana always reduced it to this.

They fell silent for a moment. Amy took a big bite of her sandwich and her mother pushed the salad around her plate with the fork.

"You're just such a *pretty* girl," Diana said finally, putting her fork down and folding her hands together. She looked at Amy as though the topic were an immense source of pain to her.

"Do you know I am one dress size bigger than Marilyn Monroe?" Amy set her sandwich down. "Literally *one*. You go around acting like I could have sunk the Titanic."

Diana rolled her eyes. "I'm only saying this because I love you. You could be an absolute knock-out if you were a little…"

"Skinnier. Thinner. Less."

Diana shrugged as though Amy had answered her own question. Amy was burning with rage but took a few deep breaths to steady herself. She didn't want a scene any more than her mother did. But she did want to make it perfectly clear she wasn't going to be body-shamed by anyone. Not even her own mother. *Especially* not her own mother.

"For your information," Amy said in a low voice, "Rick is head over heels for me. *I* asked for a break, and he hasn't gotten over it. He buys me a macaron every single morning and leaves it on my doorstep, even though it takes him hours on a round trip."

Amy took a deep breath, trying to steady herself and fight back tears. She had said too much and was annoyed with herself for using Rick's macaron as proof that he'd been in love with her. It was petty and weird and felt like a betrayal.

Her mother was silent for a long moment, toying with her napkin. "Sweetheart, I'm sorry." Amy felt a ray of hope that she'd gotten through. "You must feel so embarrassed."

"Why would I feel embarrassed?" Amy frowned.

Her mother was speechless for a moment, as though wondering how Amy could be so obtuse. "Because he's driving all over the world to bring you *cookies*."

"Would it be better if he was bringing me salads?" Amy's voice was loud and she gestured to her mother's untouched bowl. "Would that be more acceptable to you?"

"Oh, you're being ridiculous." Diana threw her napkin onto the table and held up her hands. "I simply can't talk to you when you're acting like this."

"It was a mistake to come here." Amy pulled her purse from her handbag and tossed some notes onto the table, moving to get up. "It's always a mistake to talk to you about things like this. I don't know why I haven't learned my lesson. I'm almost glad things happened the way they did with Dad so I could grow up with Pop rather than with you!"

Diana closed her eyes, as though struggling to keep her emotions in check. Amy regretted those last words. She had gone too far, and it was unfair. But she'd wanted to sting her mother as much as her mum stung her.

Amy thought Diana might apologise, or perhaps make a move to stop her as she stood beside the table, but when Diana opened her eyes again, they were hard and cold. She wasn't upset or hurt by what Amy had said, only mortified she'd said it in public.

"Tell your grandfather I send my regards," she said calmly. She picked up her coffee cup with both hands, turning to look out the window.

Sitting in the car with the engine idling, Amy fought tears as she realised something. Rick had felt more like family to her than her own parents ever had.

CHAPTER TWENTY-TWO

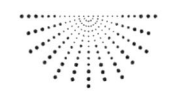

The loud honk of the other car warned Amy that she'd been about to change lanes without checking. Shaken, she took a deep breath and tried to steady herself for the rest of the drive home. It would take more than a deep breath to calm her, she realised, as she aggressively yanked the steering wheel again a moment later. It would likely take a full year of meditation, an entire bottle of whisky and a personal blessing from the Dalai Lama.

She felt close to tears several times, but bit them back. Her mother got under her skin every single time she saw her so Amy wasn't sure why she was so surprised and upset. For *once*, she'd like to see her mother get emotional, or show real support. The way Pop did. The way her girlfriends did. The way Rick had… But she needed to stop wishing for things that would never happen.

Amy hesitated at her front door, key in hand. The little yellow box she'd ignored on her way to meet her mother was still there. All she wanted to do was sit inside and mope, but it had turned into a spectacular winter day and she knew another long walk, though the last thing she felt like, would clear her head. She wasn't wearing the best shoes for walking, but if she went inside, she knew she wouldn't come back out.

On her way down to the beach, Marley called. She was nearby and they decided to walk to Bronte Beach together and treat themselves to a slice of pizza from the little authentic Italian pizzeria on the main street there. Marley walked towards Amy ten minutes later, turning heads with her oversized neon pink woollen dress, brown cardigan and orange cowboy boots. It wasn't actually the worst outfit Amy had seen on her. This was leaning more towards "fashion blogger" than "homeless fisherman" when compared to some of her other getups. She really was strikingly beautiful - tall, with honey-coloured hair, incredible bone structure and the kind of physique Amy's mother would really have appreciated in a daughter.

"I can't believe your mum said that to you." Marley angrily shook her head as they set off along the coastal walk.

It was famously picturesque, meandering along rocky outcrops, through dune scrub and past the beautiful historic cemetery, where neat rows of white stone monuments rose proudly from the lush green grass. And on the other side was the ocean, always the ocean, changing shades from bright turquoise to sea green to deepest sapphire. At points, the path was high up along cliffs, at other points it was low along the water line. The fresh sea breeze and the sound of waves crashing along the shore would keep them company the whole way.

"Yeah," Amy sighed heavily. "Neither can I. Can we talk about something else though? I want to get her out of my head."

"Sure," Marley said brightly. "Want to talk about work?"

Amy groaned. "Not really, not right now."

"Let's walk in silence for a bit then, hey? Enjoy this view."

The path was crowded, preventing them from walking at the quick pace Amy wanted to. She was frustrated by it, tsking loudly when a child strayed from its parents in front of her or a group walked slowly three abreast.

"Amy, you need to chill out," Marley admonished. "Unless you want to start tossing little kids into the ocean? You're upsetting everyone, including me."

"Sorry," Amy mumbled.

She forced herself to relax into a slower pace, breathing deeply as they looked out over Mark's Park and Mackenzies Bay.

As they reached Tamarama Beach, Marley glanced up. "Oh, is that Rick?"

Amy gasped audibly, and Marley clapped a hand over her mouth.

"Ames, it's not him. Not at all," she added, when he was closer to them. Amy could see how she'd made the mistake. The man had a similar physique to Rick, and held himself with the same straight-backed confidence. Marley put her hand on Amy's arm. "I'm really, really sorry I did that," she said.

"Don't worry about it." Amy waved her hand, struggling to get her pulse rate back to normal. They walked in silence a little longer.

"I didn't realise how strongly you still felt about him," Marley said quietly. "I thought you were over him." Amy coughed, but couldn't bring herself to say anything. "You've done a good job of hiding your feelings," Marley continued.

To everyone but myself, Amy added mentally.

By the time they arrived at Bronte, Amy's feet were aching and she was parched. But aside from still feeling shaken by Marley's mention of Rick, Amy felt better overall. It was as if the salt mist had seeped into the cracks in her spirit and sealed some of them up.

They sat outside the pizzeria at a two-seater table with plastic chairs and quickly gulped down the bottles of sparkling water their waiter delivered. Still, she'd need to take a headache tablet before bed to stave off a migraine.

"I'll have three slices of margherita, pan crust, and leave the Tabasco sauce here," Marley said to the waiter when he returned.

"That sounds perfect. I'll take the same. Don't know how much longer I'll be able to afford it," she added to Marley, once he'd left with their orders.

"What do you mean?"

"They're downsizing at work. I don't know if I'll have a job this time next month."

Marley looked horror-stricken and Amy instantly regretted having told her.

"Oh, God. I'm so sorry!" Marley reached for her satchel.

"What are you doing?"

Marley looked at Amy as though she was stupid. "We're putting a plan together, of course." She pulled out a notepad and pen. "We're going to make absolutely certain you're one of the ones they're keeping."

"Oh, no, we don't have to do that." Amy waved her hand.

Marley nodded her head vigorously, pulling the cap off her pen with her teeth and spitting it onto the table. "Of course we do. Amy, you have a mortgage. You wear expensive clothes. You like to dine out." Marley studied her, taking a hearty bite of her pizza as the waiter dropped it off. "No offence, but you'd be screwed if you lost your job." She wiped a string of cheese into her mouth.

Amy blinked. Those words stung. Trust Marley to deliver them so bluntly.

"I guess you're right," she said reluctantly.

Marley nodded, as though that was obvious, pen poised above the page. "Let's start with your motivation."

"What?"

"The reasons you love your job, love what you do, bounce out of bed for it."

Amy was stumped. Design, she loved. Still loved. Would always love. Her job? It had been a long time indeed since she'd bounced out of bed for that. The problem was Beaumont, and she knew it. He was the reason there was very little left that Amy enjoyed in her role. She'd been slowly beaten down by the way business was done at Edgerton's.

On the one hand, having this clarity about the separation between career and job made Amy feel better. On the other hand, it was somewhat depressing to realise that part of her didn't want to fight for her actual job at all. She knew she needed to. Marley was right, she couldn't survive without an income. Loretta was still just a name on a card. Sunnywoods wasn't enough to launch a business off.

She looked sadly at Marley now.

Marley sighed and leaned her head back, dipping the pointed edge of the pizza into her mouth. She chewed thoughtfully for a few moments, lifting her head to squint at Amy. "There has to be something," she said, her mouth full. "This is *important*."

"I know. It's one of the most important things there is, especially to me, or at least it always has been in the past." She sipped her water. "The problem is, Marley, I can't think of one single thing right now."

Amy picked up the little yellow box when she arrived home, sitting on the sofa to study it. The delicate scent of lemon coming from it made her stomach growl despite the pizza she'd eaten. She closed her eyes and inhaled as she opened the box, wondering if she'd be able to detect a lingering note of Rick's aftershave. She knew she was being ridiculous, but she couldn't help it. She felt a physical craving for him.

Amy thought of him getting up, God only knew how early. Getting into his car, driving all the way into the city, finding a parking spot, getting to the bakery right as they opened. Choosing a macaron. Putting it gently on the passenger seat of his car and driving all the way to her apartment block. Finding a space outside. Somehow getting into the building and tiptoeing to her door. Leaving the macaron on her mat. Getting back in his car and driving all the way back to the army base.

She had to take several deep breaths to steady herself, then dialled Lyra.

"Do you want to come over and watch some movies?"

"Romantic movies?" Lyra asked.

"Sure."

"Soppy ones?"

"Is there another kind?"

"With alcohol?"

"I'll mix cocktails myself."

"And chips?"

"All the chips," Amy said.

"I'll get a cab right now."

When Lyra arrived, she looked as bad as Amy. Pale and haunted, with dark circles around her eyes. Alex still wasn't returning her calls. Amy put her arms around her friend and hugged her tightly.

They decided on *The Notebook* and draped a blanket over their legs as they sipped gin and tonics and dipped their hands into a family-sized bag of crisps. Halfway through the movie, Amy hit pause and shifted on the couch to look at Lyra.

"Would I be an idiot if I took Rick back?"

Lyra's eyes widened. "Oh, no Amy. No you absolutely wouldn't. Are you considering it?"

Amy chewed her lip. "It would make me pathetic, wouldn't it? If I accept this lie, doesn't it set a precedent where I'll accept any other lies he decides to tell?"

Lyra shook her head, frowning. "Rick isn't like that. You know he isn't."

"Well, maybe that's what my mum thought," Amy said on a sigh. "That Dad wasn't like that. She kept pretending everything was fine. Do you know she's still in love with him? After all that? Still giving him *money?*" She shook her head, incredulous.

"And you feel like that's pathetic? And that you'd be the same if you forgave Rick?" Lyra guessed.

Amy nodded, suddenly fighting tears. "Like I'd be a complete fool. You know what else, Ly? I'm so mad at him."

Lyra reached out to squeeze Amy's arm. "I know, honey. I know."

Amy shook her head. "Not even for the lie. I'm mad at him because he's the only man I've ever really wanted. And he's forced me to give him up." Her face crumpled and Lyra pulled her close, hugging her tightly.

CHAPTER TWENTY-THREE

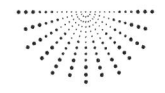

Her father's handwriting was barely legible, Amy realised, as she sat on her bed, tapping an envelope in her hand. His address was scrawled on the back. Even looking at that chicken-scratch cursive stirred up so many feelings. Anger, betrayal, pain... anger again. It also made her think of Rick. And thinking of Rick made her ache for the feeling of his arms around her, the sound of his voice, the smell of his hair.

The words from a song Pop had sung to her as a kid came to mind. *Can't go over it, can't go under it, got to go through it.*

She didn't want to see her father, but she knew their relationship had impacted the way she'd reacted to Rick. Seeing him might help her process some things. So there was nothing else to do but go through it.

When Amy finally worked up the nerve to drive out to the address, she was sure there had been a mistake. The neighbourhood was tattered and crumbling, etched with graffiti. Teens lingered on the corners smoking cigarettes and scowling at passing cars. Chain-link fences guarded weedy front gardens, rusted out car corpses and snarling dogs.

Once she was near his house number, she killed the engine and sat in the car, staring. She was half-afraid that if she left the car, she'd come back and find her wheels missing. She was glad that, thanks to daylight savings time, it was still light out. She simply could not believe her father, Sean Porter, a man obsessed with his image to the point it had cost him almost everything, was living in a place like this.

Amy wasn't sure if he was going to be home. She hadn't called ahead, didn't even have a phone number. She had an email address from which she sometimes received messages, but she'd never replied to them.

She hesitated in the car, wondering if it was smart to see him after all. She wasn't entirely sure what she was expecting. Surely nothing good could come of it. But she needed some answers if she was going to let go of the baggage surrounding what her father had done. She sighed and forced herself out of the car.

The front garden grass was patchy, with evidence of haphazard attempts at growing things. She thought it perfectly reflected her father's character. Start something, move on, never finish. Unless the task at hand was losing the family savings and house and ending up in prison, of course.

She steeled herself and rang the doorbell. There was complete silence. She waited a long moment, then rang again. Still nothing. Her shoulders slumped. She'd worked herself up, driven all this way, and now he wasn't even home. She turned back to her car and was halfway across the yard when the front door opened.

"Amy?"

At the sound of her father's incredulous voice, tears sprang to her eyes. She turned to face him.

He hadn't aged well. The last time Amy had seen him, shortly before he was sent to prison all those years ago, he'd been a youthful, handsome young man with a trim physique and keen sense of style. Now, his dark hair was streaked with grey and looked shaggy and unwashed. He had a paunch around his middle and a five-day growth shadowing his slackening jowls. His shirt was untucked and there was a dried blob of something down the front of it. He was barefoot. He was, quite frankly, a mess.

"Dad?" She ran back across the garden and onto the porch. They stared at one another sadly for a moment until he held his arms out. Amy wrapped her arms around his middle and he closed his over her shoulders. He was crying.

"Come inside," he said finally, releasing her and wiping away tears. "The neighbours are going to stare."

Amy stepped inside and felt claustrophobic with the stuffiness. She resisted the urge to go and open some of the windows or lift the blinds. Everything was dark and artificially lit. Like a casino.

"Want something to drink? A beer or something?"

She shook her head. "I'm not going to stay long, I have to get back. Can we sit somewhere and talk?"

He gestured to a beat-up sofa that she recognised as Pop's old one. It was strewn with pizza boxes which he swiped out of the way. Hung above the sofa were framed family portraits of better times. They were the same ones Amy had copies of, the ones she leafed through in her shoebox once a year. There was the shot of Sean, Diana and Amy, smiling as they walked across a beach, parents each holding one of Amy's little hands. The one where she was in her father's arms as she touched his nose with a chubby finger, gazing lovingly at him.

"How are you?" Amy tried to make eye contact with him.

It was surreal, seeing him after all this time. He kept shifting his gaze around and she didn't remember him doing that.

"I'm sorry about the mess," he said and Amy shook her head to let him know it was fine. He looked at her and a smile spread across his face. "You look really good, baby girl. I like that brooch."

Her hands flew to the banksia Rick had given her. She wore it every day. The thought of him grabbed her by the throat and she forced herself to focus on her father.

"Thanks," she replied. "You look…"

He laughed and tugged at his shirt self-consciously. "Oh, I didn't know I was going to have company, so I didn't get dressed up. Sorry."

"Dad, it's fine. I just wanted to see you, that's all."

He blinked. "You could have come to see me before, you know? It's not like I killed someone. Didn't need to be a huge part of your life, but you didn't need to shut me out. It's horrible not knowing how your baby is growing up." His voice shook.

Amy felt the truth of his words and an ugly question occurred to her. How much of her motivation in cutting him out of her life was about self-preservation, and how much was about appearances? She felt heat rise to her cheeks. Suddenly it seemed like a miracle he had opened his arms to her.

"I've tried to look you up on social media," he continued, "but your personal stuff is set to private. I can look at your design account, though. And your mum shows me pictures now and again, so I always know a bit about what's going on. Seems like you have a stellar career. I'm so proud."

"I'm not sure about the career," Amy said wryly. "But thank you." He smiled. "How are you doing? Are you working?"

"I tried. I'm trying, don't get me wrong. It's hard to get

work if you have a criminal record." He put one ankle on the other knee and picked at a loose thread in his trousers. "Not many people will take chances on you."

"I hadn't thought of that. How do you survive then, if you don't mind me asking?"

"Dole. Odd jobs. Your mother gives me a bit sometimes."

So it was true. Diana was helping Sean, with money she could only have gotten from Bill since he'd "retired her" after they got married.

Her father's gaze moved around the room. Amy did the same, and her eye fell on a sports magazine on the floor, open to the greyhound race section. Her father spotted it at the same time and swiftly kicked it under the coffee table. She looked at him.

"Are you still gambling?" She managed to keep her voice completely neutral as she asked the question.

He shook his head. "Nah. Gave all that away."

"Are you sure?" she asked, a little sharply, pointing under the coffee table. "Because that looked exactly like the kind of paper you used to buy."

He threw his hands up. "I wasn't going to say anything, but you're forcing my hand." He paused, giving her a significant look. "I'm going to get our house back, baby girl. I'm onto something good and it won't be long before your old man can make everything right again. You'll see."

"Oh, Dad." Her shoulders sank along with her heart. "You can't be serious."

He looked at her imploringly, as though he could make her understand if only he said the right thing. "You gotta trust me. It's not like before. This time I have a reason. The thing is I know where I went wrong before-"

"With gambling!" she couldn't help but shout. He looked wounded and she wished she hadn't raised her voice.

He shook his head. "You don't have to believe me, but

you'll see. I'm going to get our house back, I'm going to win your mother back and everything will be like it was before I messed it up. I promise."

The tears brimmed over as she looked at him. He really believed what he was saying. He was lost in a fantasy world, deluded. This man didn't have any answers for her. He didn't even have any for himself. He was Peter Pan.

"Okay," she whispered finally, nodding as a tear slid down her cheek. "I believe you."

His face lit up. "See! You know your old Dad would never let you down."

But you did, Amy thought. *My entire childhood was uprooted and my family blown apart because of you.*

"No Dad, I know." She forced herself to smile. "I'd better be heading home."

"Already?" She nodded and stood. "Got a fella to head back to?" he asked hopefully as they walked towards the door together. She shook her head. "Well, that's crazy. You're a knockout."

She turned and hugged him tightly, burying her head in his chest. Pretending for a moment that he was the father he saw himself as. "I love you," she whispered.

She walked out the door and across the garden, turning to wave at him before she got in the car. He waved back, his face full of joy and hope.

"Come back soon!" he called, before she shut the door. She nodded, waving and smiling. She even honked the horn as she drove off. But as soon as she pulled away her smile fell.

Her father wasn't like Rick. Two people couldn't be more different. How had she ever gotten that confused?

Amy soaked in the bathtub that evening, glass of red in hand. But she couldn't relax. There were too many thoughts swirling around in her head. She was truly worried for her father, who didn't seem to be able to separate fact from reality and who was wasting the rest of his life in that horrible house. For Diana, squirrelling money away to give to the man she'd left so many years ago. She didn't know which of her parents she found more foolish - the father who'd lost everything and still thought he could win it back on another gamble, or the mother who still loved him despite everything.

She didn't think there was any way to help her father. He was clinging to a version of things that had already cost him his wife, child, home and prison time. If that hadn't been enough of a wakeup, Amy really wasn't sure what would be. But she vowed to return his emails now and again, maybe even visit near Christmas.

What Rick had done was crappy, mean, hurtful and wrong. In some way it was understandable … and Amy knew now it was forgivable. It wasn't the same as what her father had done. *He* wasn't the same. But there was a bigger problem. Even if they managed to put his deception behind them, she had no solution for how they would make their future work. He was in the army. She didn't want to be an army wife. She didn't want to move, and he could be asked to at any time. She could lose him at any time, if he was called up to serve. It was a lot to live with. But wasn't she risking losing him anyway, by staying apart?

She took out her phone and after a long hesitation, sent Rick a message. *I still love you. I just need more time. Thank you for the macarons.*

Her message was marked as read immediately. She saw

the three dots indicating that he was typing. They appeared and disappeared several times over the course of the next few minutes. Her heart was fluttering wildly in its cage, her breath snagged somewhere in her throat. Finally, he sent it.

I'm waiting. I won't stop waiting.

CHAPTER TWENTY-FOUR

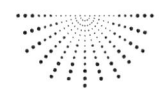

The water at Icebergs was so cold at 530am that it took Amy's breath away. Her stroke was off and she tired out quickly, pausing frequently at the ends of the pool to hook her elbows over the concrete lip and catch her breath. But by the end of her ten laps, she'd found her rhythm again. It had been far too long since she'd done this, and she decided to make it a more frequent occurrence. As she towelled herself dry, she took deep, long breaths and stared out at the golden sunrise, thoughts of Rick swirling with the current.

She finally slipped into her chair beside a worried-looking Martha shortly before 10am.

Beaumont called Amy and Kristina into his office late that afternoon. Martha looked at Amy in panic, but she felt calm.

"He's definitely not getting rid of Kristina," Amy said. "So I doubt he's getting rid of me. Yet, anyway."

They filed into Beaumont's office. Kristina stood attentively before his desk, her arms clasped behind her back like an at-ease soldier.

"Amy, did you hit some traffic this morning?" Beaumont asked.

Amy shrugged one shoulder. "I was a bit late. I think this makes twice in six years. Is it an issue?"

Kristina looked to the floor and Amy could almost hear Beaumont deliberating how to react. He decided to let it slide but Amy knew it would be filed away somewhere. Everything with Beaumont was.

"You two are going to work together on our new account, Peregrine Hotels." Amy turned to look at Kristina, who betrayed no emotion.

"But that doesn't make sense at all," Amy said. "We never put two people on accounts."

"We're trialling it," Beaumont said firmly. "And the pitch meeting is just over a week from now, so I'd like the two of you to get started right away. I'd have told you about it this morning, but Amy you were…indisposed."

"Late, Beaumont. I was late. But have Peregrine requested *two* account managers?"

"Kristina, do you have an issue with this?"

"No." Both her tone and expression were unreadable.

"Then I think we're done here," Beaumont snapped. "You're free to leave."

Amy opened and closed her mouth a few times, her face burning. She knew it wasn't Kristina's fault, but being paired in a team made her feel like she was back in kindergarten. Not like a top designer with a strong career history behind her.

As they filed out of his office, Amy pulled Kristina into one of the fish tanks, closing the door behind them.

"This is nuts, right?" Amy said, hand on hip. "We have completely different styles. Whose are we going to go with?"

"Both," Kristina said simply. "They can have the choice."

"That's not how we do it here." Amy tried to suppress a

wave of annoyance. "We pick one style and we give them a few options within that."

"Do you really think that's best for the client?" Kristina looked Amy in the eye.

The question took Amy aback. It was the exact same one she had asked Beaumont when she'd joined the company. She'd never been able to get him to change his mind. What Kristina was suggesting made perfect sense to Amy, but she found herself hesitant to admit it.

"That's irrelevant," she said finally. "It's how we do it."

"Okay, maybe that's how it's been done before. But does that mean it's how we should do it forever?"

Amy bit her lip, considering, and finally shrugged her shoulders. "*You* can tell Beaumont you're refusing to do it his way."

Kristina smiled tightly. "Why on earth would I tell Beaumont about this?"

Amy had wondered whether Kristina was as desperate for Beaumont's approval as she had once been. It seemed not, but Beaumont still clearly favoured Kristina. Amy bit back a sigh. It didn't feel like that long ago that *she* was the one Beaumont was always impressed with.

"How about whoever's design Peregrine chooses, that person takes over the entire project and then the other is free to start on something else," Amy suggested.

"Agreed."

As Amy approached her desk, Martha beckoned her towards the supply closet.

"What was that about with Kristina?" She was obviously eager to tell Amy something but curious about her news.

Amy pulled a face. "We're being lumped together on a client."

"Okay," Martha said, her face unreadable.

Amy sensed Martha wanted to say something unkind

about Kristina, so she cut her off. "What did you want to tell me?"

"They let Doug from the other team go."

Amy gasped. "His clients love him!"

"Exactly. I think Beaumont found out he was taking on clients outside of work. Doug's contract obviously has a non-compete clause, so he can't do anything for a few months unless those new clients are enough. Doug said it's going to be hard for him for a while."

"Wow. So Beaumont really is serious."

Martha nodded, her eyes round and frightened. "The culling is getting real."

Peregrine Hotels was the boutique brand of a larger hotel chain, and Amy and Kristina were supposed to work together to refresh the bar area of their inner city hotel. Amy was already home when she had the idea of driving in for a solo drink so she could assess the bar in person. She groaned, feeling too drained to head back out, but she reminded herself she was competing against Kristina. That gave her the motivation she needed to grab a leather satchel instead of one of her handbags, and toss in a sketchpad and some pencils.

On the drive over, a call from Lyra came through and Amy pressed to accept it through the speakers.

"So, I'm doing a thing," Lyra said slowly. "And I need you and Marley there with me."

"Of course. What's the thing?"

"I may or may not be signed up to sing at a food truck market in Lilac Bay on Friday."

"Oh, Ly, that's awesome news! I'm so happy for you. Of course I'll be there."

"That's not all," Lyra said hesitatingly.

Amy switched lanes along New South Head Road, glancing at Rushcutter's Bay as she passed it. "Spill then," she prompted.

"I may or may not have written a song. For Alex. That I'm going to sing for him."

Amy felt goosebumps ripple over her arms. "Oh, Lyra," she breathed.

"Is it dumb? Tell me if it's dumb. His cousin said she's going to get him to come. At least I'll know once and for all if he'll ever forgive me."

"Lyra, I think it's the most hair-brained idea I've ever heard." Lyra exhaled heavily. "And I absolutely one-hundred percent think it's going to work," Amy added.

"You couldn't have led with that?" Lyra cried, a note of glee in her voice.

Amy chuckled. "Listen, I'm on the road, but I'll be there with bells on."

They hung up and Amy pulled into the horseshoe drive of the hotel, her heart flapping wildly at Lyra's news. As a valet took her keys, Amy paused for a moment to try and ground herself while soaking up her first impressions. The hotel came across as classy but not snobby, the polished marble columns of the facade softened by golden lighting and the rounded curves of deep planters draped with trailing ivy. For a moment, she wished Rick was with her and the thought of him was a jab to the stomach that made her breathless.

Amy steeled herself, hoisted her satchel onto her shoulder and went through the foyer to the bar. It was bleak and almost empty save a few clusters of sad-looking hotel guests, distinguishable by the bright blue key cards beside their drinks. The tables were squashed together like a busy diner rather than a classy hotel lobby bar, which only amplified the emptiness. The carpet was faded, the music too loud.

She noticed the bartender right away. Cute and well-built, with slightly mussed hair and a strong jaw shadowed with brown stubble. He gave her an appreciative glance as she approached, and they had a short discussion about the whiskies on offer.

"My shift finishes in a couple of hours…" he said, eyeing her as he poured out a measure of Macallan.

Amy froze. He was hitting on her. A cute guy was hitting on her and pre-Rick, it was the kind of offer she'd have eagerly taken up. Now, it simply made her feel a little nauseous.

"I'm here for work," she said finally, hoping that was a direct enough refusal.

He shrugged. "On the house anyway." He slid the drink across the bar to her.

Amy caught it and stared into it for a moment. Then she laid a ten dollar bill on the bar and smiled politely, taking her drink to a dark back corner. She had a view over the whole area so she could take in her impressions; that was how she was able to spot Kristina without being seen.

Kristina walked briskly in wearing motorcycle leathers, her helmet tucked under her arm. Amy guessed the valet hadn't offered to park the bike for her - or she hadn't let him. She ordered a soft drink and took it to a table right in the centre of the room. She pulled out her iPad and stylus and sat, coolly appraising her surroundings. The bartender looked almost nervous as Kristina took a sip of her drink and then bent her head to take notes on her tablet.

Amy briefly considered going and saying hello to her. It felt odd not to and besides, she'd be trapped in the corner for a while if she didn't. But she wasn't in the mood for making conversation. She knew Kristina wasn't exactly the small talk type, but they weren't friends and it felt like a big effort to gather up her things and go say hello and sit beside her. A big effort that was beyond Amy right now. Besides, they needed solitude to note down their observations; that was exactly the reason Amy had come alone and she guessed it was the same for Kristina.

Amy sipped her whisky for an hour, watching Kristina and the downcast guests. She sketched a rough layout of the area onto her notepad and felt the familiar pull of inspiration as she jotted and doodled her ideas onto her pad. Lighting changes, custom display solutions for the bar, adjusting the room's layout - there was so much she could do with the place. Amy sketched and took notes until her temples began to throb from the loud music.

She packed away her note book and was trying to get up the will to act surprised as she walked past Kristina, when Kristina shoved her tablet into a backpack and walked briskly out, leaving her unfinished drink on the table.

That solved that problem.

On the drive home, Amy realised something: this was the second client project she was excited about, the first being the work she was doing for Hazel at the retirement home. The inspiration poured over into her work for Sunnywoods and she continued working on that until the small hours.

It was also a good way to try and keep her mind off Rick, if not an entirely successful one. Something about the encounter with the bartender had made Amy feel fiercely loyal to Rick. She'd been hit on plenty of times while they were dating, and she'd simply told him about it each time. He'd always nodded and smiled, as though it made perfect sense that people were hitting on his girlfriend. He wasn't the jealous type, and she loved that about him. Like she loved so many things about him…

And Lyra was going to be reuniting with Alex, Amy was sure of it. Why wasn't she doing the same with Rick?

CHAPTER TWENTY-FIVE

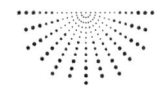

By the Friday morning of the food truck festival Lyra would be singing at, Amy's mind was made up. She lay in bed with the covers up to her chin, a smile playing on her lips. There was a lightness in her heart, in her head that hadn't been there since her argument with Rick.

When she thought about him now, the crushing pain in her chest was gone. If she called his face to mind, she was filled with desire and anticipation, simple and uncomplicated. Something had shifted and clicked inside her. All she wanted now was to hear his voice. She was no closer to puzzling out their future, but she knew for certain that she wanted one with him, and that she wanted them to figure it out together.

Her hands were shaking as she held her phone and opened up their chat history. She scrolled through their messages and it was like watching a relationship in reverse. His pleading and apologetic messages gave way to hot and passionate ones, sweet and romantic ones, and finally the very first ones, full of hope and caution.

Scrolling this way meant that what started off broken

ended up healed, what had almost ended seemed like it was only beginning.

It was the first time Amy had allowed herself to look back through all the words they'd exchanged. For a relatively short relationship, they'd definitely had a lot to say to one another. As she got to the beginning of the thread and read those early, tentative messages, she was fighting tears. *Hi.* His very first message. Her mind was made up.

Rick had never given up on her - she still opened her door every morning and found a carefully-boxed macaron on her mat - but neither had he been aggressive. He'd given her the distance and space she needed to work through everything, all the while gently letting her know he was still waiting. And she had worked through it. The parts she needed to work through without him, in any case.

She stared at his picture on her phone, her finger hovering over the call button as a grin spread across her face. It was quickly followed by a wave of anxiety. What if she'd waited too long? What if he didn't want to be with her now? Rationally, she knew that couldn't be the case. The macaron had been right outside her door yesterday, proving it. But she couldn't keep a niggling doubt from the back of her mind.

His phone went straight to voicemail and she hung up, afraid to leave a message. She paced her room for several moments, psyching herself up, and then tried again.

"Rick," she said after the beep, puffing out a shaky breath. Even the sound of his name in her mouth sent blood ringing through her ears. "I'm sorry it's taken me this long. Thank you for giving me the space. I know now. It's you I want, and I don't care if you're in the army, or the circus, or if you're really Jack the Ripper. Well, okay that last one is a lie," she laughed nervously, then turned serious again. "I want *you*, and I know we can find a way to figure it all out together. There has to be a solution. I don't know what it is, I just know I can't be apart from you any longer. Call me when you get this. I love you."

She hung up, flopping on the bed as the adrenaline slowly wore off. Once she'd stopped shaking, she slipped a jazz record onto her record player and dressed with meticulous care. She'd head straight from the office to the food truck market for Lyra's song after work, since the two places were so close. Maybe if Rick got her message in time, he could come meet her there too. The idea that there might be two reunions on the cards that night made her giddy with glee.

She paused for a moment before opening her door, wondering what colour the macaron box would be. The boxes were so often perfectly coordinated with her outfits that it was uncanny. Today, she was wearing a mauve tweed pencil dress and she was almost certain that when she opened the door, the box would be purple.

"Ah, come on, Rick," she said, smiling. "Of all the days for us to mismatch."

She picked up the green box and ate the pistachio macaron in tiny bites on the drive into the office.

"Amy?" There was an edge to Beaumont's voice and she realised the entire design division was staring at her expectantly. They were gathered around the boardroom table and discussing Edgerton's pricing model in an afternoon team meeting when she had zoned out.

Her cheeks flamed and she opened and closed her mouth. But when she scanned the autopilot part of her brain to see if she remembered anything from the previous few minutes, she came up completely and utterly blank.

Martha looked pained. "He asked if-" she began in a low voice.

Beaumont cut her off sharply. "I asked if *Amy* knew the answer."

Her colleagues averted their eyes, coughed or cast her sympathetic glances. She had been studying her phone, which she'd snuck into the meeting with her and held on her lap. She was waiting for Rick to call back, or at least send her a text, but so far there had been nothing. As the day wore on, a sense of dread loomed. Something wasn't right. He would have called her back by now. Surely.

All eyes were still on her in the boardroom.

Kristina spoke up. "Design Beam. Then Chalker & Hadfield followed by The Integron Group."

"Yes!" Beaumont said loudly. "Those are indeed our main competitors, thank you, Kristina. For paying attention. During this important time for our business. Where we're downsizing. And making decisions."

Amy knew he was saying that for her benefit and, if it was possible, her face got redder. It was a dangerous time indeed for her to be lacking concentration, especially with Kristina part of the team.

Martha reached out and squeezed Amy's hand gently under the table. Amy flashed her a quick smile. Despite that scare, she still struggled to keep up with the discussion in the room as Beaumont droned on. She could barely get through a few minutes without her thoughts straying back to Rick, and her eyes straying back to her phone.

CHAPTER TWENTY-SIX

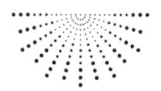

When the day was finally over, Amy heaved her handbag onto her shoulder, gave Martha the briefest of farewells and hurried outside to meet Marley. They walked down to the bay together, Amy's phone still glued to her hand.

Lilac Bay was completely transformed for the food truck festival. Lights twinkled along the shoreline, drawing the eye out through the opening of the bay and into Sydney Harbour beyond. The Harbour Bridge looked majestic in the fading light and the water shone deepest blue.

Several food trucks were parked along the pathway up from the tiny beach. A small stage had been installed and people were sitting in clusters all along the benches and on folding chairs or picnic blankets they'd brought along from home. The water in the bay was calm, reflecting the lights on its glassy surface, and everything looked so perfect it made Amy shiver.

She and Marley grabbed cocktails from the little drinks truck in the nook of the bay, near the entrance to the Secret Garden. Amy had almost forgotten the garden. They decided to take a short walk through it since they still had plenty of time before they were due to meet Lyra.

Although it was close to the city, it was so quiet inside the garden's walls that it felt distant from the hustle and bustle. Ancient, gnarled and twisted trees provided deep shade and a tight canopy through which light filtered gently, giving it an other-worldly vibe.

They sat down at one of the picnic tables as they drank their cocktails.

"What's with your phone?" Marley asked.

"Huh?" Amy feigned ignorance. She wasn't ready to talk about Rick yet, and in any case, there was apparently not much to say.

"You keep staring at it like it's going to give you the winning lotto numbers."

Amy forced a half-laugh. "I just remembered I have to send a quick message."

"Well go on then." Marley sipped her cocktail. "I might get some proper conversation out of you once it's done."

Amy nodded and flicked her phone open. She felt like an idiot for only now having the idea of texting Rick. She'd been so sure that he'd return her call, it hadn't even occurred to her. But maybe something had happened to her voice message; it hadn't reached him, or it had been corrupted and he couldn't hear it properly.

Hi, she typed, then paused, uncertain how to continue. *Can you give me a call when you get this? I'd really like to talk to you. I know now that I can get past what happened. What I can't do is live without you. It's always been you.* She hit send, but the message remained unread for the twenty more minutes that she and Marley sat in the Garden.

Then they realised they needed to hurry to see Lyra before she went on stage. Amy knew she should put her phone away, but she didn't want to miss Rick's return message or call when it came through.

They met Lyra by the side of The Pie-ganic which she and Silas had driven down from its usual spot right at the lip of the bay. They hugged her and gave her words of encouragement, then went to grab a spot with a good view of the stage.

Amy hunted for Alex in the crowd, but didn't find him. Her heart sank a little for Lyra, but at least the atmosphere along the bay was wonderful. Lyra would be singing to a relatively intimate crowd of people, all of whom looked happy and relaxed. Nothing like the crowd at Rusty's had been that fateful night.

As Lyra and Mick got onto the stage, Marley and Amy cheered like madwomen. They heard Silas whooping from inside The Pie-ganic and turned to grin at him.

Lyra started up with one of her original songs. It always seemed like pure witchery to Amy, that she could conjure up something from her soul and make people feel those emotions when she sang it. What a gift, to be able to communicate and connect with people that way.

Lyra seemed to sense that the crowd was in an upbeat mood because she and Mick launched into a series of golden oldies songs that had everyone up and dancing.

No matter that Alex wasn't there, it was shaping up to be an incredible night. Amy even forgot her own cares for a while as she and Marley danced and sang along with the rest of the crowd.

Lyra announced that she'd be singing her last song and dedicated it to Alex. Amy and Marley scanned the crowd for him and Marley spotted him, pointing him out to Amy. As soon as Lyra started singing, a collective shiver went through the crowd. Amy took one look at Alex's face, the way he was watching Lyra, and she knew. They were getting back together. And they were going to live happily ever after.

Alex started pushing his way through the crowd to get to Lyra and Amy felt herself choking up. She was so happy for her friend. This was the reunion Lyra had been hoping for, and the one she deserved.

When Lyra finished singing, she dropped the mic and jumped off the stage and into Alex's arms. The crowd whooped and cheered.

Amy and Marley hugged jubilantly and when Amy pulled back, she was mortified to realise she was fighting tears. Marley wrapped her back into a hug.

"Are you thinking about Rick?"

Amy nodded. Marley had guessed right, but not for the reasons she was thinking. Rick hadn't read her message yet. The same fear she'd experienced all day hit afresh - what if she'd waited too long?

"Why don't you get out of here?" Marley said. "Lyra's not going to notice if either of us are gone, and I can make up a story for you if she does."

"Thank you," Amy whispered, realising she wanted nothing more than to be home. She was too distracted for anything else.

She left the bay, turning once to look back on the magical scene, and then drove home, her phone on the passenger seat with the volume turned way up in case he called or messaged.

CHAPTER TWENTY-SEVEN

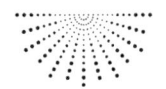

Amy didn't hear back from Rick the whole night and she barely slept. Her phone was in her hand and she was constantly waking from a light doze and checking the screen in a panic, worried she'd missed something.

At some point during the night, she grabbed her pillow and doona and went to the living room. Rick would surely make a noise when he dropped the macaron box off. She'd hear something.

She spent an hour on the sofa, but then began to worry that it was still too far away, so she moved to the door. The last time she checked, it was 4:27am.

She woke with a start at 7:19 and scrambled to her feet, kicking the doona and pillow away from the door so she could get it open.

There was no macaron. No box. She glanced down the hall, hoping maybe it was outside a neighbour's door. She even lifted the doormat. Nothing.

"Morning, Amy, looking for something?" Wilma smiled

over her shoulder at Amy as she locked her front door to head out for her morning power walk.

"No." Amy flashed her a smile she hoped was convincing. Wilma shrugged, squeaking past Amy in her white sneakers.

Amy stepped back into her apartment and closed the door. Her mind was reeling. Had she really missed him by a single day? Had he given up on her at the very same time as she had realised her mistake in letting him go?

Those macarons had been his gentle way of letting her know that he hadn't given up and that he was ready to talk if she was. He couldn't deliver a biscuit in the morning and ignore her call and message the same afternoon.

But then what? Amy paced her living room, occasionally yanking the door open in case the macaron had appeared.

With shaking hands, she made herself an espresso and sat down at her counter to drink it. She caught sight of herself in the gold-rimmed mirror opposite and felt a jolt of surprise at how stressed-out her reflection looked.

He'd met someone else. That was the only explanation. Hadn't he told her he believed in love at first sight? Hadn't he fallen for her the night they'd met? What if that was just his personality? She hadn't been *the* one for him, only *a* one.

She shook her head. No. That wasn't right. He was in love with her still, she knew it. She was being impatient. It had barely been 24 hours since she'd called and messaged. Maybe he was away on one of his field exercises, or another camping trip with no reception.

She needed to give him a little more time.

MARIE TAYLOR-FORD

By Monday, there was still no word from Rick. Amy's text sat unread and unanswered; her call unreturned.

She couldn't escape the feeling that something was very, very wrong. But that was the thing. She'd been kept so separate from every other part of Rick's life that she had no one to ask. No one to reach out to. She didn't even know Deacon's surname. The thought had even crossed her mind that she should call the army, though she knew it was ridiculous. Firstly, there was definitely no hotline for people trying to track down service-people they'd dated. The army was part of the government for God's sake. They wouldn't simply hand out information on a soldier's whereabouts to a random caller, even if Amy could find a number and a sympathetic voice at the end of the line in the first place. There was nothing at all she could do.

Except wait.

Amy wasn't entirely sure how she made it through the day at work. She certainly wasn't mentally present for at least half of it. Martha caught her in the breakout room, pouring coffee into an already overflowing cup.

"Are you having a stroke?" Martha asked, grabbing a wad of paper towels and mopping up the spill, glancing furtively around to make sure no one else had noticed.

"God, sorry, I don't know what happened." Amy scrambled to help her. "I think I was...I was thinking about the Rochester account."

"The bathroom makeover? Why on earth would that preoccupy you?"

Amy shrugged. Once the spill was cleared up, she took her coffee mug back to her desk and did her best to ignore Martha's sidelong glances the rest of the day.

At the stroke of five, she drove directly to the beach, struggling to find a park in the crowded lot. She sat down the instant her feet hit the sand, unable to go any further.

Her phone lit up with a video call from Lyra and, after a moment of hesitation, Amy slipped on her shades and answered it. Lyra and Alex had taken off on a spontaneous camping trip the day after their reunion.

"Hi, Ames!" Lyra's face lit up in a huge ear-to-ear grin.

In the background, Amy could see their tent beside a picturesque tree-lined river. Alex crouched beside a sputtering campfire, trying to bring it to life. Lyra had walked some way away from him to make the call.

"Hey you," Amy replied, turning her phone to show Lyra the water.

"Ohhhh, let's go for a long walk as soon as I'm home. I never get sick of that view!"

"Deal. So how is it?" Amy forced herself to keep her voice even, glad Lyra hadn't noticed anything amiss. "And when are you coming home?"

Lyra grinned. "In three days. We've extended it one more day because," she turned to look at Alex, who glanced up and waved, "well, because it's so awesome being out here." There was an expression of pure joy on her face.

Amy was happy for her, but couldn't ignore the tug on her own heartstrings as she thought of Rick. She knew she'd made that exact same face whenever she'd spoken about him. That giddy, headfirst, all-in, loved-up expression.

"We can see all the stars at night," Lyra continued, "every single one, it feels like. Although I have to admit we are also being eaten alive by mozzies and we have found a huntsman spider in the tent."

"Two!" Alex yelled.

Amy made a face of disgust. "That would be enough for me to burn the tent to the ground, get back in the car and never stop driving!" She managed a laugh.

"So what's been happening with you?" Lyra asked. Amy could pinpoint the second Lyra noticed something was wrong. "Oh, my God. What is it?" She dropped her voice and angled the phone away so that Alex wouldn't see or hear.

"I don't want to talk about it while you're on holiday. Let's hang out when you get home. I'll only bring your mood down."

"I'm not kidding, if you don't tell me what's going on, I'm getting Alex to pack up and take us home right now."

Amy sniffed, pulling her sunglasses off. "It's Rick," she said finally.

"Okay, what about him? Is he bothering you? Oh, Amy, your face." Lyra brought a hand to her heart.

"I'll be okay. And no, he's not bothering me. It's kind of the opposite." She filled Lyra in on the situation, her friend's face darkening in concern. "Do you think I'm being an idiot worrying about him? I mean what if it's as simple as he's over me?"

Lyra shook her head firmly. "I can tell you right now, that's *not* it. What I'm wondering is maybe he's out on some... field training expedition thing. I don't really know what it's called. But I'm guessing on those things, you don't really get much reception? That would also explain the macarons."

"I wondered that too. He has mentioned things like that before."

"I'm sure that's all it is, but I totally understand how worried you must be. Also, I know it's a bit weird to say this given the situation, but I'm *so* happy you decided to give him a second chance. You guys are perfect together. It will all work out, Ames. I can feel it in my bones."

"I'm sure you're right," Amy said, trying to be positive. She didn't want to take up any more of Lyra's time on her trip, and at that moment, Alex called out.

Lyra glanced over her shoulder and then turned back to Amy. "We're going to make some hot chocolate and toast some marshmallows. I'm also going to coat myself in bug spray. Can you message me as soon as you hear from him?"

"I will, promise. See you soon!"

After they'd hung up, Amy stared out to sea, drinking in the salty air in the last of the light. Dusk was a dangerous time for shark attacks, rare though they were. She watched as a surfer emerged from the water, peeling his wetsuit to his hip bones before he padded across the sand to the shower, surfboard tucked under his arm.

Amy wiggled her bare toes into the sand. The top layer was hot from the day's warmth, but once she dug her feet beneath the surface, the sand was damp and cool.

She decided to send Rick another message.

CHAPTER TWENTY-EIGHT

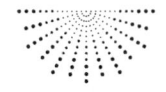

One message turned into many more over the next two days. At some point, Amy abandoned her dignity and kept trying Rick's number. Her calls went straight through to voicemail and she lost count of the number of messages she'd left. She couldn't leave any more, because a robotic voice told her his mailbox was full. If he really was away on field exercises, he was going to run a mile from the lunatic stalker she'd become.

Rather than spend another evening alone, she met Silas and Marley at the Whistle Stop that night. It was Silas's idea, and one Amy gratefully took up. Lyra was on her way home that day, but wouldn't make it in time to join them. She'd been in constant contact with Amy since she'd heard about Rick.

Around their usual barrel at the Whistle Stop, Amy, Silas and Marley's phones pinged with messages at the exact same time. Silas checked his first and groaned, rolling his eyes at Amy and Marley as he held up his screen, showing a picture of a beaming Lyra. Alex stood behind her, his arms wrapped tightly around her middle. They were at a truck stop.

"It's not just me, right? She's been really annoying this whole trip," Silas said, and the girls laughed. "She's trolling us now with all this lovey-dovey stuff. I for one am glad the trip is over!"

"I'm so happy for her." Marley's face was open and honest. She was dressed in one of her typical outfits, a combination of clothing never before seen on a human being. A billowing pair of Thai fisherman's pants, sparkly red heels and what could only be described as a blue straight-jacket. Her fringe was freshly trimmed and completely lopsided.

As Amy gazed around the bar, she spotted a young man sitting alone in the corner, nursing a beer. His back was to her, but his hair reminded her of Deacon's. An unusual shade of coppery-brown. The man stood up to go to the bathroom, his back to Amy the whole time, and she kept her eyes trained on the door for when he came out. Her heart was pounding.

"What if she gets pregnant on this trip?" Marley asked out of nowhere.

"Lyra's not going to get pregnant when her music career is about to take off." Amy's eyes were glued to the door as she spoke.

"I guess you're right," Marley said. "But she hasn't signed the contract with Teller's Music yet. Amy, why's your face so red?"

"Menopause," Amy joked quickly.

They all laughed, but Amy's laugh was forced and she hoped they couldn't tell.

"I don't even know if she wants kids," Silas said, clicking his phone off and shoving it in his back pocket.

"Sure she does," Marley said. "Everyone does."

"No, they don't," Amy said. Silas pointed his index finger at Amy and clicked his tongue, indicating she was right.

Marley looked taken aback. "Well anyway, she probably

wouldn't do it now, you're right." There was an edge to Marley's voice that Amy couldn't quite place.

"How are things with you and Ernie?" Amy asked Silas, only half her mind on the conversation. Possibly-Deacon still hadn't returned.

Silas turned down a corner of his mouth, thinking about his previous love interest. "He was into me and I wasn't into him, then I was into him and he wasn't into me." He took a sip of his beer and shrugged. "I'm waiting for him to be interested in me again. That's how this works, right?"

"I don't think so." Marley shook her head. "He's probably forgotten all about you."

Amy pulled her eyes away from the bathroom door to glare at her.

Marley pointed a finger. "He's sitting right there," she said defensively, "and I think he's on a date."

Silas spun so fast he almost gave himself whiplash. At the exact same moment, Ernie spotted him and blushed violently. The man with Ernie glanced back and forth between Ernie and Silas, a frown deepening.

Ernie stood up too fast and his table wobbled, spilling the drinks across it. The liquid splashed onto his date's pants, drenching them, and the man stood up in annoyance.

"You idiot," he said loudly, frantically brushing at his trousers. In one swift movement, Silas sprang from his seat and grabbed hold of the man's collar. Ernie flapped his hands in panic.

"Oh my God, Silas! Let him go." Amy hastily tried to separate them. Silas was eyeballing the guy, his collar still firmly in grip. Silas was almost double the man's size, much more powerfully-built and at least twice as good-looking.

"Don't you *ever* speak to Ernie like that," Silas growled.

"Okay, okay!" the guy said, holding up his hands. "I'm out of here." He picked up his jacket and quickly left the bar without a backward glance, leaving Ernie and Silas staring at one another.

"What did you do that for?" Ernie asked, trying to muster annoyance. But Amy could see the stars in his eyes and almost feel his knees going weak. "It wasn't a big deal."

"You think I'd stand there while he called you an idiot?"

Ernie looked down and Amy felt Marley touch her shoulder. She crooked her index finger and beckoned Amy away from them. It was sweet, perceptive, and very un-Marley-like.

Amy's heart was pounding, the way it always did if she was around something violent, or the potential for it. She tried to take some deep breaths, but she couldn't stop shaking. Then she looked up. Deacon - it *was* Deacon - had come back from the bathroom and was staring at her as though uncertain what to do.

"I'll be right back," she said to Marley, quickly crossing the room.

"Deacon," Amy said when she reached him, and then stopped, completely unsure of what to say. If Rick had given up on her, she'd be putting Deacon in a very awkward position, yet again. But on the other hand, if something *had* happened to Rick, she needed to know. It also crossed her mind that he must be wondering how she'd react to him, since he'd been forced by Rick to lie to her.

They stared at each other for a long moment, Amy's frown deepening and a look of realisation dawning in Deacon's eyes. "You don't know, do you?"

"Know what?" Amy whispered, every vertebra in her spine going rigid.

Deacon's eyes ran searchingly over her face. "Sit down," he said gently, and she did, hard. "Amy, Rick was in a car accident. Maybe a week ago now? He's in hospital. Actually, I've just come from there, though they're not letting us into his ward. We might be able to visit from tomorrow when he's hopefully out of ICU. We're not sure..." He trailed off and bit his lip.

Though she was sitting, Amy grabbed the edge of the barrel to steady herself, her heart hammering in fright. "Not sure what?" she whispered.

"Are you okay?" Deacon placed a steadying hand on her arm. "You look like you're going to faint."

"Not sure what?" she repeated, close to tears.

Deacon looked down. "Not sure if he'll be able to walk again. His spine was injured in the accident. Even if he does walk, it's highly unlikely..." He choked off and was silent for a moment, before he regained composure. "Rick will probably never serve in the army again. It looks like his career is over."

CHAPTER TWENTY-NINE

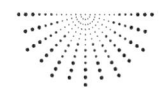

Amy would have driven directly to the hospital if she hadn't been drinking, and if she'd thought they'd let her in. Even if it was to sleep outside Rick's room. She was frantic to be near him, in any way.

After another night of very little sleep, punctuated by bouts of tears, she was up well before sunrise, using every calming ritual in her arsenal to keep her sane until a reasonable hour. She walked the beach, taking deep breaths of the sea air and watching the first surfers head out as the sun rose. Back home, she did a short but sweaty yoga session, drank far too much coffee, had a long shower, got dressed and did her makeup and changed her outfit four times. It was still only 7:15. The hands on her watch had never circled the dial so slowly.

She arrived at the hospital at 8:30, half an hour before visiting hours began. She paced the gardens outside, grabbed another coffee from the cart near the entrance, and stalked through the giftshop with so much vigour that she frightened the cashier.

Once visiting hours officially began, she found her way to

the ward block Deacon had written down for her, avoiding all the nurses' stations along the way. She knew if she was stopped or challenged, she'd be turned away.

Rounding the last corridor, she came face-to-face with a serious-looking nurse holding a clipboard. He stared up at her.

"Can I help you?"

Amy shook her head, hoping he'd go away. He continued looking at her expectantly. They were the only two in the corridor, for as far as Amy could see in either direction. This didn't seem to be a heavily-visited part of the hospital and didn't get much foot traffic. Amy realised that was probably deliberate.

"No, I. I'm waiting for someone."

"Okay," he said, sounding unconvinced. "You can't loiter around the subacute ward though. Who are you waiting for?"

"Yes. No. I..." Her face flamed. Couldn't he just get on with his business? Why was he giving her the third degree? "I'm actually here to visit someone," she said finally, after an awkwardly long moment of silence during which he did not blink.

"Which patient?" He consulted his clipboard.

"Rick."

His eyes ran quickly down the page and he shook his head. "We don't have a Rick."

"Richard," she corrected herself. "Richard Ford."

The nurse frowned and lowered the clipboard. "Is he expecting you? Are you family?"

Amy shook her head, mute. She hadn't expected to be questioned so extensively. Although, she hadn't known what to expect at all. She knew she couldn't handle being turned away when she was so close.

"Richard has only just been transferred from the ICU," the nurse said gently. "With his injuries, he's not in a position to be receiving visitors outside the family at the moment."

Tears welled and Amy could do little to stop them. "But I want to see him. Even for a second. *Please*."

The nurse pressed his lips together as though he understood her pain. Then he shook his head. "It's certainly distressing when friends are in hospital," his tone was firm but kind, "however, in Richard's current state, it's really not possible for him to receive casual visitors today. In the next few days perhaps." With one last sympathetic look, he began to walk away.

"I'm his girlfriend," Amy called, before he had gone too far. She hated herself the minute the words left her mouth. It was a desperate, manipulative attempt and she wasn't sure it would get her anywhere, but she had to try. She hadn't come this far to give up.

He walked back quickly and briefly laid a sympathetic hand on her arm. "I hadn't realised, I'm so sorry."

"Yes, I was… away and I only just found out. Please could I see him for a moment? I want to be sure he's okay."

He squinted at Amy, as though weighing something up. "He's not okay." His tone was one of practised tenderness. "I want you to be prepared for that. But you need to control your reaction and your emotions as much as possible. It's important for Richard that he doesn't think his appearance is a source of distress." Amy nodded, seeing the sense of his words. "His spinal injury is incomplete, level D." His tone suggested to her this was positive news, but she shook her head in confusion. "It means there is a very good chance he'll make a full recovery, of *all* his functions." He said the last part with a significance that made Amy blush. "But there are no guarantees and absolutely no time lines."

Her voice was small as she replied. "I'm ready. I want to see him."

Her heart hammered as she followed the nurse down the hall. She was determined that whatever shock she felt, she wouldn't react.

Before the door, the nurse paused again to look at her. "Are you certain you're ready for this?" She nodded. "I'm going to go in and ask him if he wants to see you."

"Oh!" It came out as a perfect note of disappointment. He turned to her in alarm and she swallowed a lump in her throat. "Nothing. Sorry." Silently, she willed Rick to let her in. She wasn't entirely sure what his feelings towards her would be, or whether he'd want her to see him like this.

The nurse appeared a moment later and held the door open for her, nodding. Amy exhaled the breath she hadn't realised she'd been holding and stepped inside.

The room was darkened and Rick was hooked up to several machines that beeped and hummed. One of his arms was in plaster and his neck was velcroed into a thick, moulded collar that prevented movement. As Amy approached, she could see a jagged scar that ran from his hairline, across his face to the jawline on the other side, blue stitches bristling from the raw-looking line. One eye was completely swollen shut, the skin over it a livid purple. Both legs were encased in braces spiked with protruding screws. An IV was taped to his wrist, the tube leading to two bags of fluid - one large and one small - hanging from a wheeled metal frame. A thin, clear hose fed oxygen into both nostrils.

Amy needed a moment to stifle the sobs that threatened to escape her. She willed herself forward. If Rick could survive this happening to him, she could survive seeing him this way. With the nurse's words echoing in her ears, she took a seat beside his good eye and looked into it, feeling her heart thudding so hard she was sure he'd be able to hear it. Rick watched her as she sat down.

"Rick, I only just found out." Her voice sounded odd and she coughed to disguise a sob. She remembered what the nurse had said about not showing him how shocked she was, and tried to pull it together. "Otherwise I would have been here the whole time. But I guess they wouldn't have let me in. I'm rambling, I know." She took a breath, trying to slow her pace. "I wasn't sure you'd agree to see me. I'm so happy you did."

He looked up at the ceiling for a long moment, and then back at her. "I'm having a hard day." His voice was hoarse and Amy almost wanted to laugh at the understatement. But she realised what he meant. Laying here was excruciating for him, and he could handle it some days better than others. "I couldn't say no to seeing you. Even if only for a moment."

Amy nodded slowly, willing the tears back. "I'm wearing my favourite brooch. I haven't taken it off." She touched the banksia pinned to her chest, but couldn't speak further.

He took a deep breath, and looked away from her. "I'm going to say something and I want you to listen to me."

"Okay, of course." She leaned forward.

He was silent for so long that Amy began to worry. "I want you to go, and I don't want you to come back. I don't want to be with you anymore. I've moved on, and you should too."

Amy was stunned into silence. The sound of her ragged breath was audible over the beeps and clicks of Rick's machines. "No," she said finally. "No. I won't. I don't believe you."

He kept his eyes away from hers, but when he squeezed them shut, a tear slid down his cheek. "You need to." His voice cracked with emotion. "It's the truth. I let you believe I was much more interested than I really was. Sorry."

Amy inhaled sharply, tears welling. All she wanted was to hold him. It was torture to be in his presence and not be allowed to touch him. But here he was, telling her everything had been a lie. *Another* lie. She shook her head, plugging her ears with her fingers as a tear dripped down her nose. "None of this is real," she said. "None of it."

When she finally looked up, she could see how badly he was struggling. He didn't want her there. He wanted her gone.

"It *is* real. And you need to go."

Amy puffed out a slow breath, then shook her head. "You were bringing me the macarons. I know it was you. And they were still on my mat not that many days ago. Your feelings can't have changed so much -"

"They have." He still wasn't looking at her. "I'm not in love with you now, I never was and I want you to get out."

His words were a punch to Amy's stomach. She couldn't move, couldn't find the strength to pull herself away from him, even though he wanted her gone. It was foolish, but she didn't care. She *needed* to be near him. She could deal with what he was saying later, once she knew he was okay.

He turned his eye to her. She had always responded physically to him - heart jackhammering in her ribcage, stomach doing flips, knees going weak. That had not changed one tiny bit, she realised now, no matter what had happened between them. No matter what was happening now.

"Get out!" he shouted with difficulty. "Get out, get *out!*"

Amy picked up her bag and fled the room. In the hall, she slammed directly into the nurse who had shown her into the room. "Sorry!" She stumbled blindly towards the stairwell and heard the nurse sigh behind her.

"I asked you to keep your emotions in check," he said, irritated.

She spun to face him and everything came bubbling out. "I tried! But that's the man I love lying there. And I can't do *anything*." Amy choked off.

"Then please don't come back until you can accept that."

"Don't worry, he doesn't want me back anyway!"

The nurse nodded. "That sounds like the right decision." He strode off in the opposite direction, leaving her on her own. She found her way to the nearest bathroom, burst into an empty stall and slumped down on the closed toilet lid to sob her heart out.

CHAPTER THIRTY

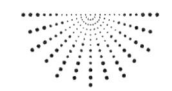

When she had cried herself out - and reassured several concerned women who tapped gently on the door to ask whether they could help - Amy unlocked the toilet stall door and came out. She splashed cold water on her face, wiped the mascara from under her eyes, and tightened her high ponytail. Her eyes were puffy and bloodshot and her nose was still red, but that was as good as it was going to get today.

She checked her phone and saw thirteen missed calls, all from Kristina. Her heart stalled as she realised they were due at their pitch meeting with Peregrine Hotels today. Amy hadn't yet missed the meeting, but she and Kristina had agreed to travel together in a taxi from the office to save costs. Kristina must have been panicking because she still wasn't there.

Amy phoned her back as she walked out of the hospital and into the sunlight, slipping her shades on. It seemed cruelly bright and warm outside, and she hated the thought of Rick missing out on such a beautiful day. Even worse, knowing that he would miss out on many more. But at least he wasn't missing out forever. At least he hadn't been killed in the crash. The thought jabbed an icy cold finger of fear into her belly.

Kristina answered on the first ring. "Where are you?" she asked, without saying hello.

"I had a… family emergency this morning. I'll meet you at Peregrine, I'm heading there now."

"Do you have your concept boards?"

She didn't. She'd taken them home for some last-minute finessing and hadn't thought to bring them with her. She checked her watch to see if she'd have time to run home, grab them and still be at the Peregrine in time.

"No," she admitted, embarrassed.

"Did you save your images onto the shared drive here?"

"Yes."

"I'll get Liza to reprint them now and give them to you there."

Amy breathed out. "Thank you."

"It's fine," Kristina said. "And Amy?"

"Yes?"

"I'm sorry about your family situation."

The line went dead before Amy could respond.

Amy tossed her keys to the valet at the Peregrine with eight minutes to spare. She'd managed to stem the flow of tears on the way over, and had swallowed one half of a calming tablet she'd been prescribed for flights. She'd randomly found the blister packet in her glove box, and desperately hoped the pill wouldn't make her too drowsy.

Kristina was waiting for her out front and wordlessly handed Amy a leather folio as she approached. Amy was touched that she'd gone the extra mile of putting her concept boards into a professional-looking folio. It would make her look much more polished and professional than traipsing in with them stuck under her arm.

"Let's head in." Kristina spun on her heel and strode ahead. They pushed through the revolving glass doors and once they were inside the air-conditioned lobby, Amy pulled her sunglasses off. Kristina flinched as she caught a glimpse of Amy's face.

"That bad, huh?"

"You don't have to present if you're not up to it. I can present your ideas too."

"I don't really think that's a good idea. I can do this."

Kristina shrugged. "As I said, I always think it's best if the client has choices. You could trust me to present yours. But it's your call."

"I'm fine. I'll tell them it's hay fever."

"That's one hell of an allergy." Kristina turned away, approaching the reception desk.

They were led into one of the Peregrine's meeting rooms and found a table filled with drinks and snacks, as well as an easel on which to display their boards. The clients hadn't arrived yet, so Amy searched around for another easel. She opened and closed a few cupboards but found nothing.

"There's only one," she said, feeling irritated.

Kristina shrugged. "You go first, I'll follow."

Amy bit back a laugh as she realised something. She felt competitive. What Rick had said to her all those months ago when they were on the beach, about competition making things interesting. It turned out he was right. Despite the fact that the ache in her heart was unbearable and almost all-consuming, she had rarely felt so eager to get a presentation started, or to convince the clients that her idea was the best one.

Amy watched Kristina for a moment, as she leaned over a bowl of M&Ms, carefully picking out only yellow ones. She looked totally unruffled and Amy wondered what was running through her mind. "Do you always do that, with the yellow?"

Kristina looked up and grinned. "It's a nervous tic of mine. Something I can control, I guess."

Amy nodded. Moments later, two executives from the Peregrine's parent company - a young, sharply-dressed man with precision-shaved facial hair, and a friendly-faced older lady in a clover-green pants suit - strode into the room.

"Jake Adcock." The man's handshake was unnecessarily firm and vigorous, and Amy bit her lip to stop from telling him to calm down.

"Amelia Blades." She shook their hands in a more rational manner before she and Jake took seats around the table. "Amy, are you..." She broke off, circling her face with her hand.

"Horrible hay fever," Amy said quickly. "I've taken tablets and it should calm down soon."

Amelia nodded, giving her a sympathetic smile.

"Shall we quickly introduce ourselves?" Kristina asked, and Amy felt a spike of annoyance that she'd taken the lead. Amy didn't want to get stuck looking like the assistant being trotted out for her first rodeo.

"Great idea. I'm Amy Porter," she began, perhaps a little loudly, before Jake and Amelia had responded. "I'm a senior designer in the commercial team and I've been with Edgerton's for six years. We've got some great ideas that we're really excited to show you. We've prepared a couple of contrasting options that we'd like to explore with you. Kristina?"

Kristina had been smiling as Amy talked and she nodded now, turning to face Jake and Amelia. "I'm relatively new to

Edgerton's. I was headhunted to join them several months ago." Amy's heart dropped at this news. She hadn't known Beaumont had headhunted Kristina, didn't know Beaumont headhunted people at all. She plastered a grin on her face as Kristina continued. "I specialise in these kinds of refreshes but there's something I'd like you to know about my style upfront." Kristina paused for effect and Amy realised she had Jake and Amelia hooked. They nodded for her to continue, both folding their hands on the table and leaning forward slightly. "I want to push you, to challenge you, take you to the limits." Kristina gestured passionately. "I might not give you what you think you're looking for, but what I will give you *works*. You told us your vision, I looked for the story beyond that. And the story I see with Peregrine is that we need a shake-up. But we aren't going to tap into your potential if we do things the same way as we've always done them."

There was silence as she finished and Jake looked thoroughly convinced. Amy suspected he was close to clapping. She was pretty impressed herself. Kristina was *good*.

"With that said," Amy began, stepping forward slightly to get their eyes on her again. "It's never wise to completely toss out the past. We don't want to lose the heritage that sets you apart in the market."

Amelia smiled and Jake nodded. "I really like what you mentioned, Kristina," he said. "We *do* need a shake up."

"But we're not here to reinvent Peregrine entirely," Amelia added. It seemed Amy and Kristina had one supporter apiece.

"Let's have a look at what we're talking about," Amy said quickly.

They first presented their agreed proposed layout update for the space. They had individually come up with startlingly similar layout concepts, but that was where the parallels in their designs ended.

Amelia and Jake both immediately approved the proposal, then Kristina stepped back and gestured Amy to the easel to present her moodboard. The gesture implied permission and Amy felt another rub of annoyance.

She slipped her boards onto the easel and stepped back to look at their faces. Amelia was nodding slowly, her eyes roaming over the imagery. Jake was squinting at it.

"I like this, it's very calming and sanctuary-like," Amelia said.

"But we don't want people going to sleep in here," Jake said, "It's pretty, but I'm seeing so much of this style lately."

"That's because it's classic." Amy tried not to sound defensive. "It has a luxe feel, which is what we want people to associate with the Peregrine brand. People will drink here and feel as though they're at an exclusive garden party. The kind you *really* want to be invited to."

Jake tilted his head at the boards. "I do really love those neon signs. Those are cool."

Amelia grinned at Amy and she nodded humbly, feeling a surge of triumph. She took her boards down and signalled to Kristina that she could load hers up.

"Whoa!" Jake said, once Kristina stepped back from her boards. "These are *awesome*."

Amelia was still taking the boards in, but Amy could see a slow smile spreading across her face. "Tell us about this," she prompted Kristina.

"Gladly. This is what I'm calling 'Mad Hatter ambiance'. A place where anything can happen, where dreams come true and where chance encounters can end in real romance. It's full of intrigue and possibility. And you want to make *sure* you've posted it all over your socials."

There was silence as she finished talking. Jake and Amelia

shared a look. "Give us a second," Amelia said. "Help yourselves to some drinks and snacks." She and Jake leaned in to one another and began whispering.

Amy grabbed a bottle of lemonade and popped the cap off, drinking thirstily. She was parched after crying out what felt like the majority of water in her body, and the bubbles felt cool and soothing against her raw throat.

Kristina slipped her company iPhone out and scrolled through some messages, tapping out a quick reply to one or the other. It made her look busy and important, and Amy was about to do the same thing when she caught herself. She didn't need to mimic Kristina to be impressive, she brought a lot to the game as she was. She realised she wasn't really used to this friendly competition thing, and wished she could talk to Rick about it. The thought brought tears pricking again, so she tried Kristina's trick of selecting a single colour from the candy tray. Green, for the last box Rick had given her. The trick was surprisingly effective.

"So, you might not want to hear this," Amelia said a moment later. "But we really like *both* of the styles. We're wondering if there's a way we can take a little from column A and a little from column B."

"These both capture some elements of what we want, but we think they'll be really special when we combine them," Jake added.

Amy and Kristina were silent for a moment, casting sidelong looks at one another. Then they both began talking at once.

"I really don't see how the two styles are compatible, I think we have to go in one direction or the other," Amy began, as Kristina said, "We're trying to achieve two different emotions here, it's an either-or kind of situation."

"Guys, guys, guys!" Jake held up his hands, smirking. "Take the win. We like both of them. Put them together somehow and come back to us with that. Make it happen, and be grateful we're not going with another firm."

They fell silent, nodding solemnly. Amelia and Jake stood and shook their hands, congratulating them. Once they'd left the room, Amy turned to Kristina.

"Well, now what do we do?" she asked. "We had an agreement that one of us would take this over."

"If there was a clear victor," Kristina reminded her, zipping her folio shut and grabbing a fistful of M&Ms - all the colours. "But there wasn't. Seems we're evenly matched."

Amy lifted her folio from the table. "So, what? We keep working together?"

"Nightmare, right?" Kristina winked at Amy as she sauntered out of the room and back into the hotel lobby. Amy couldn't help but smile at her back.

CHAPTER THIRTY-ONE

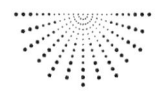

'll just go inside and have a coffee, Amy thought the next morning. She liked the idea of being in the same building as Rick, even if hospital espressos were criminally lousy.

She didn't remember having made a clear decision to drive to the hospital. She'd told herself she was going to work, but then she'd taken a long detour. Finding herself in the hospital neighbourhood, she'd decided she would simply drive around the beautiful grounds for a while. But instead, she'd steered the car into the parking lot and taken a ticket.

In the cafeteria, Amy nursed the unpalatable coffee, leafing through a design magazine she bought from the news agency gift-shop near the hospital entrance. She scanned everyone else who entered in case they might know Rick.

A text pinged through from Hazel, telling her Sunnywoods was delighted with the designs she'd presented and would be starting on them right away. Amy managed a small smile at that, then stared back into her coffee.

She stayed for almost an hour, too afraid to try visiting

Rick again. She didn't see anyone in army uniform, or anyone who bore the slightest resemblance to Rick. But then, she had no idea what his mother or other relatives looked like. If only she'd had the chance to meet them.

Eventually, she forced herself to get up and go to work.

She was hopelessly distracted once she got there. She kept hearing Rick's voice as he yelled at her to leave.

She fingered the banksia brooch and closed her eyes for a brief second, remembering the first time she set eyes on him at the Whistle Stop. If only they could go back in time. She wondered what her reaction would have been, if Rick had told her that he was in the army on that very first night. Would she still have taken the time to get to know him? It seemed unlikely. Maybe she'd have been happy with a fling, but she'd definitely have been biased against anything longer term. She wasn't the type to be rootless, or to give up her lifestyle. And she wanted to stay near her Pop, her friends and her job. Still, she'd known there was something special about him even that night.

She sighed. It was impossible to know what she would have done. It would always be impossible to know. He hadn't given her that choice.

She shook her head and forced herself to think about something else, like starting her own business. A part of her had been thinking about it since she'd taken Loretta's business card. Finding new clients took time, but she could call Loretta, ask to meet her and feel out what sort of clients she'd be willing to send Amy's way. And what they'd pay.

She could also simply start running a business from her living room for a while, but Amy knew she wouldn't be happy with that. She needed a clear line between office and home, otherwise she'd end up consumed by work.

"Earth to Amy," Martha said, from beside her.

"Yes, how can I help you?" Amy turned to Martha with a mock-prim look on her face, trying to clown away her blues.

Martha giggled. "Are you working on that laundry renovation?"

"Yeah. *Man*, it's boring." Amy glanced around to make sure Beaumont hadn't heard.

"I've got a bathroom project again. But I know Beaumont gave Kristina a client redoing an entire sandstone mansion on Lilac Bay. Why are we getting the crappy stuff and she's getting the good projects?"

Amy's heart thudded in her chest. As if she didn't have enough going on, there was this constant thing with Beaumont and Kristina. Beaumont really did have firm favourites, and he played them out hard. Amy realised now that everyone must have resented her for the entire time *she* was his pet. It was a miracle she was still friends with most of them, since she occasionally felt an urge to strangle Kristina - nice as she was.

"I don't know," Amy said sadly.

"If I never see another bathroom again, I'll die happy."

"Really?" Amy managed a grin. "Never?"

"Never," Martha repeated, firmly shaking her head.

"That is going to make your life *very* difficult," Amy said, and they giggled. "I have an idea. Why don't we do the most over the top stuff we can think of? Not this classic neutral stuff, let's create totally crazy designs."

"Beaumont won't like it," Martha said hesitantly, biting her lip.

"But the clients might. And we definitely will. We can create them as options, and see which one they go for."

"Okay," Martha said finally. "I guess it's the only way my job's going to be any fun at all today."

Amy watched her turn back to her computer screen and desperately wished it were possible to open her own company. She'd hire Martha on the spot and make sure she never had a boring day again.

CHAPTER THIRTY-TWO

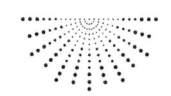

The candy pink of Marley's jumpsuit would have had teen Amy in fits of joy. The lime green polka dot t-shirt under it - not so much. Amy had invited Marley and Lyra over and when she opened her front door, she knew she'd done the right thing. She'd been keeping them updated on Rick, but hadn't had the energy to meet up face-to-face until now.

Her car had steered itself towards the hospital again that morning, and she'd sat in the cafeteria for the duration of a bad coffee, scanning the place for… she wasn't sure what. Then she'd driven into the office for a draining day of playing make-believe that she was okay. Amy needed her friends tonight.

She hugged Lyra tightly at the door. "Welcome home. Can't believe I haven't seen you since you got back."

"How are you doing?" Lyra asked. Amy shrugged, reaching to hug Marley once Lyra finally let go.

"I'm so sorry you've come back to this," Amy said to Lyra, as she fixed them all drinks. Marley was scanning the delivery menu from the local pizza place, but Lyra couldn't take her worried eyes off Amy. "I really do want to hear about your trip with Alex, and how your meeting with Teller's Music went."

Lyra waved her hand. "We can talk about that later, I can update you in about two sentences. Tonight is us supporting you."

"Please." Amy squeezed lime into Lyra's drink and gave her a meaningful look. "Tell me now, to distract me. I can't talk about him without breaking down right now. I needed you two here."

Lyra's happiness radiated, despite her obvious concern for Amy. She was unable to keep the smile entirely from her face as she spoke. "I had a really interesting meeting with Selena Teller after the trip with Alex. I kind of have big news. The label is signing me up for two albums."

Marley gasped and Amy's smile was genuine. "Oh, that is *incredible* news. You truly deserve that!"

"Wait, you said *me*? What about Mick?" Marley asked.

Lyra screwed up her nose. "He says he doesn't want this for himself. He always wanted it for me. He's got a girlfriend now and, well, we're still figuring some things out. But he'll come on board, I'm sure of it."

"Tell us more about the contract, please," Amy said.

Lyra practically wriggled with joy. She told them about the camping trip - how she and Alex had stayed up almost every night talking into the small hours, discussing anything and everything. She was completely and utterly in love and he was too. She'd also been inspired to write another song, and felt like she'd tapped into something inside her - a creative river that was starting to flow.

Amy shivered as Lyra talked. She'd seen every single one of Lyra's gigs since they'd met, and heard each of her songs. Amy fully agreed - Lyra had taken a massive step forward with the song she had written for Alex during the time they were apart. Lyra was destined for great things and Amy was incredibly happy for her, and especially glad that the record label could see her talent.

Behind her unwavering smile though, Amy was fighting a sense of panic. She had always been the one who had her life *together* among the three friends. Happiness wasn't like pie, Amy knew that. Lyra being successful didn't mean there was less success for Amy, and Amy realised it was possible to be both overjoyed for Lyra and slightly anxious for herself at the same time. But she felt as though in contrast to her friend's life taking strides forward, hers was stagnating or even going backwards.

"So, it looks like I'm going to be really busy working on these albums," Lyra said as Amy tuned back in. "It's going to be a bit hard to split my time between it all. I honestly don't know how I'm going to manage."

Amy handed the girls their drinks, joining them on the sofa. Lyra frowned into her vodka lime and soda.

"Don't worry about us. You can leave Amy and I to handle each other, as long as you don't forget us when you're rich and famous."

"Seriously," Amy added, putting a hand on Lyra's arm and looking her in the eye. "We're going to be right here whenever and wherever you need us. You don't need to feel guilty and you don't need to worry that we're getting annoyed or we're forgetting you. We'll still blow up the group chat though, to be clear."

Lyra laughed. "Thank you both, but I'm not planning on ditching my friends, that's not what I meant. Although, probably there will be times when it's hard. But," she looked at Amy and Marley in turn. "Alex knows I'm going to be crazy busy and that's whyyy…he's asked me to move in with him. It's crazy quick, but it's the only way we'll still be able to spend time together." She balled her fists up and held them to her cheeks, her expression somewhere between joy and panic.

"Oh that's amazing!" Marley leaned over to hug Lyra, who grinned at Amy from over her shoulder.

"Are you going to say yes?" Amy asked.

"I don't know." She looked conflicted. "I *really* love living with Si. I can't imagine not seeing him every day. Especially since I won't be able to work at The Pie-ganic much anymore either. To be honest, it will break my heart to move away from him. It will definitely be the end of an era. And of course, he's being completely unsentimental about it. Especially because Ernie is over basically every night-"

"So they *did* get back together after that night at the Whistle Stop," Amy said.

Lyra nodded. "They're joined at the hip now. Actually, Si wants Ernie to move in so he isn't exactly pushing me to stay."

"Everyone's moving so fast in your family," Marley said. "You'll be pregnant before you know it."

Lyra grinned, shaking her head, and Amy realised that was the second time Marley had mentioned pregnancy. She shot Marley a sidelong glance, but her face was as clear and bright and happy as usual. Amy made a mental note to ask her about it another time, when they were alone.

"Who's going to help Silas with the truck?" Amy asked, changing the subject.

"I'll do two days a week until we can find someone else, but there's a teenager named Cameron that Alex is kind of big-brother mentoring. He's turning out to be a huge help."

"That's great," Amy said. The girls heard something in her tone of voice that made them fall silent. Lyra's face dropped. "No, please keep talking," Amy said quickly, sniffing.

Instead, they both leaned to wrap her in a giant group hug. Safe within their arms, Amy let herself collapse a little.

A fter the girls left late that night, Amy worked up the nerve to call Deacon. She needed to talk to someone who was talking to Rick. She wasn't sure Deacon would answer her call - if he was even still awake. But he'd given her his number at the Whistle Stop so he must not have been completely against the idea.

It was several rings before he answered with an uncertain, "Hello?"

Amy sank onto her sofa at the sound of his voice. She'd been pacing the room. "Is this a bad time?"

"No. You can call whenever you like. I was still up." Silence hung in the air between them. "You went to see him?" Deacon sounded like he was stating a fact. Rick must have told him.

"Yes. And I guess you also know he threw me out."

Deacon exhaled audibly. "Listen, he's not in a great place right now."

"I know. God, how could he be? I'm not angry. Just sad. I really thought he was still…"

"He is," Deacon said gently. "I can tell. We've never seen him how he was after he met you. We tried to tell him he was doing the wrong thing by not telling you about the army, but he was so scared of losing you."

"That's why I never got to meet any of you."

"Yeah. We didn't think it was fair, even though we totally understood what was going on in his head. I finally agreed to meet up once, if he agreed not to make me lie outright."

"I know he *did* love me, but he seems pretty certain it's over now. I don't want to bother him, but… I wanted us to try again. I started calling him. Before I knew what had happened. But even then, I was already too late."

"Oh God." Deacon sighed. "I'm sorry, Amy. I hope you're

not beating yourself up about the accident. He *wanted* to go get those macarons for you, we couldn't talk him out of it."

Amy was silent, her eyes wide and her heart gurgling. "Wait," she said slowly, her voice shaking with realisation. "That's when he had the accident? When he was driving to get me a macaron?"

Heat burned in her cheeks and her breath came ragged. Why had it never occurred to her that he'd been injured during one of those trips? She'd assumed it had happened on the army base. Of course it had happened when he was bringing her the biscuits. He must have been tired out of his mind getting up so early, for so many weeks. Oh my God. She was an idiot. No wonder he never wanted to see her again.

Deacon coughed. "That was really dumb of me," he said, in a soft voice. "I'm so sorry. Of course you couldn't have known that. But that isn't the reason he's trying to push you away now. I'm absolutely certain of it."

"I need to go." Her voice was a whisper.

"No, wait, please. Are you going to be okay? Do you want to meet up?"

Amy shook her head, gulping several times. He waited wordlessly on the line. "Thank you for letting me know. I'll call you soon."

She hung up and sat staring out her living room window. Then she did something she hadn't done in a long time - something she had used in the past as a coping mechanism whenever she wanted to switch off her brain.

She walked to the little 24/7 supermarket halfway down her street and bought a family-sized bag of frozen French fries and a super saver jar of mayonnaise. She ignored both the chirpy banter of the teenager on the checkout and the judgmental looks of the waif-thin woman in line behind her.

At home, she changed into her pyjamas, warmed up the

oven and spread the chips across two racks. She grabbed a half-finished bottle of whisky from her liquor cabinet and slumped onto the couch, clicking the remote through the options on her streaming service until she decided on a perfectly trashy, six-season show.

Halfway into episode one, the chips were ready and she scraped them from the baking trays into a huge stainless steel bowl. She sat on the sofa, dunking the fries directly into the mayonnaise jar, sipping whisky and clicking "next" at the end of each episode.

At some point, she finally fell asleep.

CHAPTER THIRTY-THREE

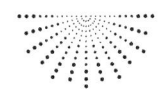

The congealed mayonnaise jar on Amy's lap slipped to the floor with a thunk, waking her. Her mouth was pasty and she had a pounding headache. She didn't even bother hurrying to work once she was showered and caffeinated, instead driving straight to the hospital and grabbing another coffee in the cafeteria.

This time she didn't buy a magazine and simply sat there, watching the door like a hawk. She didn't truly expect to recognise anyone, and Rick's words still haunted her. She'd had moments where she could make herself believe he'd pushed her away to spare her. A misguided idea, but she could almost see herself doing the same thing if their situations were reversed.

But in the cold light of day, it seemed more likely that he'd meant it. That he simply didn't want her around. Particularly now that she knew the accident had been partly her fault. She could hardly blame him. It was like a punch to the stomach each time she thought about the role she'd played - and she wasn't the one lying in the hospital bed. Amy knew she should leave Rick alone, walk away and allow him to forget her. She deserved to spend the rest of life pining for him. Except she wasn't strong enough to do it.

Eventually, she spotted the nurse from the subacute ward - the one who'd let her in to see Rick. She abandoned her coffee and walked swiftly across the cafeteria to him. He recognised her immediately. Before he could talk, she grabbed his arm, ignoring his frown.

"Listen. I need to know how Rick is doing. I don't want him to know I'm asking. I'll pay you if you want. I'm going to come in here every single morning at this time and be waiting with a coffee right there." She pointed to a table. "Just tell me how he's progressing. I don't care about anything else. And I'm Amy, by the way."

The nurse was silent for a long moment, then pulled his arm back from her hand, sighing. "I won't be able to give you specific details, and of course I don't want any money. But I can give you a general update on the days I happen to be working this shift. I have no update today, I haven't seen him yet."

"Fine. And thank you for agreeing."

He nodded. "I'm David, by the way. And I'm actually slightly afraid to say no."

Amy tried to laugh and it came out sounding wild. She worried she was proving David's point, so she politely thanked him again and left.

Work became a welcome distraction for Amy. She was oddly impressed with her own ability to compartmentalise what was going on in her private and professional lives. Although, perhaps she wasn't doing quite as well as she imagined. She often caught Martha giving her lingering, questioning glances, and she spent far too much time in the bathroom, breathing deeply and checking her phone.

Now, she stood opposite Kristina, the long desk between them littered with mood boards. It was their second attempt at a negotiation on Peregrine; the first earlier in the week was a complete disaster. They'd both pushed for their own designs, trying to get away with adding one or two things from the other. It had ended with escalating tensions and Amy walking out of the room.

This meeting was off to a much better start and Amy had to give Kristina credit for the change. She had been the first to set aside some of her design elements and agree that Amy's were a better fit. As a result, they were slowly building up trust and Amy was learning to put her ego aside.

"They liked your neon signs," Kristina said, "so those stay."

"I think your playing card theme goes quite well with them," Amy added. They moved the two boards together and found they worked well, in a quirky way. "I also like these neutral chairs with the sheepskin."

Kristina tilted her head to take it in. Then she shook her head. "See, I think your greenery will go really well with the darker, high-backed chairs." She slid two boards together like puzzle pieces and Amy could see that she was right.

"I just had an idea." Amy went to the Mac that was set up on a clear Perspex desk by the window and wiggled the mouse to bring it to life. She logged in and navigated to some files she'd saved for a previous client, opening the image she was looking for. She stood back as Kristina examined a shot of golden wallpaper featuring brightly-coloured birds and black line drawings of flowers.

Kristina nodded slowly, playing with one of her long braids. "If we use that, we can strip down some of the other stuff and I think we're getting really close to what they wanted." They smiled at one another.

"The only thing I'm worried about is their budget," Amy said. "That wallpaper is crazy expensive."

"We need it though. Let's see what we can adjust to make it work."

They spent the next two hours jiggling things around, adding fixtures here, removing accessories there. Amy was really happy with what they were doing, and it seemed Kristina was too. The time had passed so quickly that Amy was shocked when Martha knocked on the glass and tapped her watch, indicating it was time for their lunch date. Amy beckoned her in.

"Do you need a bit more time?" Martha asked, entering the room. "You guys looked pretty focused."

"We need a break." Kristina unscrewed the lid of her water bottle and took a long drink.

Amy raised a questioning eyebrow at Martha and jerked her head towards Kristina. Martha nodded, looking surprised.

"Would you like to join us, Kristina?" Amy asked.

"Sure," Kristina said, with a note of studied casualness. "I'll get my purse."

"We were going to walk down to Lilac Bay, grab some pies and then sit near the little beach," Amy added.

"I'll bring my sunnies then. Meet you at your desks." She walked off.

"I would have thought you'd rather eat your own arm, after the Evertree thing," Martha said, as soon as Kristina was gone.

Amy gave her a wry look. "That wasn't her, I told you. But is it really okay with you that I asked her?"

"Sure." Martha nodded. "We can't talk shop now, that's for sure."

"Actually, I get the feeling we could trust her."

Martha's eyebrows shot up. "Well, *you* can, but I'm not ready to." Amy shrugged, walking to her desk to grab her handbag. "I'm serious," Martha persisted, trailing her. "I really don't think it's wise to get close to her."

They fell silent as Beaumont walked past and gave them both a curt nod. He froze a few steps later and Amy felt a sense of foreboding as he turned back to look at them.

"Didn't realise part-timers felt entitled to lunch breaks these days."

Martha's face crimsoned and the look on Beaumont's face made it clear he was enjoying her discomfort. Amy opened her mouth to defend Martha, but Kristina was quicker.

"She's finalising a pitch with me," Kristina lied, coming up behind them, standing slightly in front of Martha, as though to block her from Beaumont. "It's a working lunch. That okay with you?" There was a clear challenge in her voice.

Beaumont grinned ghoulishly and held up his hands. "Can't a man ask questions in his own company anymore? Sheesh, what's the world coming to? They'll be murdering us in the streets soon, eh, these women?" He appealed to Kyle, who was sitting innocently at his desk, absorbed in a pitch document.

"Huh?" Kyle pretended not to have heard a thing.

Beaumont flapped his hand dismissively and Kyle winked at the girls once Beaumont stalked off. They managed to hold their laughter in until they were outside in the sunshine.

"Oh my *God*," Martha groaned, biting into her pie. "This is sensational."

Amy managed a smile. Without work to focus on, her thoughts had circled back to Rick. She felt guilty, outside enjoying the sunshine when he was stuck in that room. She felt the now-familiar lump in her throat and forced herself back to the present.

"They're geniuses, right?" she said to Martha. "I'll pass your compliments to the chef."

She and Martha had bought pies from The Pie-ganic, Silas and Lyra's organic pie truck. Lyra wasn't there, she was in the studio that day, and Silas had seemed slightly overwhelmed by the number of customers along the bustling promenade. He'd definitely need to get someone to help, and soon.

Kristina had bought a vegan pasta dish from Meat is Murder, the other food truck along the bay.

Amy and Martha sat side by side on the wood and stone bench facing Lilac Bay's small beach. It was peaceful and quiet, the perfect spot for lunch. All the action happened near the mouth of the bay, which fed out into Sydney Harbour. The amusement park and ferry station attracted a lot of foot traffic and a constant loud bustle.

But where they were sitting, the huge, twisted old trees threw shade on even the hottest days, and the water sparkled a clear crystal blue. The moored boats swayed gently with the light currents that rippled through. It was calm and quiet.

Kristina had apparently never walked down this way before and was sitting barefoot and cross-legged in the grass nearby, staring out over the water.

"I can't *believe* we don't do this more often," Martha said.

Amy squirted a small packet of tomato sauce onto the top of her pie. The flaky pastry was making her mouth water.

For a split second, Amy saw her mother's disapproving face in her mind, and then she deliberately bit deep into the pie. Amy still hadn't spoken to her mother, and she intended to keep it that way. Diana was definitely going to have to be the one to extend the olive branch this time.

"We used to do it all the time in the early days," Martha continued wistfully.

"Until Beaumont became a complete nightmare," Amy added. Martha said nothing, and Amy remembered her vow not to trust Kristina yet.

"What's Silas's story?" Kristina asked, a forkful of pasta poised in front of her mouth. "He single?"

"Unfortunately he is very, very taken," Amy said. "I've had a crush on him since I first met him about a decade ago when I flat-shared with him and his sister. We don't stand a chance against Ernie though. They're moving in together."

"Silas really is something else," Martha agreed with a wistful sigh.

They sat in silence for a long moment, eating and enjoying the sunshine.

"Do either of you take on work outside of Edgerton's?" Kristina asked suddenly. She turned to face them, her eyes hidden and unreadable behind her mirrored pilot sunglasses.

Martha shook her head. "Of course not," she said carefully. "That's against our contract clauses."

Kristina shrugged. "What about you, Amy?"

Amy thought about Sunnywoods for a moment. She'd spent no company time or resources planning it, doing it all after hours so that she had less time to dwell on things with Rick. But still, taking on a client meant she was technically in breach of her contract. After a moment's consideration, Amy decided to trust Kristina.

"I took on a really small client, my Pop's nursing home, Sunnywoods. Why do you ask?"

"I was just curious," she replied casually. "I wonder how many people are doing that at work. Whether all that side-hustle is enough to make a decent living off. That's all." She took another bite of her pasta and turned away from them, looking back out at the water.

Martha pressed her lips together and gently shook her head at Amy. A warning that she shouldn't have confided in Kristina.

CHAPTER THIRTY-FOUR

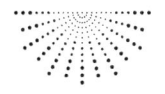

"Here you go, Amy."

"Thanks, Flora." Amy smiled gratefully at the elderly cafeteria worker she'd come to know so well, as Flora handed her a forbidden espresso from the staff-only machine. Amy slipped her a five-dollar note, which Flora pocketed with a wink.

Amy hadn't missed a single day in her visits to the hospital. And true to his word, David kept her updated. The updates were brief and hastily delivered, but Amy was reassured there was an upward trend in Rick's recovery. There were no signs of infection in any of his wounds and he was quickly regaining dexterity in his hands and upper body. It was his lower half they were still concerned about. The nature of the injury meant every function was *likely* to return, but likely and definitely were two different things.

One night after work she got a call from Deacon. "I saw you leaving the hospital today. And yesterday. Are you staking it out?"

"That's okay, isn't it?" Amy asked, panic-stricken. What if

he had instructions from Rick to make her stop? "I haven't bothered him. I like being in the same building as him."

"It's fine with me. More than fine, actually. There's something I want to tell you." He paused and Amy's heart picked up pace in the silence. "Rick told me he wants you to move on. That he doesn't want you stuck with him when he's like this. That's why he asked you to leave. He'd kill me if he knew I'd told you."

Amy released tension she hadn't realised she'd been holding. "I had wondered. But when I found out I caused the accident..."

"You didn't," Deacon said firmly. "He doesn't think you did either. You can't beat yourself up over that. Anyway, Rick is still madly in love with you, Amy. It would have cost him a lot to throw you out like that, when he would really have wanted to do exactly the opposite."

Amy swallowed hard, feeling a huge rush of love towards Rick. If *only* she could see him, tell him she didn't want to be spared from any of this. She wanted to be right beside him, helping him fight for his recovery. Making it better or easier in any way she could. "He's an idiot," she whispered finally.

Deacon gave a short laugh. "I love the man like a brother and I agree. Amy, you've got no idea how much the boys at work look up to Rick. What kind of soldier he is." Deacon's voice wavered. "He's the one you want in the trenches beside you. He's saved more than one hide. All any of us want is to see the man happy. And that means being with you."

The next morning, Amy arrived at the hospital early and paced the cafeteria. She drew strange glances from the other visitors, but didn't care.

"Please be on duty today," she muttered to herself. An

hour later, she spotted David across the room and all but ran to him, thrusting a note into his hand with a pleading look.

"Please get that to Rick. I'll be waiting in that little shop at the front of the hospital. If he has any message for me, come tell me there. Even if the message is to get lost. I know you're not a courier, but I'm really hoping you'll do me this favour."

David gave a curt nod, staring down at the paper in his hand.

I'm waiting. I won't stop waiting.

While he took the note upstairs, Amy paced up and down the aisle of the gift store full of frantic, nervous energy. She blindly pulled odds and ends from the shelves, dropping them into a basket. The cashier gave her a querying look as the total rang up at over fifty dollars. If questioned, Amy couldn't have recalled a single item in her bag.

She stood outside the shop, waiting, as the hands on her watch crept in a slow circle. She knew she'd be desperately late for work, but she couldn't make herself care.

Finally, David came back towards her, his expression unreadable. Amy's heart ceased beating as he stood in front of her, expressionless.

"Come with me."

She slumped with relief. "He'll see me?"

David nodded. "I honestly can't tell if you're a lunatic or a woman in love, but he'll see you."

"I think the answer is both."

David took a few steps and then turned to look back at her. "It's his last day in the subacute ward," he said, unable to hide a smile.

She frowned. "Is that a good thing?"

"It's a *really* good thing."

Rick looked like a different person. The stitches were gone, and although the scar would change his face forever, it would be less severe than it first seemed. His black eye was healed, and now looked bright and clear. The breathing tube and drip were gone, and his legs were free of the casings. Even the room looked better, the curtains had been thrown back to let in the bright light of the perfectly sunny day.

Rick's bed propped him up to a 45 degree angle. In different lighting, Amy could almost have believed he was slouched on her sofa, relaxing.

"Hey," she said, taking a few tentative steps towards him.

"Hi."

They stared, both greedily drinking in the details of each other's faces. Rick's pupils grew, swallowing his irises as he looked at her, and Amy knew hers were doing the same. Her breath hitched as she saw a flush creep over his face. Her heart was flinging itself against her ribcage and she let out a shaky breath, trying to steady her emotions.

Rick cleared his throat, looking pointedly at the shopping bag. "Is that for me?"

She looked inside the bag, noting its contents for the first time. "Sure."

"Sit down."

Amy scraped the heavy plastic visitor chair over from the other side of the room. It took a long time and it was loud. When she finally sat down in it, there was an amused glint in Rick's eyes.

"Are you laughing at me?"

"Absolutely." His smile stopped her heart.

She thrust her hand into the bag. "Okay, let's see what I bought for you. Oh, these are great." She pulled out the first item - a pair of novelty glasses, the wide fake eyeballs bouncing out of their sockets on long springs. "These are from the hospital's *Spring* collection." Rick groaned at the joke as Amy put them on. "They're especially appropriate if you're here to visit someone with an eye injury."

Rick's mouth quirked and she saw his chest heave as he fought against a laugh.

She took the glasses off and put them on his night table. "You can keep those. Don't worry about the cost."

"What else?"

She pulled out a pair of socks. "Now at first, these look like ordinary socks. But they've actually been personalised for someone named Dougal." She showed him the embroidered name, beneath a laser printed image of an unhappy-looking man with a bushy beard and huge glasses. "It appears this is Dougal's *actual* face. I'm guessing he left these behind and the staff decided to wash and sell them. There's no other credible explanation."

Rick couldn't help but laugh. "Dougal."

Amy placed the socks beside the glasses on his night stand. "Again, you can keep these and I don't want to hear a word about paying me back."

"I can't even guess what else you have in that bag," he said grinning.

"I'm going to be honest, neither can I." She dropped it into her lap and covered it with her hands as they scanned one another's faces again. "I can't believe I don't know what to say to you, when I've been thinking about this moment since…" She bit off the words. She'd been going to say *before the accident*, but that wouldn't come out right.

"I've been thinking about you," he said finally, looking down. "I'm sorry for throwing you out."

"No, don't be. I don't really know how to say this, but." She took a deep breath. "If you're trying to push me away because you think it's for my own good… then don't. I can handle this, Rick. I've barely thought about anything but you since the moment we started our break. I don't... there are no answers yet, about anything to do with us, neither from me nor from you. But please, be honest with me. Completely honest. Don't do anything you *think* is best for me. Let me decide."

He looked at the ceiling. "Okay." It was barely a whisper, but Amy felt a surge of hope. If he was agreeing to that, he thought they might have a future. He pressed his lips together and turned to look at her; her pulse spiked in response. "We were great together, weren't we? I'm not imagining it? We were actually really good together."

"We were something else," she agreed.

He looked at her strangely, and she realised he was holding back a laugh. "Did you just say *we were something else?* Ames, that's from a movie or something. People don't say that!"

"Excuse me, *I* said it." She grinned widely, delighted to have made him laugh. That dimple. How she'd missed it.

He coughed and reached for the water cup and straw on his trolley. Amy resisted the urge to help, and noted that his movements were slightly uncoordinated. Still, he managed it alone.

"What else do you have?" He set the cup down and gestured to the bag.

"Um," Amy pulled out a random item, studying it. "This seems to be moustache wax. It says it's 'for refined gentlemen', so it's obviously not for you. Some kind of hipster thing, I guess."

"I don't even have a moustache!"

"You also don't have eyeballs on springs, or a face like Dougal's, so I don't know what to tell you. Nothing in this bag is going to make sense."

They grinned at each other for a long moment, until the

smile faded from Rick's face and he heaved a deep sigh. Amy wanted to ask what he was thinking. But she didn't want to put a foot wrong and ruin the moment. Right now it was enough for her to be near him, and not have him ask her to leave, not be breaking down in tears.

There was a knock at the door and Rick looked past her, his eyes lighting up. "Time for my daily torture session."

"That's right," said a perky voice.

Amy turned to see a stunning young woman with light pink scrubs draped flatteringly over a knockout figure. Her thick dark hair was up in a messy topknot, there was not a scrap of makeup on her perfume-model face, and her toned arms were etched with tattoos.

"I'm here to beat you into submission again," the woman said, grinning at Rick. Amy's stomach lurched with the certainty that this woman was Interested In Rick.

"Hi, I'm Lauren. Rick's P.T." She eyed Amy and stretched out a hand. Her shake was overly firm. "Physical therapist, not personal trainer," she added, and Rick laughed.

"I'm Amy, I'm..." She hesitated, not entirely knowing how to introduce herself.

"Nice to meet you, Amy," Lauren said, before she could finish. "I'm afraid I'm going to have to ask you to leave." She didn't sound remotely afraid. "I get him all to myself for a whole hour a day."

Amy stood, feeling awkward. Lauren looked her up and down and heat flamed in Amy's cheeks.

"I was about to head out," she said. "I'm about two hours late for work anyway."

"Yikes." Lauren raised her eyebrows.

Amy gave Rick's hand a light squeeze and turned to leave. Lauren was standing at the foot of Rick's bed, examining his chart, clearly waiting for Amy to be gone. Amy had taken a few steps when Rick called out to her. She spun to face him.

"Come back tomorrow?" he asked.

Lauren watched her from behind the clipboard.

Amy beamed, nodding eagerly. "Promise," she said huskily.

"Do I get the rest of my presents then?"

Amy couldn't help but laugh. "I'll look through them and let you know if there's anything worth having!"

As she drove into the office, Amy's elation was so all-consuming that not even the knowledge she was hours late to work could bring her down. She dialled Lyra through the car's speakerphone.

"Guess where I just came from?" she practically yelled when Lyra answered.

"Okay, so I know it's the hospital, but are you excited for the reason I think you're excited?" Lyra's voice rose in glee.

"Yes!" Amy shouted, her face split ear to ear in a grin, which widened when Lyra squealed. "He agreed to see me."

"How did he look?"

"Better. Way better."

Lyra breathed out heavily. "Oh, Ames. I am *so* pleased to hear that. You have no idea."

"Yeah, me too," Amy said, turning off the freeway and into the back streets of Lilac Bay. "I'm about one million hours late for work, but I wanted to tell you."

"Thank you! I'm so glad you did. And don't let Beaumont get you down. Not today. Love you, Ames."

They hung up as Amy parked and she rushed inside. She arranged her features into a careful mix of penitent and terrified as she crossed the carpet to her desk, armed with a tale about a power outage breaking her alarm clock in case Beaumont hauled her in.

Martha looked up and surveyed her, a slow grin spreading across her face.

"Save the theatrics," she said when Amy pulled out her desk chair. "He's not in."

Amy almost collapsed in relief. "I've been saved by sheer dumb luck then. Where is he?"

Martha shrugged. "Some important meeting. Rumour has it it's with creditors, but I don't know how reliable the intel is." She jerked her head towards Kyle and Amy nodded.

Slowly, her heart rate returned to normal. She briefly contemplated the fact that Edgerton's might be facing some kind of financial trouble. Then she decided that was Beaumont's problem. She wasn't going to let anything get her down today. Especially not now that some of her own problems seemed to be behind her.

CHAPTER THIRTY-FIVE

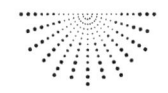

Rick was sharing his new ward with an elderly man who had the bushiest eyebrows Amy had ever seen. He was snoring rather loudly when Amy arrived a couple of mornings later, and Rick put a finger to his lips.

"I can't stop looking at them," he whispered, his eyes locked on the brows.

"They're fabulous," Amy agreed, sitting quietly beside him.

"Watch this." The man exhaled with a thunderous snore and his eyebrows trembled visibly, like a feathered headdress on a showgirl.

Amy and Rick grinned at one another and silently golf-clapped the performance. A moment later, Rick felt for her hand and held it. Amy's heart bunny-hopped around her chest and they sat in silence, watching the eyebrows.

"The army sent me a shrink, as part of my recovery," Rick said a while later. "It's a pain in the arse mostly, but he's taught me that I have a really long road ahead of me. It's not going to be easy, but I guess that part was obvious." He laughed wryly. "And I know I'm not going to take this too well a lot of the time." He looked at her as though weighing up whether or not to say something. "But I do know I'm actually lucky. My life could have ended in that accident. One tiny variable in any direction, and..." He shook his head.

Amy nodded slowly, exhaling to keep her breath steady. "I think about that all the time."

"It's taken me a while, but I'm starting to get a bit of a new perspective. If my life could end at any moment, I want to make the most of it. But," he threw his hands up, "I don't know what that looks like. I don't even know how to *not* be in the army." He swallowed, tears forming in his eyes, his voice husky with emotion. "I was in the Cadets and then joined when I was seventeen."

"Is there definitely no way you can go back?" She kept her voice perfectly neutral. "It seems like they think you'll make a full recovery and then...I don't really know anything about it, but it could be possible for you to return, right?"

Rick swallowed. "They're *pretty sure* I'll make a full recovery, as in, be able to walk again. The damage is mostly affecting my lower legs. But, no. They don't know for sure, and they don't know when. Maybe years. I don't know how much of their caution is to stop me getting my hopes up, and how much is cold reality."

Amy gulped. She hadn't really allowed herself to dwell on the extent of Rick's injuries until now. The pain on his face was unbearable.

"And I don't want any other job in the army," he continued. "I only ever wanted to be a soldier, haven't even tried for officer."

Amy toyed with the corner of his bed sheet, her eyes down while she got her emotions in check. "I wish you didn't have to try and figure those things out. I know that you can. I'm not trying to be flippant, it's just that I believe in you.

Even though I can understand how hard it's going to be." Rick nodded slowly as she continued. "This whole situation also made me realise some stuff. Like how all along... I never truly believed we'd break up. You gave me a lot to work through, but some of it was my own issues. From long before we'd met." She raised her eyes and his were trained on her face. "I went to visit my dad, to see whether that would help me process anything."

"And did it help?" His voice was gentle.

She screwed up her face. "In a way, I guess. You're not the same in any way, and what you did was not the same. Rick, I will wait, for as long as it takes. For your recovery. For you."

He swallowed audibly. "Why don't we start with you coming to visit a little more often?" he whispered a moment later.

She squeezed his hand, nodding. He squeezed back as firmly as he could, and it broke her heart to feel how light that squeeze was. A few months earlier, those same hands had effortlessly pinned her to the bed. She bit her lip to keep from thinking of those moments. She rested her forehead on their hands, her nose touching the starched white bed sheets.

There was a knock at the door and Amy quickly sat upright. Lauren. At least her knock woke up Rick's roommate and the snoring stopped.

Lauren looked even more beautiful today, if that were possible. She was wearing a smidge of eyeliner that enlarged her eyes to cartoon proportions. She stood at the foot of the bed, smiling at Rick.

"It's ti-ime," she said, in a singsong voice. Rick groaned dramatically.

Amy instantly felt like the third wheel. "I guess I'd better head off."

Lauren nodded. "Nice to see you again."

She somehow managed to make the words sound genuine.

"You too." Amy was less successful. She waved at Rick and was almost at the door when he called her back.

"One sec," he said to Lauren. He beckoned Amy closer, slipped an arm around her neck and pulled her to him for one gentle kiss. It had been far too long since she had felt the softness of his lips on hers. When she straightened up, it felt as though she was seeing stars.

CHAPTER THIRTY-SIX

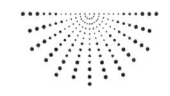

For the first time, Amy had hope that she and Rick might get a second chance. She spent the whole drive into work feeling alternating flurries of joy and fear. It was hardly ideal that they had reunited at his hospital bed, but she had a clearer picture of his recovery path now. It was brighter than she'd let herself hope during those long mornings in the hospital cafe.

The competing thought was one that sickened her. Rick might not be able to serve in the army again. He might have lost the career that had come between them and in a way, Amy was responsible for that loss. She'd meant it when she'd realised she wanted to get back together with him despite his career. And now she found herself on the opposite end of the spectrum from where she'd begun: rooting for Rick to get his job back.

She loved him, and she wanted him happy. His career made him happy. That he might now lose it was nauseating. Not that she had answers for how she'd cope if he returned to active service. She only knew she was in love, and what Rick wanted, she wanted.

Amy also wished she didn't dislike leaving him with Lauren. Dear God, did she have to be *such* a knockout? And as Lauren herself had pointed out, she had access to Rick an hour a day at least. Would his feelings of gratitude eventually turn to something else as she helped with his recovery?

Amy shook her head to keep her focus on the road and turned across a lane of heavy traffic to get into the underground parking at work. She parked in her spot, switched off the engine and sat there.

She simply couldn't find the energy to get out. Aside from Peregrine, her work bored her.

Still. She needed to eat. And pay her mortgage. And remain clothed. And she didn't want to go work for a rival firm.

She left a voice note in her group chat with Marley and Lyra, filling them in on the morning's events with Rick. It was hard to find time to meet up in person lately - it seemed Lyra was busy or stressed most days and Amy had been using her evenings for the Sunnywoods stuff. But the support was there and she felt it.

"My office, *now*," Beaumont said when she walked in. Amy cast a glance at Martha, who shook her head to indicate she had no idea what was happening - a terrified look on her face.

Amy felt many eyes on her as she crossed the open-plan floor and headed towards Beaumont's office, trying to steady her racing heart and adrenaline surge. The walls were made entirely of glass, fitting the fish-tank theme elsewhere. Amy would have thought he'd appreciate some privacy in his own office, but apparently everything he did was for an audience.

Once they were inside and Amy had closed the door behind her, she put on her best poker face. Whatever this was, she was going to get through it with her dignity intact. She had been playing with fire, coming in late each day. She hoped the burns wouldn't be too bad.

As they faced one another over Beaumont's ridiculously oversized desk, Amy brought to mind a conversation she'd once had with Martha.

"He's definitely compensating for something with that desk," Amy had said.

"Yeah, the lack of a soul," Martha quipped, and they'd dissolved into giggles.

Right now, it didn't seem quite as funny.

He folded his hands on the table and stared at her unblinkingly. He had a ghoulish look on his face and Amy realised this was the first time she'd seen him up close in a while. His forehead and eyes were frozen, as though he'd gone overboard on the Botox. His thinning hair was teased like candy floss to disguise the fact that there was barely any of it. He suddenly looked like a very sad and lonely man.

"I'm going to pay you the courtesy of not beating around the bush."

"Okay?"

"I don't need both you and Kristina. You're too expensive. I pay her less than you and she's hungrier and she's working harder. You're swanning in at any time you choose, even though you know we're in a difficult period."

Amy let the words sink in, fighting to keep the panic from rising. Despite her best efforts, she knew her cheeks were colouring. She considered her words carefully.

"Did you ever think about the fact that I'm overworked? We all are! And you're giving me crap jobs? That's not even a joke, I can't remember the last time I worked on something other than a bathroom. Maybe Kristina's hungry because you're giving her the good jobs. And let's not even mention Evertree."

Beaumont surveyed her coolly, but she saw an eyebrow

try its best to raise. He clearly hadn't expected her to fight back. Her palms were sweating and her heart was galloping; she hoped it wasn't showing too much.

"Fair point." His tone was neutral. "I have a proposal for you."

"I'm listening."

"A pay cut. You're clearly not working the hours you should be, and this way I can keep you both. Kristina's proved willing and able to handle everything I've thrown at her, so if anyone's going to go, it's going to be you. This way, it doesn't need to come to that."

Amy shook her head, heat burning her belly. "No." She hoped her voice wasn't shaking as much as her insides were. "I'm paid what I'm worth. I've brought in a lot of business over the years and I do *good* work, when I'm given the space and time. *I* have a proposal. Share the interesting projects more equally between Kristina and the rest of the team, unless you want her to burn out. And stop saying yes to so many clients. We can take on what we can take on. No more. If we can't do a brilliant job with it, the clients aren't going to come back anyway. How many have we lost lately?"

Beaumont surveyed her coolly. "Can you tell me the name of the firm, please?"

"Yeah, I get it. You're the boss. I'm trying to stop you from going under and taking those people out there with you." Amy couldn't believe the words coming out of her mouth. She'd never spoken to him like this, had barely spoken to *anyone* like this. She felt like she had little to lose and knew that was a dangerous mindset. "This business is clearly struggling, otherwise you wouldn't be firing people left and right. You-"

"*Can you tell me the name of the firm, please?*"

Amy bit her lip. She was on eggshell-thin ice and she knew it. She wasn't about to quit and couldn't afford to be fired. But nor could she afford to let anyone treat her this way.

"Edgerton's. You. It's your firm, Beaumont." Amy stood, smoothing her skirt down over her hips. "And it's going to be your funeral if you don't change something soon."

"That's the thing." He narrowed his eyes at her as his face purpled with rage. "I know exactly what needs to change. I don't think the funeral will be my own."

The threat was clear, and Amy's pride wouldn't allow her to stand there and take it. "I'm taking the day off as a leave day," Amy said. "I've got far too many holidays owing and I need to take one. I really hope that you will reconsider what you've said. I won't accept a pay cut. Can you really afford to lose me?"

She stalked out without a backward glance, snatching her handbag off her desk as she strode out, propelled by a surge of elation. Sitting in her car, the elation was quickly replaced by fear, cold and shaky. She also realised that her colleagues might think Beaumont had fired her, so she shot Martha a quick text message letting her know that wasn't the case.

***

She found herself unable to start the engine and drive away. For one thing, she felt woozy after all the emotion. For another, she had Marley's words ringing in her ears from their conversation at the pizzeria. *No offence, but you'd be screwed if you lost your job.* That wasn't quite true, but she wouldn't be comfortable either. She was several months ahead on mortgage repayments, and could reduce the due amount each month by paying only interest.

She opened her glove box, unwrapped one of her emergency toffees and then took out the pencil and paper she always kept handy for moments of inspiration.

With the drop in her mortgage repayments, plus the three months grace she'd bought herself by getting ahead, she could afford a reduced income for a little while. Reduced, but not none, she reminded herself. Still, she scratched some sums onto the notepad as she chewed her toffee. If she ate out fewer times in a week, didn't buy any new clothes, makeup, homewares, design books or magazines, cancelled a few subscriptions… she'd still be broke. She'd be *less* broke, but she'd still be broke. At least not homeless and broke, though.

She sighed and tossed the pencil and paper onto the floor of the passenger seat. Her tummy rumbled and she realised she hadn't eaten yet. She should go back inside. She should really go inside. She and Kristina were re-pitching with Peregrine Hotels soon and it would be a good idea to go over everything once more.

She tilted the rear-view mirror and studied herself in it.

"Amy Beth Porter…you get upstairs and crawl into Beaumont's office," she told her reflection sternly. It was no use. Her body wouldn't do it.

She locked up her car and strolled out of the garage the back way to avoid seeing anyone from work, weaving through alleys and laneways until she was at Lilac Bay.

CHAPTER THIRTY-SEVEN

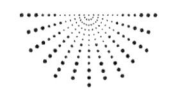

It was another picture-perfect Sydney day and Amy stood on the shore and let the warmth seep into her bones. Small waves were lapping along the pure white sand of Lilac Bay and several sunbathers had stretched out their striped beach towels, soaking up the rays. A young family was picnicking on one of the benches of the grassy park, set among the lilac bushes. The boats moored in the bay were shining white and clean in the sunlight, seagulls perched here and there atop the masts. Out beyond the mouth of the bay, ferries were crossing through the deep, sapphire-blue water and under the Sydney Harbour Bridge.

To Amy's left was the Secret Garden and if she followed the path along that way, she would end up at The Pie-ganic. She headed in that direction, passing the lilac bushes and using the track that ran alongside the disused railroad.

"Ames." Silas grinned as she arrived. Several little stand-up tables were clustered by the truck and Silas was playing music to create a nice atmosphere. Amy felt as though she could stand there all day.

"Hey, handsome." She smiled up at him. "I'll take a cottage pie and a lemonade thanks. How are things going here?"

He shrugged as he reached into the pie racks with a long pair of tongs. "They're really busy," he admitted. "I'm struggling without Ly."

"Can you get someone to help for a while?"

He nodded. "I need to talk to Lyra about it, but yeah, I think that's the only way it's going to work. I have Cameron helping me a few days a week, when he's not helping Jenny. But Alex has convinced him to sign up for a university course, so I'm not sure how long he's going to be able to help."

Silas slipped her pie onto a compostable plate and put it on top of the counter. He questioningly held up a sauce packet and she nodded.

"It's nice that Alex has encouraged him to do that. But bad news for you. Jenny looks pretty flat out as well." Amy tilted her head to the other food truck.

"Yeah. She's struggling too."

"Have you ever thought about combining your trucks?"

Silas threw his head back and laughed. "You remember all the drama about meat and veganism from earlier, right?"

Amy nodded, smiling. "But it's not really like that anymore, is it? You and Jenny get along well. Between you, you have the whole spectrum of things to offer clients."

"We call them customers here, Lady Porter."

"Customers," she corrected, smiling, "but honestly, if you did team up, you'd be able to take breaks then, and you could split the cost of some help between you."

"And split the profits."

"Well, you'd probably have more profits to share!"

He grabbed her lemonade from the fridge and sat it beside the pie, chewing his lip thoughtfully. "I wonder if that could work. Maybe I'll bring it up with Jenny and see what her reaction is."

Amy grabbed her pie and drink, leaving money on the counter. "You can keep the change and the free advice. I'm going to enjoy my pie out here."

"Aren't you supposed to be at work?" Silas frowned, checking his watch. "You never used to have time to come visit us, and this is twice in the last couple of weeks."

"I should definitely be at work. But I'm taking a mental health day."

"Good for you," Silas said, then shooed her off as a fresh batch of customers arrived from the ferry wharf.

As Amy ate her pie in the sun, looking out over the water, she thought about Kristina. The two of them were like Silas and Jenny in a way. They had opposing styles and maybe conflicting values; she couldn't really tell. But between them, there seemed to be a lot they could offer clients. Or at least, that had been the case with Peregrine. And Amy had to admit, there was something about Kristina that had made her want to lift her game. Maybe it really was time to seriously think about starting a business. The work she'd done for Sunnywoods had more than proved she could manage alone.

Before heading home, Amy stopped in to visit her Pop. She hugged Carol in greeting, grateful that such a cheerful woman worked there. It was like checking in with a sunbeam.

"To what do I owe this pleasure, Amy Beth?" Pop checked his watch. He looked her up and down from his recliner, where he was watching a Western on the wall-mounted TV. "It's only two pm!"

He clicked pause on the remote and started to lever the

chair into an upright position.

"Don't get up." She kissed him on the head and sank into the recliner beside his, throwing two bags of Clinkers onto the little table between them.

"Oh, it's a *two* Clinks kind of day, is it? Something's either gone very wrong or very right. This about your fella?"

Amy pulled the kickstand on the recliner, tilting back to the same angle he was at. "Yeah," she sighed dreamily. "Things are definitely starting to look up on that front."

"Look at your smile." Pop reached for one of the bags. "Warms the cockles of my heart. Shall we each have a bag each to celebrate?"

"I'll just have a clink or two." They chewed in silence for a moment. "Pop, I never told you, but I went to see Dad a while back."

Pop nodded slowly. "Yeah, he told me…figured you'd talk about it when you were ready. Were you okay after that?"

She considered. "Yes, I think so." She sighed. "He's sick though. He's still sick, even after everything that happened."

Pop leaned his head back in the chair and looked at her. "I know it. If you ever have kids, I hope to Christ you don't have to go through what me and Nellie went through with our Sean."

"I'm so sorry. I always think about it from my perspective, but I don't often consider how hard it has been for you."

"Well, ain't your job to consider that. And the other three kids turned out okay, if I do say so myself."

"Is it weird I'm not closer to them? I mean, I speak to Uncle Bill about his construction business sometimes, but I never speak to Aunt Peg. And I do chat to Rusty, of course. Did I tell you he gave my friend Lyra one of her first gigs?"

Pop nodded. "Smashed the place to bits, she did too, little tramp."

Amy laughed. "It wasn't her! It was some bogan guys. And

Rusty said insurance covered most of it." She chewed her chocolate. "But I've only ever seen Peg at big things, like Nan's funeral."

"It's hard keeping a family together." Pop played with a sweet and looked up at the ceiling, sounding faraway. "I think some of 'em was upset I took you in. Felt like I was doing it to exclude their kids or something. And the others always were jealous of Sean."

"Really?"

Pop nodded. "He was the best-looking one." He chuckled softly. "Might not even be mine now's I come to think of it. But he was always different. He was always trying too hard, falling in with the wrong group, working himself up to impress the wrong people. Always insecure, always something to prove." He shrugged. "He was like that."

"I get that now, I think."

"What's made you think of all that?"

"I was considering asking the bank to borrow money," she said. "Maybe starting my own business. And then, I wondered if maybe that's a slippery slope to something. I remember dad was always borrowing more. I'm surprised they kept lending it to him."

"I'm really glad to hear you're thinking about that. You'd do wonderful on your own, I know it."

Amy bit the inside of her cheek. "Even if they approve me, it's such a gamble. And those don't tend to work out well in our family."

"Well, if you want my two bob's worth, you should give it a go. I'll sell a kidney before I let you lose your house, if that's what you're worried about."

"God, Pop. I don't think it would ever come to that. But nice to know I have a backup plan," she joked, patting his arm. Loretta flashed into her mind and Amy made a mental note to call her once she was home.

"Seen the common room before you stopped by? That should have given you a boost of confidence."

"No," Amy sat forward in her chair. "They've done it already? Is it looking good?"

"Not good, *spectacular*. Let's go see it, hey? Since I take it you're wagging work for the whole day."

Amy shrugged and made a cute face as they levered themselves up from the recliners. Pop stood with a grunt and shook a handful of chocolates into his gnarled hand. They linked arms and headed down the hall to the common room.

"Shall we get Hazel?" Amy asked, as they passed her room.

"She's getting her hair blown off or something."

Amy burst out laughing. "Do you mean blown *out*? She's at the salon?"

"She's definitely doing something with her hair. Now, what'd I tell you." Pop stopped as they arrived at the common room entrance. Two workmen were still busy in the room, one painting the skirting boards and the other up a short ladder connecting a light fixture.

"Oh," Amy breathed, letting go of Pop's arm and stepping into the room. "It looks great, doesn't it?" She was beaming as she looked around. Seeing her visions come to life would never get old, but this one had worked out much better than she had anticipated.

Before her refresh, the room had aged badly. The space was large - meant for meals and concerts and meetings - but it had been fitted out once decades ago and then forgotten. Beige carpet, faded mushroom-coloured wallpaper, harsh fluorescent lighting. The dining tables and chairs looked like they'd been shipped directly from some former communist country, and one window had even been boarded over, though no one could remember why.

There was definitely a spectrum of "assisted living" but

the occupants at Sunnywoods were for the most part healthy, lucid and mobile. Many of them could expect a good few years ahead of them and Amy had wanted the surroundings to reflect that. After doing some research, she'd discovered that hospital patients recovered better with pictures of nature in front of them. So she'd decided on an outdoors theme.

The old wallpaper had been stripped and replaced on one side with a floor-to-ceiling photo of a forest, giving the impression you were actually sitting alongside the tall poplars and mulchy undergrowth. Then other walls had been repainted and left bare, to be hung with gilt-framed artwork from the residents' grandkids.

Amy had wanted to use rugs to add warmth to the space, but that was impractical for walkers and wheelchairs, so she'd settled on fresh low-pile instead. The chairs had been replaced with more comfortable and stylish ones. The tables remained but were covered with custom-made wipe-clean toppers, and Amy had included little vases filled with silk flowers. The boarded window had been liberated and a huge disco ball hung near it, casting rainbows around as the light shone in.

The transformation from dingy, depressing common room to upbeat, light-filled retreat was complete. The room was even more functional now, but it was also *fun*. Amy hoped the residents felt joyful when they spent time there.

"We all can't wait until it opens again. Three days' time. Hazel's even organised a little reopening party."

"We're not *all* happy about it," snapped a gravelly voice behind them. Amy spun to see a wizened little woman hunched over her walker. Her voice, crispy hair, mouth wrinkles and obviously false teeth were all the tell-tale signs of a lifelong smoker.

"Hello, Cruella," Pop said sweetly.

"It's *Janella*, for the thousandth time." She flicked her eyes to Amy. "Your Pop's losing it, sorry to tell you."

Amy grinned at Pop. "You don't like the new room?" she asked, when Janella simply stood and stared at them.

She hmphed. "It's okay I suppose. If you're a *koala.*"

Amy couldn't help but laugh at that. She was like a caricature of a cranky old woman. "What would you have done differently?"

She clutched a hand to her heart. *"Me?* No, love. Got no clue, me. My *grandson* does though. He should'a been given a chance to try and do this."

"He's a designer?"

"Yes. Yes, he is and he's a very talented one. They should'a asked the residents if any of them else had grandkids, and they could've split the rooms up and had different grandkids do them. That's all's I'm saying! Was a bit like nespertism."

"Nepotism? But I'm not related to the owners at all. Nor to Hazel, who suggested it. And typically, you get one designer to do the whole thing, so everything works together."

"We're sorry your grandson missed out, Cruella," Pop added. "But even you have to agree this is a big improvement."

Janella looked back and forth between the two of them and rolled her eyes, slowly turning around in her walker and heading back the way she came. Amy looked at Pop with round eyes.

"Don't you worry about her, Amy Beth. She's a right grump. Always has been."

"I'm worried about getting that old. She can't even storm out of a room!"

They laughed until Pop wheezed, then went back to his room to finish the Western and see whether Hazel returned with any hair.

CHAPTER THIRTY-EIGHT

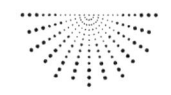

A week later, Amy was still gainfully employed at Edgerton's, although she was spending most evenings working on a business plan and had also made an appointment to speak to an employment lawyer. She wasn't quite ready to take the step of reaching out to the bank for a loan, but the more she worked on the business plan the more excited she got. And the more excited she got, the more she was convinced it could work.

Despite Beaumont's warning about the hours she was working, Amy spent every single morning at Rick's bedside. They were starting to get their old energy back, although they avoided talking about the future. It was enough for her that they were enjoying one another's company again, and that there was a lot more laughing than crying going on during her visits.

On her next visit, Amy could hear Lauren's voice before she turned the corner into Rick's ward. She peered in, neither Lauren nor Rick noticing her. Rick was sitting upright in his bed, looking ruggedly handsome. His scar gave him a kind of rough sexiness he hadn't had before, and Amy almost groaned at herself for being the real life cliche of "chicks dig scars."

His blanket was tossed to the side as Lauren pulled and manipulated his legs while telling him a story. "And so she's picking up the phone and trying to get to these voice messages by pressing four zeros, but that's the *password* for the mailbox, not how you dial into the mailbox in the first place."

Rick grinned. "Oh God. I have a feeling I know where this is going."

"Right? So the first zero gets her an outside line and then the next three zeros ring emergency services. And she's arguing with the poor person at the call centre who wants to know the nature of her emergency." Lauren lowered his leg and bent double with laughter, gasping to get the punchline out. "'Just give me my voice messages!' 'Ma'am, this is *the emergency hotline for the police, ambulance and fire service.*' And she does it like six times."

Lauren wiped tears from her face as Rick did the kind of silent laugh he only did when he was really losing it. The kind of laugh Amy had only ever seen him do for her.

Her face was burning and adrenaline coursed through her body as she marched quickly into the room, a huge grin plastered onto her face. Lauren's laugh died on her lips, but Rick beamed at her.

"Ames! Are we done?" he asked Lauren.

"For today!" She pulled the blanket back over his legs and adjusted it with a tenderness Amy found hard to take. She nodded curtly to Amy as she passed. "See you tomorrow," she called over her shoulder.

"Can't wait," he said mock-sarcastically, then shook his head at Amy. "She is crazy."

Amy leaned over to kiss him. These weren't the passionate kisses of a relationship, these were the friendly pecks of close friends, or family members. Every time she was close to him this way, she wanted to grab him behind his neck, pull their lips together and scandalise the hospital. Instead, she forced herself to sit in the seat beside the bed.

"How's rehab going?"

"Great! Lauren has much cooler ways of doing it than some of the other P.T.s around here."

Amy nodded. So Lauren was beautiful, funny *and* insanely good at her job. She hated herself for the spike of jealousy. She should be happy Rick had the best working with him. She wished the best was slightly less attractive.

Rick was watching her. "What's on your mind?"

"I want to hear about you first."

"Well, it looks like I'll be getting out of here the week after next." He was glowing and Amy felt a huge burst of happiness. "I'll need to come in a couple of times a week, but as an outpatient."

"And you're all set to be living back at your mum's for a while?"

"I wouldn't say *set* exactly. More like braced."

"At least you'll get some decent food there as well. Although I will miss playing 'guess the dish'." Amy grinned, thinking about the photos he sent her each evening of his gloopy, congealed meals.

"You forget that I'm in the defence force," he said, grinning. Then the grin turned lopsided. "Used to be," he corrected. "Either way, I'm fine with rough food."

"You've done better than I would have, that's for sure. Have you been able to practice with a wheelchair? Or do they assume you can do it?"

Rick shook his head. "Lauren and I are working on it from tomorrow, so I should hopefully be pretty good with it once I'm out."

"Could I take you to the beach?" Amy blurted, realising

she wanted more than anything to share Bondi with him again. And to be the one with him when he saw the ocean for the first time again.

He looked thoughtful, then a slow grin spread across his face. "I don't see why not. I'll have to ask Lauren when she thinks I'll be up to it. But that would be amazing." He flopped his head back into his pillow. "Oh my God, the beach," he breathed.

Amy smiled at him, feeling her heart balloon to double its size as she traced the lines of his face with her eyes. He was starting to let a bit of stubble grow and it suited him, adding to the ruggedness of his looks.

After a moment of daydreaming, he lifted his head back up and looked at her. "So what's on your mind?"

She opened her mouth and then frowned. "Are you sure? It feels weird to start telling you this stuff again."

"But I want to hear it. I love having other stuff to focus on. Besides," he added cheekily, "whatever it is you've messed up, I'm sure I can fix it for you."

"Oh, is that right?" She grinned. "Well, try this on for size. Beaumont is trying to push me out of the business, and worse, I don't care. Pop wants me to start up my own business." She fell silent. Rick was watching her closely.

"And?" he prompted.

"And what?" She threw up her hands. "That's not enough?"

"No," he shook his head. "I mean, and what do you want? You didn't mention that in there at all."

She puffed her cheeks. "Yes. I would really love to have my own company. I daydream about it, and I'm taking some practical steps. But," she traced a finger over the seam of her dress. "I've always been worried about the business side of things. All the costs and the inventory and keeping track of that. And making sure I have enough clients, but not too many. I spoke to this woman I met at my step dad's birthday, and she has a few clients she could recommend me to."

"A few clients? Is she mafia?"

Amy chuckled. "No, she kind of has a network of women that she connects with one another. It sounds weird, but it's a passion project. She doesn't really need money. She and her husband are rich as far as I can tell. She said a lot of women in her circle were starting to want to get out from under their husband's shadows. She started off making a few introductions here and there, and she's accidentally made a business out of it."

"Huh. Sounds smart. What else would you need to worry about?"

"Paying rent on a place and having employees and dealing with the legal stuff like contracts and HR. Probably a million other things I haven't thought of."

"You know what?"

"What?"

"You've had a huge smile on your face the whole time you've been telling me about those challenges."

"Have I? Well, I don't know why. They're all scary and overwhelming. I mean, where would I even have a place?"

"Why don't you walk around the neighbourhood you like, I'm guessing Lilac Bay, right?" She nodded. "See if there's anything for lease. Or look online. Start there."

"But it will take a few months to get set up, and I don't have a ton of savings to be able to support that, let alone for the cost of making a place into offices. I don't have that kind of money."

"Amy," Rick said, sounding serious. He took her hand and set her pulse on an uneven rhythm. She watched his mouth as he spoke. "Do you remember our trip away to Hotel D'Montvue?"

She nodded, her cheeks staining with colour as she

thought about all the time they'd spent together in bed that long weekend.

"Not that stuff." Rick smirked as though he could read her thoughts. She noticed his face was a little heated as well. "Amy, you jumped out of a *plane* that weekend. Do you remember that?"

She nodded, a smile slowly beginning to spread across her face. "I do," she said. "I jumped out of a plane, didn't I?" Rick nodded, grinning. "Even though I thought I was going to die, I did it, didn't I?"

"You only needed a tiny little nudge. Do you think you'll die if you start your own business?" She shook her head. "Do you think you're completely incapable of finding investors? Or that your business plan is so bad the bank will turn it down? No? Then consider this your tiny little nudge."

She sat staring at him with a silly grin on her face. Then her eyes filled with tears without warning. "God, I miss you so much," she said, her words catching in a sob.

"Come here," he said, and she leaned forward in her chair. He reached a hand out and she was hoping he would touch her face. Instead, he ran a hand unsteadily through her hair. It wasn't the kiss she was aching for, but somehow it felt as though he was taking all the problems out of her world with each stroke.

CHAPTER THIRTY-NINE

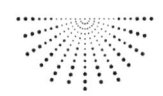

"Where have you been?" Martha hissed as Amy walked towards her desk. She turned her head back to her computer before Amy could answer, tapping randomly on her keyboard like a bad extra in a movie.

"I had a medical appointment," Amy lied, putting her bag down and pulling out her chair. She'd been going to the hospital before work for weeks, so she wasn't sure what the big deal was. She was still getting all her work done on time. She glanced around to see whether Martha was under surveillance, but couldn't see anything unusual.

Martha tilted her head to look at her. "No you didn't."

"Okay, fine. What's the problem anyway?" She wiggled her mouse and typed her login credentials when the computer came to life.

"Beaumont's been looking for you."

"Why?"

Martha shrugged and kept her eyes trained on her computer.

"Amy," Beaumont's voice boomed from across the room and Amy jerked involuntarily. She cursed herself, knowing he'd have enjoyed that reaction.

"Yes." She spun to face him. "How can I help you?"

"My office. Now."

Amy shot Martha a sidelong glance, and she gave a worried look back. Amy knew this was it. The meeting where he fired her. She'd been mentally preparing for it, but she found that was no use now. The blood was ringing in her ears as she took a seat opposite Beaumont and stared at him expectantly.

"Did you carefully read your contract when you signed it?"

"I did," Amy said confidently. "Anything else would be foolish."

"It would! You're right. So, you're familiar with all the clauses in it?" She tilted her head in assent. "So, you know that you're expressly forbidden to financially benefit from work of the same nature as what you perform for Edgerton's, for a third party client that you are not engaged with via Edgerton's as per section eleven part two."

"Paragraph three," Amy added. "I am."

"And yet, you've taken on the client…" he consulted a piece of paper on his desk, "Sunnywoods Lifestyle and Retirement Village. Is that correct?"

Amy was stunned and could feel her face burning. Why had she ever believed she could trust Kristina? Martha had warned her, but Amy had chosen to give her the benefit of the doubt. She'd thought they were getting along so well. They'd even won their re-pitch with Peregrine, and were working well together on the account. Or so Amy had thought. Now she felt the cold thrust of Kristina's knife in her back. It hurt more than she could have imagined.

"It was a favour to my grandfather," Amy said finally, her voice impressively level. Beaumont didn't like it. He wanted to see her sweat.

"But money has changed hands. You've been paid for the work and they are a third party client."

"They are," she agreed. "But according to the contract, for me to be in breach of the terms, I need to have directly financially benefited from the arrangement."

"They paid you. There's no clearer demonstration of direct financial benefit than being paid."

She grinned, knowing she had him on a technicality. "I accepted a payment of zero dollars. And in return, they deducted a fixed amount from my grandfather's residential costs. His rental rate will be significantly reduced for a few months. I was not paid a penny. And I can prove it."

Beaumont's face was reddening. He didn't like the way this was being flipped around on him. "You can't prove it, because you took the money, and you're in breach of your contract!"

She shook her head, smiling sweetly. "Shall we call the Sunnywoods accounts department right now? As it happens, I know their number off by heart."

Beaumont sat staring at her for a moment longer, fury etched into his features. He got himself under control, but was obviously uncertain what move to make now. He'd assumed he had her.

"May I get back to work?" she asked, keeping her tone neutral. She knew she should be flooded with relief at the narrow escape. But instead, she was filled with indignation.

He nodded once. "But first, head to the boardroom for a meeting I'm about to call. I think it's time I gave everyone another stern talking to. I want all the focus on the work we do here. And I'm going to tighten up the contracts for the future."

They headed out of the room together and Beaumont called for a yachting meeting with the traditional "all hands on deck!"

Everyone pretended they'd been hard at work, instead of staring into the fish tank to see what was happening between Amy and Beaumont.

As they filed into the boardroom, Martha caught her arm. "What happened?" she whispered.

"Kristina ratted me out."

Martha turned pale and Amy shook her head to indicate she didn't want to talk about it anymore. There was one thing left on her to-do list for the day. An item she had spontaneously added.

"Sit down, everyone, find places." Beaumont stood at the head of the large boardroom table as the stragglers came in. Kristina entered the room and smiled at Amy, who frowned back. Kristina blinked in confusion. She clearly didn't know the jig was up.

Once everyone was settled and quiet, Beaumont opened his mouth to speak.

"May I say a few words beforehand, please, Beaumont?" Amy asked quickly, standing. "As you know, I learned an important lesson this morning and I'd really like to share that first-hand with the team." Beaumont hesitated a moment, then held his hand out, gesturing that she could proceed.

"Hi, everyone." Amy looked around the faces at the table. Faces she'd worked with and grown fond of over the last six years. Faces she would miss. Hope from IT, Liza from printing, Martha, Kyle, Amber from her team, Emily from payroll. "My boyfriend was almost killed in a car accident recently." A collective gasp went up, and Amy shook her head. "He's recovering. That's not why I'm telling you this. But he said something that really stuck with me. He said 'If I could go at any moment, I want to make the most of the time I have.' And I realised how smart that was." She slowly exhaled to steady herself. "And that I want to do the same. So I'm announcing that today will be my last day at Edgerton's." There was a hiss as sharp breaths were taken in and her colleagues spun to glare at Beaumont accusingly. He looked thrown. "He didn't fire me," Amy said quickly. "Although he's definitely trying to push me out. I *want* to leave. Because I have grown to hate it here. I hate the way we do business, the way we screw over clients and cut corners. I hate the way we are made to compete against each other."

"Amy, *sit down*," Beaumont said, finally finding his tongue.

She continued in a louder voice. "There is a better way to do things. A way that's better for clients and better for all of us. And I'm leaving because I want to do it that way. I don't know yet if I'll join another house, or if I'll start my own. If I do start my own business, *not all of you* will be welcome to join me," she looked witheringly at Kristina, who had a huge smile on her face. The smile faltered and was replaced with a frown as she took in Amy's words. "But for now, I just want to say thank you for being awesome colleagues. It's been a wonderful six years. Mostly," she added, shooting Beaumont a look. His face was so red that for a split second Amy worried he might actually have a heart attack. "Thank you all. Now, Beaumont, you don't need to cut anyone else from my team."

Martha's mouth was hanging open, her eyes shining with pride and awe.

Amy walked out of the room, which was so silent she could almost hear Beaumont's ears whistling. It felt as though she was watching someone else, or she was inside a dream as she collected her handbag, pushed her desk chair in one more time and strolled out of the office, into the sunshine.

It was only when she had reached the shore of Lilac Bay that she collapsed into shaky tears.

CHAPTER FORTY

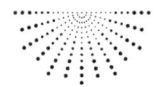

Amy slipped her sunglasses on and sat on the wood and stone bench that looked out through Lilac Bay and into Sydney Harbour.

She felt giddy. She was free of Beaumont, but now she was also unemployed. Drastically so. Her finances weren't exactly shipshape, as she was all too painfully aware, and she wasn't sure at all what the future held for her. It was a kind of dizzy freedom, like tipping headfirst over a cliff. Or jumping out of a plane.

She pulled out her phone to ring Rick. "Guess what!"

"Hold on a sec." Rick could hear a crackling noise as his hand covered the mouthpiece. "Can we finish later?" he asked someone in the room with him.

"Yeah, sure. I'll come back around three," Amy heard a female voice reply, and her heart beat faster. *Lauren*.

"You there?" Rick came back to the call. "What's up? You sound excited."

"I guess I am…I quit my job!"

"Ames," he breathed, and she could hear the pride in his voice. "That's the best news I've had all day. Well done! I'm *so* happy for you."

"Thank you." She felt the butterflies of anxiety and hope in her stomach. "Although, I have *no* idea what comes next."

"We'll figure it out," Rick said, and a huge smile broke over her face. *We*. "The important thing is that you took that first step."

"That's true." She realised her hands were shaking. "I'm going to ask the girls out for a drink tonight to celebrate." Instantly she felt horrible for talking about a part of life that Rick was still separated from.

"That's awesome," he said after a pause, and the happiness rang slightly hollow.

"I'm sorry." She bit her lip.

"No, don't be. I'm honestly really happy for you. And I'll be out of here soon so I can slowly start doing things like that again. At least the Whistle Stop has wheelchair access," he said with a short laugh.

They fell silent for a moment. "I'll come and see you again tomorrow morning. And I can stay until you kick me out. I'm a lady of leisure now."

"I guess you are. Can you switch on your video for a moment? I want to see your face."

"It's a mess. I've been close to tears for a while."

"I've seen you crying tons of times," he chuckled. She switched on her video, pouting at him for the comment. "Take your sunnies off."

She did so. They sat and beamed at one another for a long moment. Then he shook his head. "God, you're beautiful. I missed looking at that face when we were apart."

"Shut up or you'll make me cry for real," she said, her voice wobbling. "I missed your handsome face more than you'll ever know."

"My Frankenstein face." He traced a finger over his scar.

Amy shook her head. "It makes you even hotter, if that's possible." It was the truth.

"Alright," he said. "That's enough sop. Got some food here I need to choke down." He turned the phone's camera to face a dish of unidentifiable meat drowned in a brown sauce, congealing beside a scoop of packet-mix mashed potato. A small plastic pot with three cubes of unripe melon sat beside it.

"I'll bring you some pies from The Pie-ganic tomorrow morning."

"You'll be driving all over town, that's ridiculous."

"You did it for me." A lump formed in her throat as she thought of all the macarons he'd left, and all the hours of driving to get them to her. Tears threatened. "I'm so sorry!" She wafted her hand in front of her face.

"Don't be," he said gently. "You're a weeper. Some people are born that way. Nothing to be ashamed of." He chuckled when she pretended to swat him through the phone.

When she ended the call, she sent a text to the chat group with Lyra, Marley and Silas, announcing she had quit and that if anyone had a job for her, she was all ears. She'd meant the last part as a joke, but moments later, Silas wrote back with a string of celebration emojis. *Come work at The Pie-ganic?*

Amy laughed out loud and texted back that she'd let him know if she needed any shifts. Marley rang then, and Amy instantly swiped to answer her call.

"Oh my God, Amy!" Marley was so loud that Amy had to hold the phone away from her ear for a moment. "You did it!"

"Yes," she answered, cringing. "I did it."

"I am so proud of you!"

"Are you really? I didn't follow our plan at all. Not even a bit."

"Well, then this is what you needed to do. And it's always important to follow your heart. And it'll work out, I know it."

"I guess." Doubt began to flood her. "But design isn't like singing was for Lyra. I'm not about to get awarded a big contract for following my heart."

"Listen to me." Marley sounded serious. "You know how much I love Lyra. But she didn't *do* anything to get that contract."

"You're kidding, she sings like an angel!" Amy was indignant.

"Oh, yes," Marley said quickly. "I don't mean she isn't talented, or that she doesn't deserve it. But she didn't actually pro-actively put herself out there and start marketing herself and knocking on doors. Basically she got that contract through connections. And backed it up with outrageous talent," she post-scripted.

"I really don't want to compare myself to Lyra." Amy felt awkward. "I don't like talking about her behind her back, either."

"Oh, I'd say this to her face," Marley said, and Amy knew with certainty that she would. "But I'm talking facts. She deserves to be where she is. But she got there by pure chance. You, on the other hand, are a fighter, Amy. I know you'll end up making your mark. Whether you open your own company, or you go join a different one. I'm so proud of you for taking a step that so many people dream about but never actually do."

"I guess I did do that, huh?"

"Yep. And if you're free tonight, I'd love to meet at the Stop and buy you a drink."

"I was going to suggest that. It's Wednesday so I usually meet Pop, but I'll call and explain."

"He'll be delighted for you."

"You're right, he will." She grinned, thinking of Pop's reaction. "Thank you, Marley. I really needed this pep talk."

"See you tonight!"

After the calls, Amy hoisted her handbag onto her shoulder, dipped her sunglasses back down and set off for a walk around Lilac Bay.

She wasn't really dressed for it, in peep-toe heels, a fit-and-flare sundress and a complete lack of sunscreen, but she knew it would do her good. She didn't feel quite ready to get back in the car and drive home to Bondi yet.

Lilac Bay was relatively small as far as suburbs went. It scooped a neat little bite out of the Sydney Harbour shoreline and between the Secret Garden, the old railway line and the ring of mansions set back from the shoreline, there were only about ten or twelve blocks of suburb left.

Amy walked almost every street of them, pacing until her shoes pinched her feet and she felt faint from the lack of water. She'd been half-looking for a property available to let, as Rick had suggested. She knew it was a pipe dream, but it seemed she was taking chances today, so she figured it couldn't hurt to try.

It was several hours later when she finally gave up and took a shady outdoor seat at a cafe with a sandstone facade, comfortable mesh chairs, and harbour glimpses. She groaned as she slipped her shoes off under the table, rubbing her bruised and blistered feet against one another.

"I'll have sparkling water and an espresso," she said to the friendly, red-headed woman who came out to serve her. "And a slice of your very best cake."

She grinned. "One of those days, is it?"

"I'm property-hunting."

She snorted. "In Lilac Bay? Good luck to you."

"I know." Amy rolled her eyes. "But a girl can dream, can't she?"

The woman suddenly looked thoughtful. "Are you looking for something commercial or residential?"

"Commercial. I'm apparently about to start my own business."

"Oh, congratulations." The waitress smiled. "I do actually know someone who's giving up a commercial place, if you'd be willing to look slightly outside the Lilac Bay perimeter."

"Oh?"

"My husband runs a CrossFit gym and they're relocating to a bigger venue."

"So, it's a garage or something?"

"Sort of. But it would be big enough for a little set of offices. And it's pretty much a blank canvas at the moment so no walls to rip out or anything. He made a flyer. Shall I grab it for you?"

"Sure!"

"I'll get your drinks. And it sounds like you've had a red velvet cupcake kind of day," she added with a wink.

"I have indeed." Amy smiled up at her.

Once she was gone, Amy sat and breathed in the air. She did so love Lilac Bay. It was different from Bondi. Less salty, less crowded, more refined and more delicately scented. You could catch the smell of lilacs from almost any point in the suburb.

She thought about Kristina. She couldn't deny that she felt hurt by her betrayal. Kristina would get to work with Peregrine alone now, probably what she had wanted all along. But something was niggling at Amy. Kristina's betrayal didn't really make much sense. She was already the top cat with Beaumont. She was already getting the best work, the juiciest clients, the freest reign. Why would she need to push Amy out? There was a puzzle piece missing, but Amy couldn't quite figure out what it was.

She told herself it didn't matter anyway. It wasn't like she could go back and ask for her job after such a spectacular exit. She sighed. It was onwards or nothing.

The woman came back out then, bringing her drinks and cake on a small gold tray.

"I thought you could use a scoop of vanilla ice-cream to go with the cupcake," she said, setting the tray down. "On the house, of course."

"You're an angel." Amy reached for the water before it hit the table.

The woman pulled a flyer from her back pocket and placed it in front of Amy as she drank.

"I'm not going to do the hard sell, but he'd love to see this place go to someone reliable. The rent's a bit below average - it's owned by an elderly lady who doesn't really need the money, she wants no-fuss tenants. She'll take anyone my husband recommends, or at least strongly consider them. Have a think about it, his number's on the back."

"Thank you so much." Amy took the flyer up. "I really will. And thanks for the ice cream. I need to come here more often."

She nodded and smiled, heading over to a couple who'd just sat down. Amy examined the flyer. The photo was black and white and grainy, she couldn't really tell what the place was like. The square meterage was perfect, if Amy factored in a large reception area and then one or two smaller office rooms. The flyer listed a kitchenette and small bathroom as facilities.

And if Amy sold her body as well as both Pop's kidneys, she might be able to afford a few months' rent there.

CHAPTER FORTY-ONE

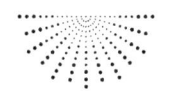

Martha called as Amy was getting ready to meet Marley at the Whistle Stop. Amy put her on loudspeaker as she freshened up her makeup and Martha told her what had happened after her grand exit from Edgerton's.

Beaumont had made very specific threats about what would happen to anyone he found out was having professional contact with her.

"Professional contact?" Amy repeated.

Martha chuckled. "I know. What even is that, and how does he think he's going to police it?"

"Oh, Beaumont."

"Oh! And Kristina collared me after the meeting and dragged me into the supply cupboard."

"*What?*"

"I know! She demanded to know why you left. I told her we both knew what she'd done, telling Beaumont about Sunnywoods."

"My God. What did she say?"

"She stalked out, didn't come back to the office the rest of the day."

"Wow." Amy wondered what that meant. Surely if Kristina's goal had been to get rid of her, she was done now. She didn't need to bother Martha. "I'm sorry she did that. I saw some missed calls from her on my work phone, but I haven't listened to her messages. I need to give the phone back to Hope. I'm going to wipe it and get you to take it in, if that's okay?"

"Sure, no worries."

"I have to run, but thank you so much for calling me. I'll talk to you soon."

They hung up and Amy caught a taxi to the Whistle Stop, an expense she could ill afford, but she was considering it a last hoorah. The driver turned on the car radio to an obnoxious commercial channel. She was about to ask him to change it, when the DJ's voice caught her attention.

"Next up, we have a song from a rising local talent! We're excited to be one of the very first stations sharing the first single from Lyra and we are *huge* fans over here at WMXFM. This song is called *The Right Notes*. Why don't you give us a call after hearing it, tell us what you think? Here it is folks, *The Right Notes*."

Lyra's song started up, the one she had played for Alex at the Lilac Bay Food Truck event the night they had reunited. The song that had started it all for her.

It had already been magical when she had sung it on the tiny stage with a second rate sound system. Professionally produced, it now sounded like a smash hit. As the chorus struck up, Amy shivered.

The cab driver glanced up at her in the rear-view mirror. "Good song, huh?"

"That's my best friend singing," Amy said proudly.

"Psht," he scoffed in disbelief, rolling his eyes at her and returning them to the road.

She didn't bother arguing, wanting to hear every note of Lyra's song.

Marley may have been right about Lyra not fighting tooth and nail for years to get a contract. But she was no less deserving than someone who had. She'd spent all that time gigging in tiny bars, putting up with crappy, unappreciative crowds, pouring her heart and soul into her music and song writing. Now, she'd finally be recognised for her breathtaking talent.

Amy wanted to call her right away and cry to her about how amazing she was. But Lyra still hadn't read her message in the group chat announcing she'd quit her job. She must be at the studio. Amy hoped she was taking care of herself and not letting the record label burn her out.

She walked into the Whistle Stop to find Marley already waiting at their usual barrel, wearing what looked like a chiffon nightgown.

"I just heard Lyra's first single in the taxi!" Amy said.

Marley squealed. "I'm jealous. I haven't heard it on the radio yet. What station was it on?"

"WMXFM."

"I'll tune into that at work tomorrow, I hope they play it again! What huge days you and Lyra have had!" She hugged Amy tightly.

Amy began to laugh, and it came out as the same rapid-fire machine gun sound she'd made when she landed after skydiving all those months ago.

Marley's eyes widened in alarm. "Oh no." She laid a hand on Amy's arm. "You're losing it."

"I'm not losing it!" But the laughing continued.

"Amy, that's a really embarrassing laugh," Marley said in a low voice, when the machine gun continued for a moment longer.

"Sorry." She tried to control herself. "I think maybe I am

losing it. A tiny bit."

"You're going to be okay. I know it." Marley smiled at her reassuringly and Amy desperately wanted to believe her. "And in the worst case scenario, you can go work with Silas. Can't beat that view!"

Amy nodded, taking some deep breaths. She was right. Amy wouldn't starve. Even if he couldn't pay her much, Silas would feed her at least. Thank God she had those several months of grace from her mortgage payments. Their phones pinged in unison and Marley glanced at hers.

"Lyra's on her way in to join us!"

"I really miss her," Amy said, as their drinks arrived. "She's been so busy lately, the poor thing."

Marley nodded. "But things evolve. We're all still best friends. It's inevitable that as we get partners, win recording contracts and launch our own businesses, we're going to have a little less time for one another. We just have to make the moments where we do get to hang out count more."

Amy looked at her. "You are so ridiculously wise sometimes."

She grinned and then shrugged. "I was raised by a wise woman."

When Lyra turned up soon afterwards, Alex was with her. Lyra ran straight over to Amy and pounced on her for a hug.

"I am so proud of you for walking out of there," she said into her ear. Amy hugged her back.

"And I cried in a cab because I heard your song on the radio." They broke apart, laughing as Marley went to fetch two new stools. Alex looked around, a puzzled smile on his face.

"This is where you guys always come and hang out?" he asked. "What's so special about it? Looks like a bit of a dive if you ask me."

"We didn't ask you." Lyra slapped him.

"And it's the Whistle Stop!" they added in unison. Alex shook his head, grinning.

Amy felt a tug of sadness, wishing Rick was there with her. This was a huge moment in her life, and he'd been the one to give her the last nudge she needed. She let her eyes drift to the booths where he'd been standing when they first met. As the others arranged the stools to fit round the barrel, Amy shot Rick a quick text message.

Can't wait to see you in the morning.

Same here, he immediately replied. *Best part of my day.*

Amy tucked her phone away and looked at Lyra. She looked a little thinner than when Amy had last seen her, slightly pale and with dark shadows under her eyes. The record label was working her hard, that much was clear.

"So, what's the next big step with work?" Lyra asked Amy, once she and Alex had their drinks.

"Oh, God. I wish I knew. I'm still coming to terms with the fact I actually did it! I keep thinking I'll wake up tomorrow and head in like nothing happened. Maybe I should."

Marley put her hand on Amy's arm and Lyra shook her head firmly. "Nope. You did the right thing. The universe is going to work it out for you."

Amy pulled out the flyer she'd been given at the cafe and slapped it on the table.

"I've never started up a business before," Amy said, "but I do know I don't want to run it out of my living room. And for that, I need premises. This is the most reasonable place I've been able to find, and it's totally out of my price range. I need a huge cash injection to get something up and running, buy the equipment I need, not to mention hire the manpower to redo this place." She dropped her head into her hands. "I'm going to meet with the bank next week, but it would all be so much easier with a business partner. Except everyone I know is still at Edgerton's and I have nothing to lure them over with. And there are some I wouldn't want anyway," she added, thinking of Kristina.

"I still really have a great feeling about it all," Lyra said.

Alex nodded and picked up the flyer, considering it for a moment. "If you wanted help converting this place, I could actually be useful," he said thoughtfully. "I'm still officially unemployed but I've flipped houses before. I could save you a lot of money, and then what I did for the houses was get licensed professionals to double-check the wiring and plumbing and sign off on it if it passed their inspection. They don't sign off unless they're happy putting their name to it."

Amy's eyes bulged and she looked to Lyra, who shrugged happily. "It might stop me feeling so guilty when I get stuck at the studio for hours longer than I said I would." She smiled up at Alex lovingly.

"Alex, I wouldn't have any idea how to compensate you for that," Amy said. "It might be a long time before I can pay you what your time would have been worth."

"I wouldn't have offered it if I didn't mean it. I love projects like that. It would be cool to have something to do while I figure out my next move."

"Well, it would be a huge help, obviously. But don't decide anything now. Right now, another round of drinks is in order. If I'm going to crash my whole life, I might as well do it in style!"

Hours later, as they were all heading home, Lyra pulled Amy aside. "Give me a call tomorrow, alright? I think I've got an idea I want to run by you."

CHAPTER FORTY-TWO

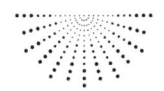

Amy opened her mouth on her first morning as a free woman and felt like she'd spent the night in a sandstorm. It took two full glasses of water before the feeling was gone, but the grit in her head wasn't so easily vanquished.

She slipped her gown on and cranked her espresso machine to life, scrolling through the messages she'd sent Rick last night. She groaned at the soppiness of them, sinking into the sofa with her espresso when it was ready.

She tucked her feet beneath her and clicked to dial him.

"How's the head?" he asked, picking up on the second ring. There was a smile in his voice.

"Oh God. I'm so sorry I bombarded you with all that!"

He chuckled. "Don't be. I enjoyed every single word. Listen, I'm about to start P.T. Are you heading over later?"

"Yes," she said quickly. "I might have to catch the bus, but I'm coming over. Don't expect any fancy presents this time though. Ah crap, I won't be able to get the pies. I'll get them another day soon, is that okay?"

"Amy." His tone was serious. "You gave me boggle-eye glasses and Dougal socks. I'm set for life."

They laughed and Amy was hit with an overwhelming desire to be snuggled up against him, feeling his chest rock as he laughed, his arms around her, his breath on her face. She hung up before she got too teary and spent the morning dragging herself around to get ready. She sat down at her computer and set up a job alert after half-heartedly searching for a few moments. She needed a backup plan, but maybe today wasn't the day to start firing off her resume.

When she arrived at the hospital several hours later, Rick's room was empty. His shirt hung on the bathroom door and Amy ran the fabric between her fingers, then brought it to her face, taking a deep inhale of his scent. The nightstand was crowded with presents and cards. She assumed he was at an appointment and shot him a text to let him know she'd arrived. His phone vibrated inside the bedside table drawer.

The bed was freshly made and looked soft. Amy wandered around his room for a while, struggling to keep her eyes open. She sat on the edge of the bed and examined some of the items on the side table. She smiled when she caught sight of the novelty glasses, and felt her heart swell when she saw several items that were obviously from army friends. A small bronze statue of an officer stood proudly beside a gold ring inscribed with the army's motto.

She laid on the bed, thinking about Rick's friends and how badly he must be missing them. She felt exhausted. She told herself she'd just close her eyes for a few moments until Rick came back. Then, feeling chill, she pulled the blanket up around her chin and fell sound asleep.

Sometime later, she woke to quiet voices in the room. Rick and Lauren. It sounded as though they were going through some technical details on Rick's wheelchair. Amy was about to open her eyes when Lauren's voice stopped her cold.

"Does she know yet?" she asked, her voice barely above a whisper. Amy's heart thudded heavily against her ribcage.

"No." His voice was quiet.

"You can't keep it from her forever, you know?"

Amy's stomach churned and she felt a wave of nausea sweep over her.

Rick sighed. "I know. But I want to keep it between you and I for a bit longer. Until I know it's real. Please. Don't say anything to her. I have to be the one to tell her."

"Of course I won't." Lauren was sympathetic.

Amy lay statue still, her heart hammering and her skin prickling. She concentrated on keeping her breath even so they wouldn't realise she was awake. The discussion moved onto other topics but Amy couldn't hear anything over the blood rushing in her ears.

A few moments later, she sat bolt upright, stunning them both, and jumped off the bed. She barely managed to lock the door to the attached bathroom behind her before she was sick from the tips of her toes.

"Are you okay in there?" Rick knocked gently on the door for the third time. "Can you let me know you're okay?"

Amy rinsed her mouth again and spat the water out. She gripped the edges of the sink and looked at herself in the mirror. Her skin was blotchy, her eyes red. She stared at her reflection unblinkingly for a long time. She couldn't quite believe what she'd heard. Had she been an idiot not to worry more about Lauren? Surely not. Rick wasn't like that. He'd tell her if there was someone else. *He did say that*, she reminded herself. But he'd said that to push her away, he'd admitted as much. There had to be another explanation for their conversation. One that would make perfect sense. She would ask him. But not today. She couldn't handle anything today.

"I'm okay," she said finally, straining to keep her voice light. "Just badly hungover."

She wiped her face with a paper towel and opened the door. Rick was in his wheelchair, frowning with concern.

Amy felt her heart cartwheel through every kind of emotion, seeing him in it for the first time. They were silent for a moment, trying to read one another's faces.

"Can you do tricks in that yet?" Amy asked finally. He grinned.

"Lauren's taught me one or two things. I'm keen to try them out." At the mention of Lauren, Amy's smile wavered. "You really don't look well, Ames. How much did you drink last night?"

"I guess more than I thought. Are you allowed out? Do you fancy going outside for some coffee or something?"

He glanced at his watch. "Yes. I have another appointment in about forty five minutes."

"Let's go."

Rick was much better at manoeuvring the wheelchair than Amy had expected him to be, although the physical exertion seemed to cost him. It was a strange feeling to get used to, being taller than him. She wondered how he felt, but could read nothing in his expression aside from determination.

A little girl hugging a stuffed rabbit to her chest and holding her mother's hand paused to watch as they headed toward her. Amy felt her stomach lurch, wondering whether she'd say something awkward.

"That man's got a chair like Daddy's," she said after they'd passed, and Amy inwardly breathed a sigh of relief.

Without thinking, she turned to head down the stairwell, used to taking that route. She quickly swerved back into the corridor, hoping Rick wouldn't have noticed. She could tell from his frown that he had. It was the kind of mistake Lauren definitely wouldn't have made.

The woman in the coffee cart at the hospital entrance smiled warmly at them as they approached.

"What can I get for you both?" She kept her eyes firmly on Amy.

"Espresso, please." The woman nodded and waited, still looking at Amy.

Rick was scanning the chalkboard menu. "Latte, I guess."

"What kind of milk would you like?" Amy wasn't sure whether she was imagining it, but it sounded as though the woman was talking a little slower with Rick.

He frowned. "Cow's?"

She smiled and lifted up several packs of milk. "We also have almond, oat and lactose-free." She pointed to each of them in turn.

"*Cow's*," Rick said, slowly and emphatically.

The woman reddened and made their coffees in silence as Rick and Amy exchanged amused glances. Then Amy picked up both cups, realising Rick couldn't work his chair and hold a cup at the same time.

They made their way to a shady spot under the huge spreading oak tree in the hospital's beautiful grassy grounds.

"I need to get you a cup holder," she said, handing Rick his latte as she sat in the grass at his feet.

"Don't bother," he said. "I'm going to be throwing wheelies in this thing all the time. It'll only spill."

She laughed. "Sorry about that woman at the coffee cart." She took a sip of her espresso.

Rick twisted his mouth. "Thanks for not saying anything to her."

"I very nearly did. I mean, she's working at a hospital. Why's she speaking to someone using a wheelchair as if they're slow?"

"I'd really prefer you didn't. I don't want anyone jumping in to defend me. I think it's a conversation I'm going to have to have with my mates as well. And my mum," he added.

"I can't guarantee I'll be able to hold my tongue. But I will always give you first punch and first comeback rights. And I'll try to follow your lead."

"Sounds like a plan." He grinned at her.

She leaned her head against his legs. "How do you feel about getting out?" She stared into the distance and tried to keep her voice level. She kept hearing Lauren's words. *Have you told her yet?*

He sighed. "It's a mix. I'm scared, not afraid to admit that. And relieved. There was a time I didn't think I'd ever get out. Lauren is honestly a miracle worker. That woman really knows her stuff. I can't believe how much better I'm getting every single day because she's working me so hard."

His phrasing brought unwelcome images of Lauren and Rick to Amy's mind. She shook her head to rid herself of them. "That's good," she managed finally, hoping her voice didn't sound as flat to his ears as it did to hers. "It's a shame you won't see her every day anymore."

"Oh, I will." Amy's stomach lurched. "She's actually taking me on as a private patient. The army's paying. She's even using up some of her vacation time to keep working with me daily."

Amy didn't trust herself to speak for a long moment. "I'm glad," she said finally.

Her phone rang. She left it going for a moment and, when she finally picked it up to flick it off, she saw that it was Lyra. Amy dimly remembered Lyra saying she had something to tell her today.

"Do you mind?" She held the screen up for him to see who it was. If Amy had ever needed to see Lyra's face, it was now.

"Of course not. I'd like to say hello to her."

"She'll be delighted to see you. She's always been Team Rick."

Amy swiped to answer and Lyra squinted into the camera, trying to figure out where she was and who she was with.

"Rick!" she shouted gleefully, and he grinned into the camera.

"Long time no see."

"Alex is here too." Lyra shifted the angle to include him in frame. Their first video double date. "Amy, I really can't wait to tell you this, I'm so sorry if it's inappropriate in front of Rick, and I'm sorry that it's not face-to-face."

"Oh, God. What on earth are you going to say?" She covered her face with her free hand.

"That I want to help you set your business up." She was almost wriggling with glee.

Amy peeped through her fingers. "*What?*"

"Alex and I talked about it. I have this chunk of money just sitting there from the record deal. We don't want to use it right now, so we thought it could be more useful to you. Then you don't need to get banks involved and you can get that place you showed us the flyer for. Alex can help you with the renovations once you've drawn them up. Ames... you could really do this!"

Amy was speechless for a long moment. "No!" She shook

her head firmly. "I can't let you do that! You could use the money to put a deposit on a house or something."

Lyra and Alex exchanged a happy look. "I already own my place. But we will buy a place together," Alex said. "I want to flip it, and now's not a great time for that. I'm taking on a part-time job, but in between it would make me really happy to do this for you." He smiled. "I also have an ulterior motive. I want to take lots of pics when I do your place up. I'm going to get a website going, offering my services to other people who are flipping houses and need help."

Amy was still shaking her head in disbelief. There was no way she could accept. "Guys, I can't let you do this."

"Sure you can! If it makes you feel better, we can draw up a contract or something. It could be a loan, or me owning a stake in the business or whatever you think would work best for you. I wish I could afford to give it to you," she said with a little laugh, "but I'm not quite there yet."

Amy turned to Rick, who was beaming at her. "Lyra's a grown woman," he said. "She wouldn't offer it if she didn't mean it. Neither would Alex. I think it's the answer to all your problems and you'd be stupid to turn it down."

"*Thank* you, Rick," Lyra said. "Maybe she'll listen to you!"

"Alex, could you use another pair of hands with the renovations?" Rick asked. "Not entirely sure what I can do yet, or whether I'd get in the way, but…"

"That would be great, man," Alex said confidently. "Between us, we'll definitely figure out a way to put you to good use."

Rick grinned at Amy. "Lauren's going to think that's great for rebuilding my fine motor skills and my strength."

Amy smiled tightly at Rick and then turned back to Lyra and Alex.

"No crying!" Lyra said, noticing Amy's face was crumpling. Alex slung an arm around Lyra's shoulder. "I'm so happy I can do this for you," Lyra said, her own voice wobbling. "You're amazing and this is going to be incredible for you."

Rick and Alex rolled their eyes at one another. "So, power-tools?" Rick asked, and Alex laughed.

"Or ideas on how to best insulate from floods of tears?"

CHAPTER FORTY-THREE

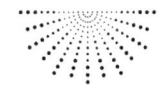

The following two weeks passed in a blur of phone-calls, appointments and far too many open browser tabs. There was so much to organise with setting up a business, more than Amy could have imagined. She was glad she hadn't known when she made her dramatic exit from Edgerton's, or she'd likely never have had the courage to do it.

First on the list was convincing the landlady that she was the perfect tenant for her place. Amy called the number on the back of the flyer and spoke to the woman at the cafe's husband. They met up, and he agreed to support Amy's application. She sweated on whether it would be a yes or a no, and was delighted when the old lady called herself to tell Amy she wanted to lease the place to her. Amy signed contracts the next afternoon.

Second on the list was finding a lawyer to draw up the contracts for Lyra's loan - something Lyra was adamant was unnecessary, but which Amy insisted on. She would never get over Lyra's generosity, but she could make sure the gesture never caused issues between them.

Amy registered her business on the official roll, which should have been more fulfilling than it was. She had champagne chilling in the fridge that she'd pictured herself popping once the paperwork was filed. She hadn't realised the process was entirely online. The champagne sat unopened as she squinted into her laptop during the small hours, re-submitting the forms multiple times after technical issues on the website.

She also hadn't really thought about the fact that her business needed a name, until she'd come to that field in the form. *Porter Design* wasn't very creative, but it was the best she could do after round six of trying to create a suitable password for the online registration system.

Insurances, tax accountants, social media handles, expense tracking software, invoicing tools, the list ran on and Amy doggedly ploughed her way through it.

She'd reached out to a few architects she knew and one had been able to work with her on short notice. With Rick and Alex's help, they'd developed plans for the office layout. It wouldn't be anything fancy - a huge, open-fronted reception area that doubled as a showroom, one small office and a storage room, as well as a refresh for the kitchenette and a bathroom.

Then had come the fun part, the interior design for it all. Amy found herself thinking of Kristina as she worked on her ideas. She thought of how they'd managed to come together so well for the Peregrine account, and she was hurt afresh at Kristina's betrayal.

Amy briefly thought about that moment at Lilac Bay, where they'd eaten pies together. If she was given a do-over, would she tell Kristina about the side-hustle at Pop's home? She decided she would. After all, that had been the catalyst for Amy finally walking away from Beaumont and deciding to start her own business. Something she was less nervous and more excited about day by day.

Amy had a short conversation with Martha, who told her things had gone from bad to worse at Edgerton's. Morale had tanked and sick leave was at an all-time high. Kristina was frequently away from her desk, but had stopped trying to convince Martha to give her Amy's personal number. That was something at least.

"Oh, and remember those crazy bathrooms we decided to design that day?" Martha asked.

"Yeah."

"The clients went nuts for them. Totally ate them up."

"Oh God, you are *banned* from talking about bathrooms. Ate them up?" They laughed. "But I'm really glad to hear that."

"Yeah," Martha said proudly. "I think I'm going to get a new account out of it, so thank you for the idea."

"You're most welcome. I have to go; I'm working on my logo design. But let's talk soon."

They hung up and Amy rubbed her temples, wondering where to even begin on the logo. She needed a break. So far, the only breaks she'd been taking were to see Rick an hour or two a day in hospital. The visits were sweet torture. Amy badly wanted to kiss him, and constantly found excuses to touch him, sometimes daring to grab his hand with no excuse at all. She loved the feeling of his huge, rough palm against her smooth one. Their kisses were still chaste, and it took every ounce of willpower Amy had not to gently curl her fist into his hair and pull their faces together.

She hadn't yet worked up the courage to ask Rick what he and Lauren had been talking about that morning. It played on her mind constantly, startling her awake at odd hours of the night. She comforted herself by reading Rick's texts. They were sweet and sometimes flirty. Rick wouldn't send her messages like that if he was interested in Lauren. But she'd run through a thousand other possibilities in her mind and still not found a credible one. Was it that Lauren was in love with Rick? Even if he didn't return the feelings, Amy needed to know. Because now, each time she visited Rick and Lauren was there, her annoyance at the other woman ratcheted up a notch.

She thought about Rick as she doodled logo ideas on a sketchpad, eating an entire bag of toffees at the same time. By the bottom of the bag, she had thought of the perfect design. She couldn't wait to get it done.

Amy's first decision as her own boss was to give herself the following Monday off. She needed it. Her brain was swirling and she was developing tension headaches from being hunched over her computer far too many hours a day. There was still so much to do for Porter Design, but she knew she needed to take a rest or she'd fall apart before it was done.

It wasn't exactly going to be a "break" in the truest sense, since she was due to meet Rick's mother, Pam for the first time, but still. It would get her away from screens and forms and decisions, at least.

She was certain Pam was going to hate her. How could she not? Amy was part of the reason her son had spent so long in hospital. Amy blamed herself, and the guilt was another thing that kept her up at night. Whatever Pam decided to say to her, Amy knew she'd deserve it.

She dressed with greater care than usual. She needed something that said "respectful and successful" but that also wouldn't get ruined at the beach, since the plan was to drive Rick back to Bondi with her for a few hours. She settled on a calf-length, off-the-shoulder red gingham dress with white sandals. She fixed her hair into a high ponytail and kept her makeup light.

When she pulled up outside the address, she found a neat red brick single-storey with a petrol-green door and imitation shutters painted the same shade. The yard was well-maintained, with thick grass and rows of pale purple hydrangeas brushing the bottoms of the grid windows. There were two cars parked on the concrete drive and Amy's stomach dropped. One was a green Nissan Micra that almost definitely belonged to Pam. The other was a vintage and well-used Holden ute, red in colour with black stripes along the bonnet. *Lauren.*

Her suspicions were confirmed when she rang the doorbell. A tall, attractive older woman with a white-blonde bob opened the door and Amy could hear Lauren's rich laugh coming from another room, the deep bass of Rick's voice rounding out their perfect duet.

Pam wore high-waisted jeans and a white t-shirt loosely tucked in, a combo that showed off her waspish figure. Dabs of gold - a round pendant on a long chain, ball earrings, a slim watch - along with a flawless classic-red manicure elevated her outfit. Amy instantly knew Pam's sons would have been teased for having a "hot mum".

"Pam?" Amy asked unsteadily.

"Amy." Pam gave her the tightest of smiles. It wasn't a warm welcome, but at least Pam hadn't slammed the door in her face. Amy took a deep breath and plastered on a beaming smile.

"It's so lovely to meet you, finally. Rick's told me all about you."

"Really?" Pam raised an eyebrow, not moving to let Amy in yet. "From what I heard, you didn't even know I existed."

"Yes, well. Once I knew about you, I mean."

Pam surveyed her. "I was wondering what type of woman would make Rick feel he had no choice but to lie about what he did for a living." She let the sentence trail off, as though she wanted Amy to mentally complete the thought. *And I'm surprised it was* you.

It wasn't the reproach Amy had been expecting, but rather an entirely new angle she hadn't even considered. She didn't think it was fair of Pam to blame her for Rick's lie. She raised her arms in a "nothing to hide" gesture and smiled again.

"Mum, let her in for God's sake." Rick appeared behind her in his chair, a deep frown on his face. Amy's heart flipped. He was dressed in shorts and a t-shirt that showed off his muscular arms. They'd lost some of their definition during his time in hospital, but that was slowly changing. Amy thought about those arms wrapping around her and felt heat colouring her cheeks. Rick caught her look and grinned.

Lauren stood beside him, a rolled up yoga mat tucked beneath her arm. She was even more beautiful out of scrubs, and Pam's face lit up when her gaze fell on her. *Great*, so she not only despises me, she loves Lauren, Amy thought.

Rick moved to Amy as she took her shoes off and leaned to kiss him. It was an awkward gesture, partly because she still wasn't used to his height in the chair and partly because she wasn't used to an audience.

"Oh, shall we all have an early lunch before you head off? It's mostly done, anyway." Pam brought her hands together and looked beseechingly at Lauren. Amy had the feeling it was something the two of them had discussed in advance.

"Sure." Lauren shrugged casually, but the sudden pink in her cheeks gave her away. Amy wondered why Pam wanted the four of them to have lunch so badly. Maybe she thought Rick needed a chance to assess both women simultaneously.

"Is that alright with you?" Rick asked Amy, frowning. Pam and Lauren looked at her.

"Uh, of course," she said, not really feeling she had a choice. "No rush. The beach isn't going anywhere."

"Great. Lauren, could you help me in the kitchen?"

Pam and Lauren disappeared, and Rick rolled his eyes apologetically at Amy, moving onto the carpet and gesturing to her to take a seat on the sofa.

"Sorry, she's a bit weird today," Rick said. "We seem to have hit peak 'Mum' now that I'm home."

Amy smiled to let him know it was okay, and took a proper look around the room. It was like being on the set of a sitcom about a cosy, loving family. A big, worn sofa hugged the edges of the room, framing a wooden coffee table stacked with a selection of magazines, several remotes and a Rubik's cube. The carpet was thick and plush and the television was mounted between wooden shelves filled with paperbacks and jigsaw puzzles and framed family portraits.

"I like this place."

He glanced around as if seeing it for the first time. "Yeah. I guess it's okay. I never really pictured myself back here once I'd moved out, you know?"

Amy nodded. Relaxed laughter floated out from the kitchen and she pressed her lips together.

"Don't worry about them," Rick said. The "them" didn't help matters.

"It's fine. I get it. She wishes I was Lauren. Hell, sometimes *I* wish I was Lauren."

"I don't," Rick said gently, taking her hand. Her heart rate spiked in response. His hair had grown longer and Amy liked it that way. Between the scar and the hair and the stubble he'd decided to keep around his jaw, he was starting to look like a modern-day Viking. "She doesn't know you yet, that's all."

"She knows I caused a car accident for her baby."

"But you didn't."

Amy swallowed the lump in her throat and changed the subject. "How was your session with her today?"

"Ah, you know." Rick sounded dismissive, and Amy got the distinct impression he was hiding something. Her mind was already running wild with the possibilities of the overheard conversation, plus she was sleep-deprived, over-caffeinated, mentally burnt out and had just come face-to-face with Pam's very distinct preference for Lauren.

"Let's head into the dining room," he said, pulling his hand back from hers and winking. "And eat really quickly so we can get out of here."

Amy managed a small smile, trailing him. The kitchen and dining room were combined into one large, light-filled space that smelled like fresh-baked bread. The table was large and scarred, made of solid wood and set with a centrepiece of flowers from the garden. It looked big enough for a family of twelve, but was inviting nonetheless. As was the kitchen, with its wood-topped island and homely cupboards. There was nothing designery about the place, and Amy was having trouble reconciling the icy Pam with the warm and unpretentious surroundings. The women looked up as she and Rick entered. Lauren was stirring something on the stove and Pam was draining some pasta shells that had come off the boil. She grabbed a bottle of olive oil and drizzled some over the pasta, tossing it through.

"Can I do anything to help?" Amy asked.

"No, all good," Lauren said, and Amy bristled. Why was she acting like the woman of the house? It wasn't enough that Pam clearly preferred her? "Pammy, that's the bread done," Lauren said, as a timer went off on her phone and she flicked to dismiss it. *Pammy?*

"I'll get it." Amy stepped towards the oven but Lauren

abandoned the stove to intercept and pulled open the oven door, puffing steaming air into Amy's face and making her cough.

"Oh, sorry," Lauren said, eyes big with alarm.

"Rick, can you help me find the serviette rings?" Pam asked.

Rick blinked. "Mum, we're eating and running. We don't need serviettes, let alone serviette *rings*."

"Please," she said, and headed out of the room. Rick mouthed a "sorry" to Amy and followed Pam out.

Amy and Lauren fell into an uneasy silence. Lauren turned off the stove and opened the cutlery drawer. She clearly knew her way around the kitchen and Amy wondered how that could already be the case, given Rick hadn't been home from hospital very long.

"Do you come here a lot then?" she couldn't help asking.

"A bit," Lauren said, smiling enigmatically. Amy watched as she opened another drawer and pulled out four placemats, heading over to the table with them and the bundle of cutlery. "I guess you want to sit beside Rick?" Lauren asked, looking up. "Or would you prefer opposite?"

"What do you want?" Amy said suddenly, surprising herself with the venom in her voice. "Do you want Rick? Is that it?"

Lauren's eyes widened in surprise. "Uh, I want to know where you want to sit?"

"Oh, cut the crap," Amy said in a low voice, shaking her head. "I can see straight through you."

"Okaaay. Then you'll know I'm just asking where you want to sit." Lauren looked genuinely taken aback and Amy realised she was either a brilliant actor, or more conniving than Amy had thought. There was also a chance she was telling the truth, but that wasn't an option Amy wanted to consider now that she'd waded in up to her waist.

"You've been sniffing around Rick for weeks!"

Lauren lowered the cutlery and narrowed her eyes. "If by sniffing you mean 'providing P.T.' then yeah, I guess I have been."

"I can tell you want more than that though. And what, now you've made friends with his mum to try and get on his good side?"

"I'm already *on* his good side, so no. Pam and I became friends at the hospital-"

"So you make friends with all the parents of your patients?" Amy cut her off. "You must have a packed schedule!"

"Actually, I don't make friends with them," Lauren said. "I'm usually busy working. But Pam-"

"Is Rick's mum and you fancy Rick. Yeah, I get it."

"Amy?" Rick's voice was odd, and Amy realised with a crushing wave of embarrassment that both Rick and Pam had entered the room without her noticing. God only knew how much they'd heard. Now that she'd snapped out of it, she was mortified. What had gotten into her, attacking Lauren that way? She rubbed her forehead, not daring to look back up. She could sense that Pam's face was a thundercloud.

"I'm sorry, Lauren," Rick said sincerely, and Amy's blood set afire. He was *apologising* to Lauren? On behalf of her, like she was some unruly child?

"It's fine. Really." Lauren sounded so magnanimous that Amy wanted to cry. How had she managed to come off looking like the bad party when Lauren was openly chasing Rick? Amy had to remind herself that she and Rick weren't officially "back together" and that technically, anyone could chase anyone at any time. Calling Rick her boyfriend in her resignation speech at Edgerton's and wanting it to be true didn't make it so.

"I think Amy and I will head off to the beach now," Rick said in a low voice. "Sorry about lunch, Mum. See you tomorrow, Lauren."

"I think that might be best," Pam said tightly. "Or perhaps Amy heads off and Lauren can drop you at the beach later, if you still want."

"Bye, Mum."

CHAPTER FORTY-FOUR

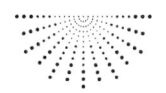

Rick heaved himself from his wheelchair into the car seat and Amy folded down the chair to place it in the boot. Once they were clicked into their seatbelts and Amy had peeled away from the curb to drive slowly down Pam's street, Rick turned to her.

"Okay, do you want to tell me what the hell that was all about?" He didn't sound as angry as she had feared, so she took some small comfort from that. But she still didn't trust herself to speak.

"Let me get to the beach first. Please." That was all she could choke out, and she was relieved when he didn't object. She turned on the radio and Rick rolled down his window, closing his eyes as the wind tossed his hair around and the sun shone on his face. Amy could barely keep her eyes on the road, he looked so sexy.

When they arrived at Bondi, Amy manoeuvred into a park at the north end of the beach and shut the engine off, turning to look at him. He watched her expectantly, a frown knitting his eyebrows together. "So tell me what's going on, and why you were tearing strips off Lauren."

She took a deep breath. "I heard you talking with her that day at the hospital when I threw up. You thought I was asleep but I wasn't. You said… you said you wanted to keep things between you and Lauren, until you knew it was real. And that you had to be the one to tell me."

"You heard that?" Amy nodded, feeling his eyes on her. Rick puffed out a breath. "Ah, Ames. And you thought?"

"I haven't really known what to think, to be honest. But now your mum hates me and loves her, and she's so pretty and I made a fool of myself. And I want us to get back together so badly."

"Hey, hey, hey. Stop. Rewind." She looked up at him and met his tender expression with her worried one. "Is that really what's been bothering you? I could tell something wasn't right. But I thought it was stress about your new business. Or maybe my situation."

"Your situation?" When he didn't answer, Amy realised he meant the wheelchair, his recovery, his injuries. *"Hang* the wheelchair," she said emphatically. "Not really, but everything it represents. Well, not hang it… argh, this isn't coming out right. Nothing is today." She rubbed her temples with the tips of her fingers and tried again. "I mean, that isn't what was bothering me. I was upset by what I heard."

Rick nodded. "I can explain everything, I'll show you once we get out of the car. But Lauren definitely isn't using Mum to get to me. Mum asked about her tattoos one time and they went to visit Lauren's friend, who's also her tattoo artist. Mum got some stuff done."

Amy's eyes bugged. "Your mum got a tattoo?"

"Yeah. It's kind of embarrassing. She got my dad's name-"

"That's not embarrassing, it's a really sweet tribute to him."

"And my name."

"Oh."

"And my brother's. In fancy cursive script. On her bicep. I guess she and Lauren went for a few drinks afterwards and they genuinely seem to have become friends. Half the time they hang out, I'm not even there. But…" he looked out to sea, then back at her, "yeah, Mum does wish I'd fancy Lauren. The thing is, I don't."

A surge of elation washed over Amy at those words and instantly, she felt magnanimous. "I guess I owe her an apology. Well, both of them really. That's going to be fun."

Rick grinned. "Well, you will go around acting like a loon." She glared at him in mock-anger. "Come on, let's get out. I want to smell the air properly."

Amy nodded and brought his wheelchair around. He swung himself into it, the motion still slightly awkward and jerky. She'd parked north so they were near the wide ramp and purpose-designed mat that allowed wheelchair access part of the way down the beach. There would still be a long gap between the end of the mat and the sand, but Amy wasn't sure Rick wanted to go nearer the water. She hoped he'd feel as uplifted seeing it as she always did.

"Let's stop here for a moment." He paused at the top of the ramp. Amy sat on the low concrete wall beside him and they both stared out to sea. Rick took long, deep breaths and tilted his face to the sun. "Oh my God. I get it now," he said a moment later. "Your fascination with the beach. I get it."

She grinned and watched him staring out over the water. She could almost see his soul refilling after those long weeks in the hospital. They sat in comfortable silence as he drank in the salt air. Amy was glad her beach looked so beautiful today. Crowded, but not insanely so. A gentle swell, a handful of surfers carving up the waves, the sand shining gold.

"This is what Lauren and I were talking about that day," Rick said a while later. He pointed to his feet. Amy looked down at them and, after a moment of intense concentration, Rick's left foot twitched. He repeated the movement several times, with both feet. Amy gasped and clapped a hand to her mouth.

"Yeah." He looked up. "It doesn't mean a lot, at least not yet. But I didn't want Lauren to say anything to you. I wasn't sure how you were processing everything. To be honest, I'm still not sure how *I'm* processing everything. The spinal shock has subsided and we're starting to be able to properly assess the damage. It does look positive, but as they keep telling me, it'll be slow. If it's important to you that I walk again, I didn't want to get your hopes up."

Amy reached for Rick's hand, tears blurring her vision. "I just want you. I want us to get back together, *properly*. I want to call you my boyfriend, I want to be able to make plans for our future. But I don't want to put pressure on you to do that if you're not ready, or if it's not me you want. I didn't truly think you were having a thing with Lauren, but at the same time I couldn't get the thought out of my head. You know she's interested in you, right? You can never convince me she wasn't keen to hang out with Pam in the first place because of you."

He shrugged. "I'm not sure about that. But it wouldn't matter if she did my therapy naked. You've got *nothing* to worry about." A pause. "You've had nothing to worry about since the first night I ever met you." His voice cracked and a bonfire lit in Amy's chest as she looked at him. She wanted to fling herself into his arms, but he turned to look at the water. They both took heaving breaths, hands twined together. "In a really weird way, I sometimes have flashes of gratitude for the crash," he said. "Or at least, I'm happy it brought us back here."

Amy frowned. "I'd already called you. I'd already asked to get back together."

He stared at her. "Before you knew I might not be able to be in the army?"

"*Yes!*" She shifted to square her shoulders to him. "Oh God, Rick, yes. That's not the reason I came back. I can't believe you've been thinking that. Even if you can go back to the army, I know we'll figure something out. I called you before I even knew about the accident at all. It must have been almost at the same time. You didn't get my messages?"

Rick shook his head, puzzled. "The phone was broken in the crash. I had to get a new one and the SIM didn't bring any of the messages over. Although honestly, I hadn't thought to check voicemail. I definitely didn't get any alerts."

Amy groaned. "Well, don't listen now. I'll sound like a complete nutbar. I must have left fifty messages."

"You're kidding."

"I wish I was! I kind of lost it when you didn't get back to me right away. If you didn't already think I was a loose cannon after I had a go at Lauren, you'll definitely think so once you hear them!"

"Come here," he pulled her to him. His huge, warm hand cupped her face and he stared into her eyes. Her breath was ragged as his lips touched hers and they kissed. Not the friendly pecks they had been exchanging. But like lovers, like the first night they'd ever kissed. Like she'd been wanting to kiss him for weeks. Someone wolf-whistled at them, but they didn't care. Amy lost all track of time and had no idea how long they'd been kissing when they finally came up for air, both breathless and red-cheeked.

"Oh God," Rick said, hunching down in his chair. "Give me your cardigan."

Amy saw what he was trying to cover up and threw her cardigan at him, grinning. "So it's not just your feet," she said, and he ducked his head.

They sat holding hands, staring at each other with identical goofy grins.

"I was thinking about what you said at the hospital one time," she said a few moments later. "About how you realised your life could end at any moment, so you want to make the most of it." She turned to him smiling. "It not only pushed me to leave Edgerton's. It made me realise that for me, making the most of this life means being with you. No matter what your career is."

She saw his jaw tighten and his Adam's apple bobbed as he swallowed. He squeezed her hands and it was a few moments before he could reply. "And I've been meaning to tell you…there's one thing they don't think I'll ever recover from."

She looked at him in alarm. "What is it?"

"It's pretty serious actually. Terminal, maybe."

"Rick?" Her heart had stopped.

"They don't think they can fix the fact that I'm in love with an idiot."

"God you're awful!" She exhaled, swatting him. "It's a weird coincidence actually. So am I."

CHAPTER FORTY-FIVE

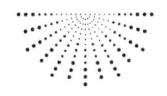

"Your pop's been missing you," Carol from reception said, her eyes glued to Rick with a decidedly thirsty look on her face.

Aside from feeling a powerful urge to slap the look off Carol's face, Amy was overcome with a wave of guilt. Though she'd been speaking to Pop almost daily on the phone, it had been far too long since she'd seen him in person. She didn't know how much longer she had him for, although there was no reason to think he was going anywhere soon. The very idea of him being gone one day made her heart bottom out. At least this time she'd brought Rick with her. Pop had been asking to meet him for a long time.

As she and Rick got out of the lift, Amy ran ahead and all but burst into Pop's room, waking him from a doze in front of the TV playing an old Western.

"I've missed you so much." She wrapped him in a tight hug after he struggled to his feet. Rick came in, smiling at the scene.

"You're going to miss me a lot more, you keep barging in

like that." Pop clutched his heart dramatically, but he was chuckling.

"I won't ever let it be this long before I visit you again."

"Don't you worry about me, I've been yakking it up with Hazel." Pop gave her a cheeky smile. "You must be Rick. Percy."

They shook hands and Amy felt her chest tightening. Her two favourite men, finally meeting one another. They all moved to the table and chairs and surrounded Pop's latest puzzle.

"That's quite the image," Rick said, casting his eyes over the Rembrandt of a woman getting out of the bath. Only the surroundings were missing, Pop having completed the nude figure first.

"It's his thing, doing these naughty puzzles."

"Nothing wrong with appreciating the female form. Don't you agree, Rick?"

"Wholeheartedly." Rick grinned as Amy swatted him.

"Oh! I almost forgot," Pop said. "I've got a present for you."

Amy beamed at him and he rifled through his bedside table before presenting her with a little box. She opened it to find a beautiful necklace inside, featuring a single large pearl on a gold chain. She looked up at him, open-mouthed. "Was this Nana's?"

He nodded, a faraway smile on his face. "She asked me to find the right time to give it to you. Was going to be either this or your wedding day." Rick coughed and Percy frowned at him. "Should I wait?"

"Is this your way of asking me what my intentions are?" Rick asked.

"I'm more worried about hers, if I'm honest with you. She usually gives 'em the flick pretty quick. Never seen her like this over anyone before," he added with a wink.

"Stop!" Amy said, blushing. "Put the necklace on me."

Pop did so, then turned her back around to examine her. "Goes perfectly with your outfit," he said, cupping the pearl in his hand for a moment. "Nellie would've burst with pride."

"Like you're doing right now," Hazel said. Amy turned to see her standing in the doorway, looking rather emotional herself.

Pop sniffed, nodding his head. "Yeah, I did an alright job with her, didn't I?"

"The best." Amy polished her knuckles on her chest. The others laughed.

Hazel introduced herself to Rick, then came forward to give Amy a hug. Amy realised it was the first time they'd done that. It was comforting.

"I've also got a bit of a surprise for you, Amy," Hazel said.

"What on earth could you give me? You've already done so much. Working on the redesign here was what really got me thinking about starting my own business. I'll be eternally grateful for that opportunity."

"That's wonderful to hear," she said, taking a seat at the table, while Amy sat on the bed. Pop pulled a packet of Clinkers from his bedside drawer. "Because I have a big client for you."

"*What?*"

"You still need to pitch, but my recommendation has a lot of sway." Amy shook her head in amazement as Hazel continued. "It's the law firm I worked at early in my career. I'm still in close contact with most of the partners. They have several projects coming up, including completely redoing their office suites."

"*Hazel.*"

"That's awesome!" Rick said, beaming.

"I asked you to do Sunnywoods as kind of a test," Hazel

continued. "I wanted to help Percy's girl, but I also didn't want to recommend a lemon to the lawyers."

Amy smiled at that. "I take it I passed the test?"

"With flying colours."

"Wow. I honestly don't know how to thank you. I know I still have to pitch," she added quickly, "but the chance alone is something I wouldn't have been able to get right off the bat. I wouldn't have got a look in. And having a client like that on my website." She shook her head. "It would be such a big boost. Really, Hazel, *thank you.*"

"Good, ain't she?" Pop said, reaching across the table to squeeze Hazel's hand. Amy's heart swelled. She looked at Rick, who was smiling proudly at her.

"There is one thing I wanted to mention though," Hazel said, holding a business card out to her. "When you pitch, they'll want to know how you can handle all their business. Resources, I mean. I've told them how amazing you are, but I've been vague on the fact that you're a one-woman show. You might need to consider bringing on a temp, or even partnering with someone, if there's someone you can think of."

Amy nodded and took the card, her mind racing. Rick was biting his lip and frowning at her, realising her conundrum. There was no one. She decided to call Martha when she got home. Maybe there was a way she could convince her to leave Beaumont and join Porter Design. It seemed unlikely, but Amy didn't really have any other options.

CHAPTER FORTY-SIX

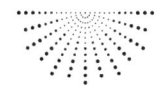

Nervous butterflies tickled Amy's stomach as soon as she woke. She, Alex, Rick and Marley were starting renovation work at her office, and Amy could barely wait. She'd also asked Rick whether it would be a good idea to invite Lauren to join. Not exactly a Nobel Peace Prize-winning gesture, especially as she knew Lauren was busy. But she wanted to do something to mend the bridge she'd set fire to between them. To her surprise, Rick supported the idea, and Lauren told him she'd be delighted to pitch in. Deacon had also volunteered an afternoon here and there.

Amy smiled at her reflection in the mirror as she sipped her morning espresso. She was really doing it, she was starting her own company. It was slightly surreal. Thanks to Loretta and Hazel, she wasn't starting with a blank slate either, and had already held preliminary meetings with some potential future clients.

She made herself a quick breakfast and called Rick when she was on her way to pick him up. Her flat wasn't wheelchair accessible and Amy hadn't yet made amends with

Pam, so she and Rick were spending their nights apart. Amy had extended an olive branch and asked whether they could meet up and discuss everything, but apparently Pam "wasn't ready" yet. Amy was embarrassed and unhappy about the situation and she hoped Pam would agree to speak to her soon.

Alex was already standing out the front of the building when they arrived. He grinned sheepishly. "I'm kind of excited."

"Me too." Amy held up the key. "I can't thank you both enough for this. Let's do it!"

They stepped inside and immediately looked at one another in horror. A very strong, very foetid smell assaulted their nostrils.

"Oh, God." Alex plugged his nose. "What *is* that?"

"I swear it didn't smell like this when I came in for the inspection!" Amy was trying not to retch. Rick pulled his shirt up over his nose. "What do we do?" she wailed. "This is unbearable."

Alex blew out a long breath. "It has to be coming from somewhere. Let's go look around."

"Look around where?" Amy asked, her voice rising in panic. "It's all one big space."

"There's some nooks and crannies." Rick's voice was muffled through his shirt. "We have to inspect them before we get knocked unconscious."

The space was large and empty, covered in spongy, stained gym flooring. There were almost no internal walls and the exposed brickwork gave the space an industrial feel that Amy was hoping would look chic once they'd finished renovating.

First, though, they had to hunt down the source of the abominable stench.

"Okay, first one to find the stench…finds the stench!" she yelled.

They laughed as Rick headed toward the bathroom at the back and Alex started peeling up squares of the gym flooring to check underneath. Amy made her way to an abandoned set of metal lockers. She picked up a discarded umbrella that she found in the first one, and used it to gingerly open the others.

A moment later, Rick called out. "It's a dead possum!"

Amy put her hands to her cheeks in horror and Alex laughed. "I'll get it out of here," he said.

She covered her eyes as he took the carcass outside, feeling overwhelmed with everything they needed to do. They had to rip up the flooring, build the plasterboard to wall off the rooms, add doors and paint. Since the only windows were at the front and the back of the building, Amy had designed some false skylights to give the appearance of natural light. It would look great, but meant they also needed to create a ceiling to cover the exposed beams and mess of silver air-conditioning ducts.

The bathroom was currently in a miserable state with cracked tiles, a stall door hanging from its hinges, dripping sinks and a rusted out toilet bowl. They'd have to completely rip it out and redo it. Then they needed to run wiring through the whole space, hang the lighting fixtures and artwork, lay the thick cream carpet in the office area, polish the concrete for the reception, add the furniture she'd ordered, and install all the tech.

Amy closed her eyes and tried to imagine the front space as she'd designed it. Rugs layered over the polished concrete, stylish sofas scattered just-so with throw pillows centred around a beautiful walnut coffee table, behind which there was a marble-topped kitchenette with a proper espresso machine. It would be finished off with lots of greenery and a floating bookshelf filled with design books.

She opened her eyes to find Rick looking at her quizzically. "Did you power down?" he asked.

"No, it was a private memorial for the possum," she joked. "A minute's silence."

They laughed and got to work ripping up the flooring. Rick used the old umbrella to get purchase on the squares and Alex finished ripping them off. Amy had hired a dumpster to toss all the rubble and rubbish into, and she took on the task of carrying the flooring out once it was up. She dusted off her hands on her vintage denim dungarees and adjusted the Rosie the Riveter-style kerchief that was holding back her hair.

Marley had texted to say she was running late as her bus had broken down. She still hadn't arrived by the time the three of them were ready to take a break, but Lauren was on her way. Amy was nervous about seeing her again.

"Do you think the smell has gone, or our nostrils are burned out?" Amy asked, as they sat down on the dirty concrete floor.

"I can't believe I didn't bring any water." Alex smacked his lips. "Rookie mistake."

"I could murder a pie," Rick added.

Amy pulled her phone out and checked the surrounding area on her maps application. "There's a bakery within walking distance, or an Afghan restaurant but that doesn't open until six, or…there's a juice bar."

"Bakery," Alex said.

"Agree," said Rick.

"I'll go." She groaned as she got to her feet. "Orders please."

When she came back, juggling several paper bags full of croissants and sandwiches, as well as a tray of coffees and a huge bottle of water, Lauren was standing outside, head bent over her mobile. Amy came to halt before her and Lauren wordlessly tucked her phone away and took a few of the bags to help her. Amy cleared her throat and Lauren raised an eyebrow, a small smile playing on her lips.

"You kind of lost it at me," she said.

"I know." Amy was glad Lauren had spoken first, and that it wasn't to scream at her. "I'm sorry. I've had a lot on my mind, but it was no excuse."

"Rick told me you overheard our conversation that morning. I can kind of see why you got the wrong idea."

"Yeah." Amy shook her head. "I should still have asked outright."

"And the Pam thing… she's just being overprotective. She asked me to join at lunch so I could give her my opinion on you. It was always going to be positive."

"Was?"

Lauren grinned, then tilted her head at Amy. "You know he's completely mad for you, right? Like in one of those hopeless, forever kinds of ways."

Amy breathed out, shook her head. "Well, he and I both. Am I forgiven?"

Lauren nodded. "Of course."

"Great, thanks." They stood staring at each other a moment longer. "Put in a good word for Pam with me?"

Lauren grinned. "Not sure I'd go *that* far yet." They chuckled. "Come on, let's go inside."

Alex and Rick were hunched over the plans, discussing something so intently that neither of them noticed as the girls walked in.

Amy stopped, watching Rick's face. He was animated and

passionate about whatever it was they were discussing. He looked full of purpose and, despite a frown of concentration as he nodded and listened to Alex, like he was having a lot of fun. Her heart ballooned as he looked up and their eyes caught. She thought about kissing him and her stomach flipped. There'd been a few repeat performances since the kiss at the beach, usually while they were sitting in Amy's car outside Pam's place. They felt like naughty teenagers, which somehow made it even hotter. But she was aching to lie beside him, wake up in his arms, sleep with him again. She needed to get through Pam first. Rick had said he'd speak to her again that night - he was becoming as frustrated as she was and kept trying to send Pam out of town to visit his older brother. Pam was having none of it though. Amy hoped their discussion went well. She didn't know how much longer she could stand being apart.

"Is this the whole team?" Lauren asked, helping Amy clear a spot in the middle of the room to set down the refreshments after she'd been introduced to Alex and given Rick a quick hug hello.

"Almost. My friend Marley should be here soon. You can't miss her. Loud mouth, louder dress sense."

"And one hundred percent awesome," Alex added, heading to the clearing and sitting on the dusty concrete floor to start tearing into the food. "Ham and cheese, or tomato and mozzarella?" he asked Rick, as he lifted the sandwich tops with the corner of a napkin.

"Ham and cheese."

Amy caught the grateful expression on Rick's face as Alex handed the sandwich over and tossed him a bottle of water. Amy and Lauren sat down on the floor beside them.

"I really timed this well, didn't I?" Lauren bit into a croissant.

Amy grinned. "Pretty sure it's the least I owe you."

Rick's phone pipped and he swiped to check a message. "Deacon's on his way in."

"Maybe we'll get done today, with this many pairs of hands," Amy said, awed at the way people were stepping in to help her.

Alex snorted. "You've never seen *Grand Designs* then, have you?"

Everyone chuckled and Amy heard Marley call out. "Come in!" she hollered back.

Marley took a few steps into the space, looking around with wide eyes, and then stopped dead, staring at Rick. Lauren looked between Rick and Marley, an amused smile on her face.

"Whoo, that scar!" Marley puffed out a breath and shook her head. "That *really* does something for you. Right, Ames? And the hair. And the *stubble*." She turned to Amy, her eyes wide and her pupils dilated.

"Are you seriously making a move on him right in front of me?" Amy was grinning.

"What am I, chopped liver?" Alex added, pretending to be offended.

"I'm not remotely interested in either of you. I'm just stating facts." Marley shrugged.

"You have to be Marley," Lauren said, getting up to shake her hand. Marley spotted the pile of croissants on the floor and moved to grab one, joining the circle on the floor.

"Well, at least that answers the question about the smell," Alex said, and Amy burst out laughing.

Deacon turned up soon after their lunch break and Amy dropped what she was doing to wrap him in a tight hug.

"Thank you for helping me," she said in a low voice. "And I don't just mean today."

Deacon patted her back, giving her an embarrassed laugh. "Of course. Anything for Rick's girl." He stepped out of her grip and grinned at Rick. "Sweet wheels, man." He walked over and high-fived a smiling Rick.

"Thanks." Rick turned a tight circle and finished with a ta-da of his hands.

"Pssht. That all you've got?"

"I'm teaching him more," Lauren said, her eyes trained on Deacon, "gimme time."

Deacon looked up at Lauren and Amy almost felt the electricity spark between the two of them. Rick noticed it too and he raised an eyebrow at Amy, smiling. *Well what do we have here?*

For the rest of the afternoon, Amy caught flirtatious glances going back and forth between Lauren and Deacon, despite an oblivious Marley's accidental attempts to come between them.

"Oh, Lauren, I was doing this patch. I went to grab some water. Why don't you go over there?" She pointed to a far corner as she tried to resume her place beside Deacon.

If Amy thought for a moment Marley was interested in Deacon, her loyalties would have been firmly with her friend. But she was simply being Marley, so Amy felt comfortable swooping in and guiding her over to that far corner, absorbing her in conversation so she would stay out of Deacon and Lauren's way. Amy couldn't hand on heart say that her motivations in seeing them get together were purely altruistic. If Lauren was with Deacon, she knew she'd worry a lot less about the other woman's friendship with Pam, and the one-on-one time she spent with Rick. Amy knew they were her own issues and insecurities, but a Lauren-Deacon romance would take care of at least one of them. So she was gratified when Lauren announced she'd be leaving a few hours later and Deacon offered to "walk her to her car."

"What is it with you army boys and your 'walking women home'?" Amy asked Rick once they'd gone. "Is that something they teach you? How to handle weapons, how to defend from a foreign invasion, gentlemanly courtship 101?"

Rick chuckled and held up his palms. "What can I say? It works, doesn't it?"

Amy spent an extra long time kissing him farewell in her car that evening, despite the fact they were both covered in dust and sweat.

"Please convince Pam to talk to me," Amy pleaded as Rick straightened his t-shirt and smoothed down his hair. "Otherwise I think I'm going to do something right here in the car that will scandalise the neighbourhood."

He grinned at her, leaning to tuck a strand of hair behind her ear and brush her lips with his. Amy's body beat with desire. "I'll do my best. As you may have noticed, I'm pretty motivated myself."

CHAPTER FORTY-SEVEN

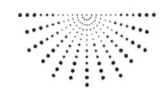

A week later, Rick, Alex, Marley and Amy were surveying their work at the offices. The progress was mind-boggling to Amy. It already looked like a different place.

The gym matting had been pulled up and the concrete polished. Most of the internal walls were in, as was the false ceiling. The bathroom had been gutted, new walls installed to make the space bigger. The tiles were laid, the sink and toilet installed. There was still a long way to go, but at this pace, Amy estimated she'd be able to open her doors in under two weeks.

She'd been holding meetings with new clients on their premises, feeling pangs of guilt that she was leaving the others to do the renovations while she was gone. They all assured her they didn't mind and she believed them, but it still didn't sit right. She had met with Hazel's lawyer friends and had convinced them she'd be able to bring in the resources to take on their work. But Martha had turned Amy down, too nervous to leave Edgerton's without proof of Amy's success.

The four of them were breaking for lunch when there was a rap on the street-facing windows. Amy frowned, wondering whether a neighbour was coming to complain about the noise.

Alex was the closest and he disappeared behind the plastic sheet they'd set up to keep debris from flying into the street. He brushed back through a moment later, leading Kristina into the room.

"What are *you* doing here?" Amy asked sharply. Rick and Marley others stared at Kristina, uncertain who she was and why Amy was speaking to her that way. To her credit, Kristina didn't look remotely intimidated.

"It wasn't me," she said.

Amy lowered her sandwich, narrowing her eyes. "It had to be you. The only other person who knew was Martha, and I *know* it wasn't her."

Kristina shook her head. "Of course it wasn't her. I've spent ages trying to get to the bottom of it. The whole time since you left, actually. It was Kyle."

It took Amy a second to process what she was saying. "*What?*"

Kristina nodded. "His grandmother is some woman named Janella, and she's at the same nursing home as your grandfather."

"Oh God. I know that woman," Amy whispered, remembering the way Janella had confronted her and Pop when they were looking at the changes to the common room.

"Yep," Kristina said. "She was peeved that Kyle wasn't asked to do the work, and she told him all about it. When she mentioned the name Amy, he did some digging around and found out it was you. He knew Beaumont had to cut someone from the team, so he was trying to make sure it wasn't him."

"This is like a spy movie," Marley said, looking back and forth between Amy and Kristina.

"I'm kind of only half getting it, but I agree," Alex said.

Rick was watching Amy, trying to determine how to react to Kristina.

"How on earth did you find that out?" Amy asked finally.

Kristina cleared her throat, looking sheepish. "I may or may not have broken into the room where HR stores their files. I uh, I looked through yours. I didn't see anything except the complaint," she added quickly, as Rick sucked in a quick breath. "But his name was on the paper as the source."

Amy slowly shook her head. "I don't know whether to be impressed or afraid of you."

Kristina grinned. "Maybe both is smart."

"I feel horrible that I thought it was you," Amy said. "And I sincerely apologise. But…" She frowned. "I don't get why you tried so hard to find that out. I'm gone. What does it matter if I thought it was you?"

Kristina looked awkward for the first time since arriving. She focused on a spot by her feet and cleared her throat a few times, scuffing a toe on the plastic sheeting covering the floor. "Remember how we got thrown together on the Peregrine account?"

"Yes?" Amy said, thinking back on how irritated she'd been with Beaumont over that.

Kristina looked up. "I requested it. I wanted to work with you. Maybe this is going to sound weird, but I accepted the offer at Edgerton's in the first place because I wanted to work with you. I've followed your career for a while. I was excited to be on the same team as you. But…" she trailed off and looked at the floor again.

"But it didn't really go to plan," Amy finished. She could barely believe that Kristina, rising star of Edgerton's, had been wanting to work with her all along. It was incredibly flattering.

"I thought you'd kill me after I found out that Evertree had been your client. But you were so chilled about it."

"Rebecca wouldn't have been open to a change if I'd been doing my job properly with her. The truth is I was burnt out at Edgerton's. I wasn't following up with my clients enough."

Kristina shook her head. "How could you, with everything he piles on us?"

"Well, now this woman *has* to join you," Marley said flatly, voicing an idea that was dimly beginning to form in the back of Amy's mind.

She and Kristina looked at each other.

"I have savings that might help," Kristina said. "I can probably put in half of what we'd need to get this off the ground. Maybe more," she added with a grin, "since I can't imagine you're paying these guys what I'd estimated for office fit-out."

Rick chortled and Alex raised his eyebrows. "Does that mean a raise for us?" he asked.

Amy hesitated. "Kristina, you could have a really great career at Edgerton's. You need to be sure this is what you want."

"Wouldn't be here if I wasn't." She shrugged. "We work well together. Look at what we did with Peregrine. We nailed it. I think we make each other's work better, and it was always my goal to start my own business. This is a bit sooner than I'd planned, but it feels right."

Amy nodded slowly. Joining forces with Kristina would be a massive boost to her fledgling business. With relatively big industry names, not to mention the fact she'd be able to split the start-up costs, they would really get noticed. Maybe they'd even frighten Beaumont.

Amy raised her eyes to Kristina, decision made. "What will we call ourselves?"

She grinned. "Well, Lucas Porter sounds like some dumb guy. *Porter Lucas* sounds like a very successful design business."

Amy walked from around the table and held a hand out to her. "Deal."

Rick, Marley and Alex broke into applause.

"This is better than TV," Rick said.

"Great!" Marley said, handing Kristina a brush. "You can start on that wall."

Amy took the brush back off Kristina, who looked amused. "I have a better idea," she said. "Come look at the blueprints with me. See if there's anything you'd like to change before we get too much more done." Kristina nodded once, looking pleased. "And after that, I have a bottle of champagne that's been waiting for the right moment to be opened." Amy smiled. "I think we found that moment."

"I have one more suggestion," Kristina said. "Martha."

Amy raised her eyebrows. "I asked her, but she said no."

"She's not ready yet. We might need to prove ourselves for a while, but we'd truly let her keep to the part time hours. I think that's the most important thing to her."

"Then we'd be a three person company." Amy couldn't keep the smile off her face as she said it.

"And that would be just the beginning," Kristina said, beaming back at her.

CHAPTER FORTY-EIGHT

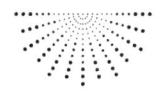

Her eyes still closed and her head still foggy with sleep, Amy slapped at her buzzing phone until it fell silent. Then she realised it was Sunday and they weren't working on the office, so she hadn't set an alarm. She squinted at the screen and saw that she'd missed a call from Rick. He rang again immediately.

"Morning," she croaked. "Why are you harassing me?"

"Because I'm bored and you've been asleep far too long. We really have to do something about spending nights apart."

"I couldn't agree more." Amy sighed. "But your mum isn't budging."

"That's what I'm ringing about. She budged."

"She *budged?*" Amy's eyes widened and she propped herself up on one elbow.

"She did. Unprompted, I swear," he said. "Well, unprompted since the last argument we had about it. Which was last night. She asked if you want to come over for dinner tonight."

"Is she going to poison me?"

"Probably. But the food will taste great on the way down."

Amy chuckled. "I can't believe this is happening. I'll be there."

"Great," he said. "Be here at six. Oh, and Ames?"

"Yeah?" She beamed into the phone.

"Bring your overnight bag."

She hung up the phone and stretched luxuriously, kicking her feet under the covers in delight.

Pulling up outside Pam's place with a packed overnight bag brought on the closest thing Amy had ever had to a panic attack.

She video called Lyra while she was still sitting in the car, desperate for a pep talk. Lyra answered, but Amy could see she was at the studio and looked beat.

"God," Amy said, taking in Lyra's face. "I wanted a pep talk but I might need to give you one."

Lyra laughed tonelessly. "Tell me I was born to do something else, please," she whispered, stepping into some sort of cupboard and closing the door behind her.

Amy grimaced. "I'm really sorry but I can't."

Her shoulders slumped and she rubbed her forehead. Amy had never seen her looking so tired. "Alex loves working on your offices. I wish I could be there too."

"You're there in spirit," Amy reassured her.

"What did you need a pep talk about? Tell me. It might help get my mind off the drama here."

Amy sighed. "I'm outside Rick's place. He asked me to stay the night. His mum has been freezing me out since I made a peanut of myself about Lauren. But we're about to have to have dinner together."

"Oh my God." Lyra laughed. "It's like we're nineteen

again. Remember how panicked you were about meeting that French guy's mum? What was his name again?"

"Guillaume." Amy put a hand over her eye and laughed at the memory.

"Guillaume!" Lyra hooted. "Didn't you tell his mum you were studying French or something?"

Amy groaned. "Why did I do that? She kept wondering why I never progressed far past *merci*. And she corrected me every time I said Guillaume's name."

They wiped tears from their eyes as they got their giggles under control. "How bad can this woman be, compared to Guillaume's mum?"

"I don't know. I'm about to find out, I guess. I so badly want this to work out. I'm so in love with him. I just want all this stupid stuff behind us."

"You got this. I believe in you. Ah crap, I think I've been found-" Lyra cut off and Amy heard a stern voice talking to her. She winced at her and Lyra discreetly rolled her eyes. They waved at one another and they hung up.

Amy plucked her overnight bag out of the car and rang the bell.

CHAPTER FORTY-NINE

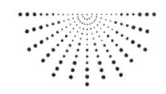

"Do you drink a lot?" Pam asked, as she hovered over Amy's glass with the bottle of red. Rick cast Amy a sidelong glance and she wondered whether he was telepathically sending her the right answer.

"Only on stressful occasions," she answered, and both Pam and Rick smiled. Pam topped her glass up and sat back down in front of her plate of spaghetti bolognese.

Dinner was turning out to be an odd experience indeed. Pam had prepared a delicious meal, and the jazz piping through the speakers seemed more fitted to a relaxed atmosphere. But she was also serving red wine like it was going out of style, constantly adding more to Amy's glass, perhaps hoping it would act like a truth serum.

Amy was also starting to think Pam had had military training from her son, the way she was trying to flank her with unexpected questions. But when Amy saw how Rick was smiling at her from over his wine glass, she'd have happily walked through an actual battlefield.

"And what about your parents?" Pam asked. "What do your mother and father do?"

Rick froze and Amy coughed, taking a sip of wine to buy herself some time. She decided to go for honesty. Or as much of it as she cared to share. "I'm estranged from my father." Amy registered the shock on Pam's face, but kept going. "My mother is a nice enough woman, but we're not close. I was raised by my Pop." At the thought of him, Amy put her hand on her heart.

"He's a great guy," Rick smiled. "Go on, Amy, tell Mum your high school grades as well."

"Straight A's."

"Nerd." Rick grinned.

Pam sighed. "Alright, message received," she said curtly. "I'm not allowed to ask questions. But I thought this was about getting to know one another."

"You can ask me whatever you like." Amy smiled warmly at her.

"I'm kind of enjoying the grilling." Rick shot Amy a wicked look over his wine glass.

"Oh, Richard." Pam smiled at him affectionately, putting a hand on her son's arm. Her eyes welled up and she waved a hand in front of her face. "Sorry."

"Mum, it's okay." Rick laid his hand on top of hers.

"When I think about you in that car…"

"I'm here now. And I could have been going *anywhere* in the car. It wasn't Amy's fault that I was bringing something to her. You have to let go of that idea."

"This feels like a conversation I shouldn't be here for," Amy said awkwardly, setting her wine glass down with a gulp.

"You should," Rick said firmly. "Because I know this is a thought you've had too. I want both of you to know. This was a random accident. *No one is to blame.*"

Then Amy choked up. She hadn't realised how much she'd wanted to hear those words, hadn't even really admitted to herself that she was carrying so much guilt.

"Thank you," she whispered, and he nodded.

"I suppose I'll get used to you," Pam said a moment later, giving Amy a sidelong look. It was no standing ovation, but Amy was pleased. She sensed it was the best she was going to get from Pam - for a while anyway.

"I wish I hadn't redecorated," Rick said, as they closed the door behind them in his room. It was sparsely furnished to accommodate the wheelchair, holding little aside from a double bed, a small bedside table and a wall-mounted TV.

Amy's eyes widened. "Please don't tell me Pam did that thing where she kept your room exactly the same as when you moved out!" Rick nodded and Amy covered her eyes with her hands.

"It was a *shrine*." They chuckled.

"Oh! I can't believe I forgot to show you!" Amy sprang up and grabbed her laptop from her overnight bag. "I got the proofs back from the graphic designer for my logo."

"Your logo," Rick repeated proudly. "Get a load of you, Amy Porter."

She grinned, sitting on the bed and tucking her feet beneath her as she scrolled through her emails for the one she was looking for. "Are you ready?" she asked, once she'd found it. He nodded. She spun the laptop around and he stared at the screen, a slow smile spreading across his face.

"A banksia."

"For you. Lots of people gave me the push I needed to do this, but your faith in me is what got me over the line. Thank you. Seriously. Thank you."

He nodded, looking at her with that expression. The one that made her heart flip flop. "You're so welcome."

He dimmed the light in his room and got beside her on the bed, sitting up against the headboard. She tucked her laptop away and leaned her head on his shoulder. They sat in silence for a long moment, as Rick traced his finger up and down her arm, sending tingles shooting through her.

"Wanna fool around?" he murmured in her ear.

"I thought you'd never ask."

The next morning, Amy woke to find Rick sitting up in bed, watching her. There was a serious expression on his face.

"Why are you looking at me so weird?" Her voice cracked with sleep.

"How dare you? That's my face." She giggled and snuggled into him. "Ames, we need to talk."

"Okay." She yawned and stretched. "Where's my coffee and breakfast in bed?"

"I woke up about an hour ago and remembered you said you'd left me those messages."

"Oh, God," she whispered, covering her eyes. "Don't tell me you listened?" She peeked through her fingers and he nodded. "Right, I'll go pack my bags?"

"Please don't go anywhere." He pulled something from his bedside table and slid down beside her, throwing the sheet over their heads to create a tiny, private universe. Amy lazily traced his scar with her finger as he ran his thumb over her lips.

He looked into her eyes and took a deep breath. "I wanted to do this on our trip to Hotel D'Montvue. But I also worried that it was way too soon and you'd think I was mad. Plus, I needed to clear up the situation first, and...uh, I didn't really know how to do that, as we've established." Amy lay still, watching him, her heart beginning to thud. "Then I decided I wanted to wait until I could walk again, so I could do it properly and get down on one knee."

Amy's eyes widened as she suddenly realised what he was going to say. "Yes! Yes. Yes."

"I haven't asked you anything yet, " Rick said with a grin. "I decided I don't want to wait until I can walk. Because I don't know if I ever will, and also because that isn't really important. What's important is us." He placed a small jewel box into her hand. "I know I said I wasn't ready and I had nothing to offer. But after I heard your messages, I realised what I already knew deep down. I trust you enough to know we can do this together. I trust *us.*"

"I don't care if you haven't asked me anything yet, it's a yes."

"Open the box, Amy."

"Okay," she whispered. She carefully lifted the lid and one of the fake eyes from the glasses she'd given Rick in hospital bounced out. She threw back her head and laughed so much she started to wheeze. He was laughing with her, so hard that for a while no sound came out of him.

"You're so mean!" She wiped tears from her eyes and rested her head on his chest. "I changed my mind. My answer is no."

When they'd gotten their laughter under control, Rick handed her a different box. She looked questioningly at him, unsure whether it was another joke. His smile was nervous and his eyes were shining. She knew this one was for real. Inside, on a navy velvet cushion, was a beautiful vintage diamond engagement ring. It was exactly the kind of thing Amy would have chosen for herself and she was thrilled that he knew her style so well.

"Oh, *Rick,*" she breathed. "This is stunning!"

"It was my great-grandmother's," he said proudly. "And I knew it would be perfect for you. Do you really like it?"

"Are you kidding me? I've never seen one so beautiful. Can I try it on?"

They lay side by side on their backs, the sheet still over their heads, as he gently tugged the ring free from the box and held it over her finger.

"Amy Beth Porter," he said, his voice shaking with emotion. "Will you marry me?"

"Well, it's awkward now because I really want the ring but I'm still mad about the eyeball."

He swatted her. She moved her finger into the ring and he slipped it down. It fit perfectly.

She shifted onto her side, staring into his eyes. They were crinkling in the corners with his smile, his dimple visible even beneath his stubble.

"Richard Ford," she said, running a hand through his hair and pulling him to her until their lips were brushing. "My answer is yes."

Marley's overcome so much in her past, and her secrets haunt her to this day. She wants a fresh start, but can she move past her trauma to find her happily-ever-after with the handsome, smart Finn? Read the heartwarming *New Beginnings at Lilac Bay* to find out!

AFTERWORD

Dear Reader,

THANK YOU for reading this book and supporting my dream, it means the world to me!

If you enjoyed reading about Amy and Rick, please tell your friends so they can experience the uplifting warmth of Lilac Bay (which is based on a real place!).

Reviews are invaluable in helping other readers find my books as well. I'd like to say a personal thank you if you take the time to write one, just email me the link at authormarietaylorford@gmail.com

Have a great day, and check the next page for a free short story :)

THE STRANGER FROM LILAC BAY

YOUR FREE EBOOK

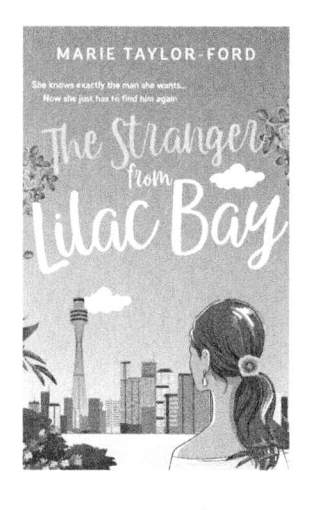

When a hot paramedic saves Hope's life, she's instantly smitten. Afraid she's just feeling grateful, Connor gives her his number and tells her to make the first move. She meant to hit save, not erase ... for a girl who works in IT, it shouldn't have been that hard.

In a city like Sydney, will she ever be able to find him again?

Get your FREE copy:
https://marietaylorford.com/strangerlilacbay/

ABOUT THE AUTHOR

Marie Taylor-Ford is a wife, mother, knitter and devoted carboholic - not in that order.

Born in Wales and raised in Australia (Newy forever!), she recently returned to her seaside hometown with her husband and two boys, after a decade in Munich, Germany.

If she's not writing, she's probably hanging out with her family or friends, knitting, reading, or doing yoga.

She'd love to connect via social media:

- amazon.com/author/marietaylorford
- bookbub.com/profile/marie-taylor-ford
- facebook.com/marietaylorford
- instagram.com/authormarietaylorford
- tiktok.com/@authormarietaylorford

ACKNOWLEDGMENTS

So many people helped shape this book, and I feel crazy lucky to have them all in my life.

HUGE thanks go to the following people for endless advice, re-reads, tips, comments and invaluable input: Hannah, Anthea Kirk, Sophia Oßwald, Shelby Shukaliak, Sylvia Muller and especially the most awesome sis in the world, Catherine. To my test readers who are also two of my best friends, Sarah and Claudia <3.

Thank you to my wonderful editor, Katharine D'Souza and my talented cover designer, Ana Grigoriu-Voicu.

Thanks also to my husband, for his unending support and encouragement. To my baby, Wyatt, for being my motivation and my delight. To my awesome in-laws for their support and wicked sense of humour. And to my Mama, who is eternally missed.

Thank you to all my friends, family and the readers who supported me with Hungry Hearts. I really hope you enjoyed this book as well!

Printed in Great Britain
by Amazon